DISTANCE LEARNING

LYN DOWLAND

Bella
BOOKS
2013

Bella Books, Inc.
P.O. Box 10543
Tallahassee, FL 32302

First Bella Books Edition 2013

Editor: Katherine V. Forrest
Cover Designed by: Linda Callaghan

ISBN: 978-1-59493-367-7

About the Author

Lyn Dowland is a pseudonym. She is a professional musician living in the UK. Despite many poems, some short stories, an occasional magazine article and a couple of plays, written to amuse herself, this is her first adventure into the world of novel writing.

Acknowledgment

With thanks to those of our friends and family who help to keep our feet upon the ground through the challenges of life, gratitude to my experienced editor and to everyone at Bella.

If you can't get rid of the skeleton in your closet, you'd best teach it to dance.

—George Bernard Shaw

PRELUDE

It was never part of the plan to be dependent upon anyone. Freed from the restrictions of her childhood and the expectations of parents, Alex had expected never to need anybody ever again. She had worked for this, striven not to have to lean on anyone, but the resolve had crept beneath her skin becoming a hidden mantra for self-sufficiency to the point of isolation.

Perhaps it was not entirely self-induced. Everyone had always presumed she was independent. But it had become a necessity. She had yet to find out why. Mistakenly, others had confused the ability to spend hours on her own for resourceful self-reliance. But true independence worked only when there was the power of choice.

It was misguided of her parents to place her on her own with unknown host families on childhood tours in other countries when she had not been old enough to know anything much. That was frightening to her. Not to speak the same language or understand strange, boisterous children and to be at an address she could neither find her way to or from without being driven in a car that reeked of unfamiliarity.

Alex was painfully shy at that stage. They had confused the ability to spend happy hours in her own company with the reluctance to spend uncomfortable moments struggling to communicate with other people. And perhaps it was her mistake too. She had pretended not to be like that, sometimes forcing an unnatural gregariousness to cover herself, although mostly only when in the safety of close friends.

The error made her withdraw and hide. The foreign families must have thought she was equally impenetrable. Sullen, her nose sunk in the pages of some book or other, an uncommunicative child whose fingers forever fidgeted, while longing to be somewhere safe, familiar. Actually hiding in the book to be away from prying eyes and inquiring words. Wanting to be left alone.

Thank goodness *that* was no longer an issue. That was in the distant past. Although some socializing was often necessary, at least now she could leave and return to solitude.

At least there is an adult choice now.

CHAPTER ONE

The Late Call in January

"Hi darling, it's me."

Josh's voice purred with its habitual warmth down the receiver, raising the temperature of a flat, post-Christmas night. Although it was soft, intentionally appealing, it was a voice that betrayed a touch of insincerity and on this particular night it was simply too late to be calling; Alex was far too tired to be playing his game.

"You're past my curfew. It's gone ten thirty." Her vain attempts at lightheartedness fell coldly across the ether.

"Yes I know. You sound sleepy."

"I am...sorry." It was not a heartfelt apology. Again, he managed to turn his intrusion around without fail, so that *she* felt the need to apologize. Disgruntled, she reached for a mug from the cupboard.

"It's just a couple of pieces of news I thought you'd want to hear, about the tour. Make yourself a cuppa and bear with me for a moment."

This apparent kindness caused her to scowl into thin air, forever hating that he knew her well enough to guess her actions so easily. "Aha. Go on." *But do we have to do this now?*

"Everything's finalized, including the Victoria arrangements. You'll simply love the ferry, it's spectacular."

I know Josh, you've said so already. "Great, thanks, I will… and?" A helpless yawn overcame her feeble efforts at being approximately polite; a wayward piece of hair fell across her face causing her to juggle the mug and the handset. "Really, I am sorry. It's just that I've been practicing for hours."

She transferred him to the speaker, bracing herself. He was leading up to something, perhaps paving the way for a disappointment.

"And that always makes you grouchy. Believe me, I know! We've secured one of the suites at the first hotel after all, despite the Oscars clash. I don't know what the delay was, and they're finishing off the arrangements for the Steinway and…something more, that is going to interest you. Alex, stop yawning! I've just had another call from the fixer and it turns out you have more interest over there than we realized, needing you for a last-minute booking. Pay attention now…"

She stopped what she was doing, biting her lip at being turned into the obedient schoolgirl.

"…they want you for two stints as guest pianist at…wait for it…the Post-Awards Party, coinciding with your first available night. I don't know what strings she pulled."

Suddenly Alex was upright, alert. The mug fell from her grasp, on the cold, hard tiles, along with her apathy. *Okay Josh, now you have my full attention.*

"What was that crash?"

"Oh! Um, nothing vital. You *are* joking?"

"Would I, about something like that? Fabulous, isn't it?"

"Which one?"

"Oscars of course, you fool. It's massive."

"But surely that was fixed ages ago?"

"Of course. However they've pulled the plug on someone at the last minute. Some scandal in the papers, a sordid affair, rehab, so I hear, I don't know."

"Who could that have been?"

"No idea. They weren't opening up. But I suspect it's Charlie."

"That's not unlikely. Last time I saw him he could barely stand up."

"Exactly."

"Will you call them back right away? I wouldn't want to appear to be stalling. And you're quite sure it fits?"

"Absolutely, darling. Just needed to double-check with you. I've told them it should be fine. I know you adore all that, the film world. So I must love you and leave you then. I'll e-mail through the draft schedule by the morning…I'll be up late tonight."

Guilt irritated her conscience. He had a good reason to be calling after all. "That's terrific. You're a star."

"Sweetheart, you're the star. I'm just the dogsbody."

"Ha-ha, very funny. Josh, you are simply brilliant!"

"Yes, I know. Speak to you tomorrow then."

* * *

Her unassuming cottage was tucked beside the road, part of a sleepy woodland village in Surrey, an unintentional gateway to the future. The home-counties: reputed to be the haunt of the wealthier London overspill, where glamorous former manor houses rubbed shoulders with humble workers' cottages squeezed onto the roadsides on a spare handkerchief of land, now hot property to be fought for.

City-weary commuters escaped to dive into their pools or perhaps dig their own vegetables in a place with a view and a gasp of fresh air, preferring the pace of life away from the unnatural hubbub of the city, somewhere down the leaf-dappled, root-tangled lanes, among those who have known its natural delights for generations. A piece of lingering nostalgia, unchanging, conventional. It would be quite easy to see this part of the world as the end of a journey, a place from which you would never wish to depart, rather than its beginning. To be unaware of the hypothetical slippery serpent's slither beneath the façade, its passage smothered by the leaf mold, camouflaged by the mask of social graces.

Someone had been ambiguous and named this cottage *Nightingale's End*. Meaning the nightingale's final destination? Its demise? Or perhaps its home? But actually it's *her* home. Sometimes when she stopped to think about it she supposed she might have escaped from London too. She thought it was definitely a possibility that she may have made a feature of escaping from people along the way. Someone had once, quite rudely she thought, mentioned the overbearing attention of her pushy parents. Perhaps it was more...neglectful, rather than pushy. A simple solution to childcare. She *had* disappeared into hours of practicing the piano. It had reaped its rewards, eventually earning her a place and winning prizes at music college that progressed to opportunities afterward; a series of concerts, promotional tours, appearances at the BBC Promenade Concert series and all the associated publicity, perhaps leading her toward too rapidly ascending the wobbly ladder from obscurity. But it was fortunate timing. The resulting financial independence had allowed her necessary escape from a fellow student, having not realized how deceitful he had been until it came to her notice that he'd maintained a string of equally blindsided girlfriends. One day in the interval at a Festival Hall piano recital, she had bumped into him, when he was supposed to have been elsewhere, with yet another one proudly on his arm. It was the final straw. He may have been charming, verging on the genius, but it wasn't that hard to leave him behind, although it had left its own bleeding wound for a while, one of those aching leaps in growing up that are forced upon everyone from time to time.

It was easier, less damaging, and more rewarding to disappear into work.

Everyone had always assumed that she could cope. She wasn't so sure. And about that time her Mum died suddenly. Her supportive mother, who had only wanted the best for her, or so Alex had always thought then. To see her daughter be able to choose and not be cornered in the way that she had been.

After all that she needed to have a place to hide. And the enclosing canopy of branches afforded by sleepy, Surrey lanes appeared to be the perfect hideaway.

The performing successes attracted agents, one of whom was a high-flying producer, who fought for and secured a decent contract. Subsequently, under the victorious Josh's guidance, she released a series of recordings and a particularly popular Cocktail Pianist disc and at that point it was possible to buy this home, this bolt-hole. Surprising really, this success, even though it had been half-hoped for, idly daydreamed a decade ago. Not an achievement to take for granted either, or so she had been told, in the current competitive music climate where bands fought for media precedence.

And the flip side? She had spent most of her life so far, too long one might say, on her own, hidden away, eroding her too short fingernails down continuously on the keys of a grand piano like some strange hermit, expected to burst forth and shine when required, a butterfly equivalent. The reality being far from glamorous. Missing out on the normal habits of passing into adulthood, having spent too long cooped up with only a piano and a piano teacher for company. Perhaps she really was a social liability. Whenever the potential melting pot of a social gathering or a post-concert party bubbled up, she was not unknown to be inclined to freeze, afraid of saying something stupid or worse, blurt something out to fill the awkward silence, unused to easy-going conversation and the babble of background voices. It is a skill that requires practice too. She knew she tended to be better with people on a one-to-one basis. It was so much easier to interpret what was going on, what the hidden messages were. Perhaps half of her was too shy to fully enjoy the exposure, while the other half was too restless to find life fulfilling without the challenge. Too much time in thought, too much time spent in her own company, enjoying pacing the countryside, planning, traveling. She could spend the whole morning practicing the piano and the whole afternoon strolling the surrounding countryside. So therapeutic. And life had been easier without the added complications of other people. The jealousies and confusions that ensue.

Work had been a consistent friend. The piano her only rock-solid, unchanging companion waiting at home. A demanding housemate, leaving little time for others, but still reliable and infinitely interesting. And the cottage? A place to curl up and hide away from the intrusive alter-ego of that other life.

So, when she had been asked *why* does she prefer to live alone, the answer for her seemed straightforward. *Why* should she *need* to live with anyone else?

CHAPTER TWO

Mazurkas

Broadcasting House had been a peculiar processing experience.

Alex had been greeted in the foyer by a polite, efficient, but rather officious young assistant and escorted up to a waiting area where there was coffee to be had while perusing the proposed list of questions. *Nice to be forewarned.* It was peculiar to watch the human, digital and cellulose cogs of the greater BBC machine whirring sympathetically in motion, people scurrying past carrying wads of paper or tapping mysterious messages.

The producer popped in briefly to verify everything was well and then she was left waiting for a while longer before being ushered in to the recording studio, little more than a large booth. Could she manage to be a fluent socialite today? Fear of stumbling was making her nervous, sick in the pit of her stomach in the way that only a lack of preparation could. Playing was fine, but talking…? The female interviewer greeted her politely enough, chatting to break the ice and then they waited quietly while the introduction was piped through, listening as an excerpt from one of her recordings was played, Alex's heart pounding. Then suddenly, they were recording the interview:

Welcome to my guest today, the pianist Alex Palmer, who is about to head out to Hollywood.

Hello.

We're delighted to have you with us. So what was it like to be invited to one of the most prestigious Oscars parties in town?

Oh, a surprise. A terrific surprise and a pleasant change from my usual commitments.

Different, in what way?

Well…it might sound glamorous to be a busy pianist, but usually it involves a lot of traveling, repetition and…er…hard work. The Oscar Party will be some glitz, with most of the hard work already done. Thank heavens! Although I've given myself extra work arranging some of the film themes for the first set, which was challenging enough.

Sounds inventive. Do you often do that?

Sometimes. A bit of improvising too.

I imagine it's enjoyable to be more spontaneous sometimes.

Yes. But even in the older masterpieces you're living in the moment, being creative at any given point, well, hopefully trying to find some new way of communicating.

And are there any actors you'll be particularly keen to see?

Any of them will do! To be honest, I'm not entirely sure who will be there and I'll be working most of the time. But it would be fun. It will be peculiar to see them in reality. Um, I mean, don't they just exist digitally? Don't they just keep them in little glass boxes and let them out for good behavior or when the right part comes up?

Ha-ha. Well, we hope you meet some A-list stars and can come back to tell us about them. I wouldn't mind meeting a few myself. Perhaps you could help to persuade some in for a discussion!

Not a bad idea, if I can come too. I'd be pleased if my powers of persuasion ever stretched that far.

But I don't suppose you have much time to see films.

Actually I am a huge fan of films, but only of a certain genre. A bit of a romantic, you might say. And I do manage to fit in a few, sometimes there are substantial gaps between rehearsals and concerts, especially on tour.

And music? What styles do you enjoy?

Well, just about anything, if it's good. An eclectic mix. Obviously the material I cover, the sheer wealth of the classical library, but anything else, if it's well done, great songs too. But it would be impossible to choose my desert island discs.

What about the reception of your recent CDs? Do you think that's contributed to your recent success and this party invitation?

We seem to have hit a hole in the market, which is hard to achieve these days. Most things have already been covered. It's harder to be original with such a canon of work from others behind you, but this has expanded my recognition in the States, too. Presumably, that's the tie-in.

I've heard you on the BBC stations, so hopefully we've helped.

You've helped. Thank you. Feel free to keep it up! It's important that people just feel any music is accessible and not that some styles are rarefied, unapproachable subjects, only for the connoisseur. It's relaxing. It transports you to another dimension. You don't have to just fix on one style.

Absolutely and this is what you've been helping to achieve. But this is only part of your US tour?

Actually, separate from it. It came in additionally at the last minute. The tour's already busy with ten concerts over a three-week period on the West Coast.

We wish you luck, of course. It's always great to have a female ambassador for the nation's arts. Has it been a difficult field to break into?

It's hard to say. Reaching the heady heights wasn't the initial aim. You just start and keep going. The success has come progressively and incidentally to the hard work along the way. Lucky really. I'm sure many don't have the right opportunities at the right times.

But you've broken the glass ceiling?

Meaning…?

There aren't that many women at the top of the ladder, are there?

I don't know. I'm hardly at the top. It's a specialist field where women have always had an opportunity. I can think of any number of solo violinists, singers and pianists in particular. It's traditionally an acceptable occupation for a woman or at least an acceptable accomplishment for a woman. There's a history of female musicians and it's not like I'm unique in modern times. But it's not without certain sacrifices.

Sacrifices?

The time involved in being professional. You give up certain more normal ways of spending your spare time.

Such as?

Oh, I don't know specifically. A normal home life. A reliable social life. The ability to keep a pet. But *c'est la vie*. It goes with the territory, the choice.

Who is closest to being your role model then?

Ha! Role model? Er, I suppose that would have to be someone like Clara Schumann. I like the feminist streak there—eight children, an unstable husband and an international career as a pianist, an intriguing lifelong relationship with Johannes Brahms, and considered pianistically as capable as a man. She was a pop star of her day. Maybe not the eight children for me though…and preferably not the desperately ill husband. I don't know how she managed it all. She must have been supremely organized and unbelievably stubborn.

I really admire the quick-wittedness of comediennes too: Sue Perkins over here and Ellen in the States…they're funny, clever and brave all at the same time.

These days it must also help to be a young and good-looking starlet in your field, such as yourself.

Well thank you. (*Laughing*) Er, I am? Um, yes I suppose it helps. It would be ridiculous to think it didn't—but it probably always has been a factor. Everything's about marketing these days. Your appearance has to be good enough to compete with girl bands or the models or the film stars.

Mmm. Looks prevailing…

Yes, it's a bit of a worrying trend—I mean, looks predominating. People want to imagine, perhaps more than they should. The visual impact should be so much more important? Should we not be digging a little deeper for evidence of talent?

Engaging the brain a little more fully? What about the millions of others who don't have that, but have something else amazing to be recognized in them? I'm grateful to be able to walk down the street and not to be recognized. Anonymity has its advantages. There's this headlong race for fame sometimes. You wonder what it's like for some of these actors, not to be able to make a move without someone being fascinated, so well-known that you are recognized absolutely everywhere.

(Laughing) *That's something I can sympathize with, especially when I've had a difficult interview with someone. It's useful to be able to keep your head down.*

Exactly, radio has that too, there's still some privacy to be had. So necessary.

And that's another program's worth of discussion there. One to be considered. Thanks to my special guest today, Alex Palmer, who is shortly on her way to play in Los Angeles, let's give them all one last morsel of what Hollywood's finest will be listening to.

Thanks again. Thanks for having me along.

* * *

It had ended abruptly. The producer's voice was heard: "Marvelous. Well done. Nice and efficient. We'll be airing tomorrow. Wait while we just check something please…"

They waited, listening.

"Okay. That worked. Bravo. Good luck, Alex." That was it.

Her gentle interrogator shook her hand politely. "Well done. That was enjoyable. Perhaps we can have you back when we have a panel discussing some of those issues."

"Fine. That would be interesting. It's been nice to meet you."

"Best of luck on the tour."

And with that, it was done. She was escorted back to the lobby and sent on her way without any further fuss and was suddenly out into the chill air and bright sunshine, with the vague feeling that she may have said too much. She lingered a while in the BBC shop. Had she waffled on a bit? How eternally clever interviewers were at luring out some extra detail. She must bear it in mind for the TV appearance, especially as Ed Smiley was allowed to be cheekier.

She had been back in her house only a few minutes and was starting to catch up on the practicalities of a late lunch when her neighbor knocked at the door, carrying a package. Pauline and her husband, a reliable, wholesome couple, kept an eye on the house for her when she was touring; and when she was home, apparently they enjoyed hearing her music spilling out into the garden, never complaining when she could be heard practicing into the night or early in the morning.

"There you are, dear. This came quite early, but after you left for town."

"Oh hi, how're you? Have some tea."

She took over pouring the tea at the table, while Alex struggled to open the package. Inside was a note from her father and stepmother. They had each written their good luck wishes and sent a tiny digital camera. *A good luck gift from us. See if you can take some interesting pictures while you're away.*

"Oh, aren't they sweet?" Pauline clucked kindly.

"Yes…sweet." Alex turned the camera over in her hands, thoughtfully. "I'm going from midmorning tomorrow. It's a bit of a change of plan, so I'll be dropping the keys in earlier if that's convenient. You might like to take a peek at the Ed Smiley Show tomorrow night. They've thrown it in at the last minute. Oh, yes, and they're airing the Woman's Hour tomorrow morning."

"Lovely, we'll tune in."

"And you have Josh's number and my mobile if you need us. I'll reimburse you if you have to call."

"Of course. Don't you worry about a thing dear—there'll be supplies in the fridge when you get back."

"Thank you. You're always so kind." Her supplies stretched way beyond a pint of milk, to homemade cakes and pies. "I'll bring you something back from the States as a thank you." She knew that quietly they relished their brushes with the edges of her other world, but they could also be relied upon not to communicate private details to strangers.

They settled to their cups of tea, a contrastingly domesticated moment to what would follow over the next few weeks, so removed from the abrasive world of reviews and publicity.

Later the afternoon would need to consist of more practice and Alex would have to finish packing and call her dad to say thanks. They were currently on good terms. It was a complicated history. Marred by the sudden death of her mother some years previously and his overly hasty remarriage. A Cinderella arrangement from which she was thankfully in a position to have escaped. Today she was grateful, appreciative even at the moment, for the early years of obsessive processing by her parents that had steered her toward this career path. This was not always the case.

It has been the lull before the storm. The brief passing luxury of time on her hands. Teetering on the verge of commencing the real roller coaster ride.

CHAPTER THREE

Outward Bound

She spent a blissful afternoon hidden away at the Sanctuary, floating aimlessly round the pool followed by a massage that pummeled places she had forgotten she owned. It was a therapeutic antidote to the anticipatory buzz of the tour and the aching muscles from heaving the large suitcases. How unglamorous traveling threatened to be—again! As the afternoon wore on she found herself reluctant to exchange the white towels for stepping outside, back into the rat race.

Heaven. Thanks, Josh.

When she left and went to pick up her hand luggage from Jenny at the office, she felt warm and limp with relaxation.

Lucky there's a car. I don't think I can move.

* * *

She was completely relaxed after the spa, and ready for her appearance on Ed Smiley. The makeup artist, Hilton ("I know," she explained to Alex's raised eyebrows, "named after the location") commented on her peaceful state as she attempted to tame her unruly hair, which had sprung into coils after the sauna.

Ed blew into the room after a peremptory knock, looking like he had just stepped out of a holiday camp in a bright green suit, spray-tanned with his hair slicked back, stooping to plant an enthusiastic kiss on her cheek.

"Careful," Hilton teased.

"Now, now!" He joked. "You know the format?" he inquired, springing around energetically. "We're the warm-up act today too. I'll introduce you, you can play one of your specialties and then I'll quiz you. Time is of the essence, so John has asked me to do a quick run-through and then we'll take it in one if we can. The audience is drizzling in already. Fabulous dress. You wearing that to the Vanity Fair do?" He nodded toward her strapless indigo gown.

"Not sure." She barely had time to answer, as he gave her the thumbs-up and escaped through the door.

Five minutes later, John had taken her through the moves and the now settled audience had applauded her lighthearted practice of "Twinkle, Twinkle Little Star," not Mozart's or Czerny's version, on the grand piano and she had to go back to the wings to hover for the real thing.

In no time at all it was over. She was actually grateful to breeze through "It's Wonderful," not having had a chance to play all day. The warmth of essential oils and sauna coals floated her through a funny interview, in which Ed joked cheekily that she must have secret Hollywood connections or had slept with someone on the casting couch to gain such an invitation. To which she had answered, "If only…" Going on to explain the demanding toll that her career took on her time. It was harmless banter, coming from him. He was witty and sparkling. It was not hard to see how he maintained his professional reputation as he closed the interview with a dazzling smile and good wishes, drumming up a warm reception from the studio audience. Then they sat there, temporarily like lemons, until John confirmed it was in the can and she could go. After much handshaking and wishing each other well and a good deal of applause, she was whisked on her way, quickly changing, collecting coat and hand luggage from the dressing room and being escorted out to a waiting car.

* * *

Some hours later, after a fitful sleep, Alex awoke, briefly disorientated, wondering where she was.

The noise and chilly air of the plane were a swift reminder. She shook herself awake and went to the bathroom to wash and reapply makeup. She must have been in and out of sleep half the night. Whenever she was half-awake, music ran through her head like an unstoppable recording and her fingers rustled automatically to cover the notes, like a writer feeling the words through an imaginary keyboard. It was a subconscious reaction and her constant, restless companion.

The plane descended smoothly to Los Angeles and she was fortunate to disembark quickly. After only a small delay negotiating baggage and immigration, she was walking through the greeting area, looking out for a sign in the crowds and listening for her name. She glanced at her time-adjusted watch.

Still evening! It would be a long night.

"Alex! Alex!" A voice penetrated through the hubbub of the crowd.

She was intercepted suddenly by a jovial, beaming girl in her twenties—blonde hair bouncing healthily around her face in an enthusiastic welcome. She wrestled the luggage cart from her grip.

"It's so good to see you! Welcome to Los Angeles! We have a car waiting," she bubbled as she led the way through the airport crush, and Alex gratefully followed her away from the noise and hubbub.

"I'm Abi, by the way. Orchestral Assistant for the LA Phil."

"Hi, Josh told me to expect you." They shook hands as they walked.

"That Josh, is he as good-looking as he sounds?"

"Mmm. Better. Probably. Anyway what's the plan? I'm afraid I'm a bit dozy from the flight."

"You can doze if you like. Vladimir, you know, your conductor, is suffering from jet lag and has put tomorrow morning's rehearsal back an hour, so you're not needed until eleven thirty. We'll go straight to the hotel now and your time's your own. There'll be a car for you in the morning, about ten."

By now the cases had been loaded into the car by a chauffeur who could have played American football in a former life and they were settled in the air-conditioned luxury of the back. Alex drifted in and out of Abi's stream of information, taking in glimpses of palm trees and high-rises as they moved away from the drabness of the airport.

At the hotel, Abi deposited her into a plush armchair in the foyer while she checked her in and then escorted her to her room along with her luggage.

"Wow, this is fabulous!" Alex exclaimed as she was let into the balconied suite. There was an immaculate full-size Steinway Grand in the middle of the living area.

"So there you are," Abi said, "hope everything will be to your liking. Here's my card with a direct line if you need me. The hotel management will help with everything. See you tomorrow."

And with a final wave, she was gone.

She was grateful for the sudden silence and solitude. She consulted her watch. Too early to phone the UK yet. Out on the balcony it was cool and the soft light of the day was fading. She checked the room service brochure and ordered a snack. Would it be okay if she practiced, she asked. She was connected to the duty manager, who assured her that the room was specifically soundproofed and that it would be fine. *Excellent.*

She took a shower and changed into a silk nightie. She opened the piano and raised the lid on the short stick. She tried a few scales. It was soft toned and responsive and soon she was engrossed with experimentation and reviewing her memorized repertoire for the next few days.

* * *

Sometime later the phone rang. She picked it up to hear the familiar, soft tone of Josh.

"Hello, sleepyhead. How's it all going?"

"The journey was fine. Comfortable, efficient and Abi was very welcoming and organized. The hotel's great. Thanks."

"Great. Glad to hear it's fine so far. Don't let me keep you. I've sorted you out with a photo shoot for the Oscars in your hotel room, tomorrow afternoon—so you don't have to trek around. They want you for the post-Oscar publicity and gratification."

"Oh, well. Thanks. 'Night then," she ended a little flatly.

"See you."

And so it goes on, she thought. *Best rest up while I can.* She took her glass out onto the balcony and had a passing twinge of regret for her cottage garden, no doubt brought on by the continuous events of the past few days and the contrasting panorama as she looked out over city lights and the scurrying lights of moving cars. And yet exciting too. A city full of ambition.

After a while, she closed up the balcony, drew the thick blackout blinds, switched the bedroom TV on, tracked down a suitable film and nestled under the blankets.

CHAPTER FOUR

Rehearsals

The blackout blinds worked too well. She surprised herself, sleeping late despite a wakeup call and had to rouse herself into action quickly. She snatched mouthfuls of room service breakfast in between scales and dressing. There was a phone call promptly at ten to confirm the waiting car and she grabbed her music bag, a last swig of coffee and fled, still in a disorientated state.

A half-hour's drive in the LA traffic delivered her to the concert hall where she was greeted by Abi and shown to an airy dressing room with a warm-up piano and private bathroom. Abi supplied her with another pot of coffee. She settled down to run over a few passages.

Vladimir Dimitriochev poked his head in during the orchestral break, his long, graying hair flopping around his face. "Sounding marvelous. Greetings darling!" He strode in and hugged her like an old friend, although they had only been introduced once before, at an after-show party.

"Any tricky corners we need to negotiate? Though I'm sure we know Tchaikovsky like the back of our hands, eh?"

She extricated herself cautiously, returned the greeting and then started to point out a couple of the more spacious rubatos that she was planning to take at the end of some of the solo passages.

"And I'm doing the usual cadenzas..." she concluded.

"Of course. One would. Do go onto the stage and take command of your instrument. The orchestra has drifted off, just a couple of horns and an oboe left. Feel free. We start again in ten," he added with a touch of unintentional poetry comically softening his pomposity.

She smiled as he left, the dust almost visibly settling from his whirlwind departure and shortly afterward she followed to try out the piano and the acoustics.

Disney Hall was composed of beautiful wood treatments, an intimate, ultramodern hall. The acoustics were currently sympathetic and reverberant from all the wooden paneling, but she knew it would change when the audience filled it on Monday. She tried the Steinway, a little more brilliant in the high register than she expected, but warm and chocolaty as it descended through the tenor register and into the bass range. The oboist who was still sitting, adjusting his reed, gave her an admiring shuffle with his feet as she flourished through a particularly fiddly passage and then tried out the double octaves. She returned a grin and he freed a hand from his reed-scraping work to give her a thumbs-up sign.

The orchestra was drifting back from its break, some with drinks, tucking them under their seats and picking up instruments. Vladimir bounded back onto the platform, cardigan flapping out like coattails behind him. He made up in energy what he was losing in youth.

"Right. May I introduce Alex Palmer, recently arrived from England?" he called across the orchestra. There was a polite drop in the noise levels and then tapping of bows on stands and light applause from the musicians in welcome. "So, let's get on. Alex would you?"

She played the piano A and the oboe took it, passing it on to the rest of the orchestra, tuning section by section like a wave moving through the place.

Soon all were ready and Vladimir launched himself at the horn section to begin the piece. It was an exciting rehearsal; the orchestral A-list was on, all the best players, and the ensemble was synchronized with the familiarity of years of practice. It was rich, powerfully blended and passionate, the warm, full sound expanding out into the hall. They had only to touch up a few corners—where the syncopated rhythms in the second movement nearly threw out the flute and oboe ensemble and the synchronization of the final tutti with Alex at the end of the first cadenza, as she had not bothered to play the whole thing in the rehearsal.

At the end, Vladimir indicated a bow for her and she called out thanks as the orchestra erupted into applause, not only for her playing, but also for her efficiency enabling the rehearsal to finish early.

"See you all on Monday," Vladimir called out as he pored over the score briefly with Alex. The leader, a dishy, Hollywood-style Californian, patted her on the back and murmured "Fabulous!" into her ear.

She gave him a grin. "Looking forward to Monday," she replied.

Vladimir reminded her, "I'll only need you at five on Monday; we don't want to do the whole thing. Too exhausting and this was excellent. And there's the reception after the concert for the sponsors, so I'll see you there too?"

She agreed and they parted company.

Back at her hotel room pandemonium had broken out. Her anticipated oasis was heaving with photographers, a lighting setup and a fussing interviewer. Flowers had been arriving during the morning and were stacking up on any available surface.

"Adorable," the interviewer purred, hurrying forward as she came in. "The flowers are a great backdrop. So pleased to meet you. Are you changing right away? Your dress would make a perfect working shot at the piano…"

The manager was at the door. He beckoned her over.

"So sorry, ma'am. They insisted they had permission through Joshua Pembroke, and I tried to hold them off, but she insisted we call him and he said he had confirmed it all with you."

She smiled weakly and shrugged. He gave her a salute and tapped his watch, indicating that he would call back in an hour to keep things brief.

She endured several different dresses and angles and an interview which repeated many of the same old questions, but tried hard to link her with famous Hollywood names. The mother-hen interviewer was soon happily clucked out and ushered away by the manager, again issuing his apologies for the intrusion and she closed the door gratefully.

She went for a delicious shower in the marble bathroom. After slipping on the prerequisite white hotel robe, she drifted around the room admiring the flowers and reading the cards.

One from the LA Phil, Josh, and her father had sent her an Interflora basket with more good luck wishes, there were greetings from Vanity Fair and then her heart thudded a beat—a typewritten card which said, "*Are you feeling beautiful tonight?*" Anonymous. She scrabbled through the flowers for an explanatory note. Nothing. Feeling a little disgusted, she tore up the card and took the display out of her room to a little nook in a nearby corridor.

* * *

Sunday dawned in a more leisurely fashion. She breakfasted on the balcony in her robe, enjoying the fact that no one could see her. The rest of Saturday she had frittered away, secluded in her room and catnapping with jet lag. Today she thought she would be a little more adventurous. She should not let her feelings be dented by some weirdo without the confidence to confront her directly. It was peculiar that the sender knew her hotel, but perhaps it had been sent via the LA Phil. Even their website was publicizing her trip. She spent the morning on the beach, watching some die-hard surfers searching for decent waves. The air was cool but still, the breaking waves comforting. While she rolled the fine sand through her hands, listening to the regular click, click of the Rollerblading on the promenade, the red carpet was being unrolled, nailed and tapped into place elsewhere in the city. Later she lunched at the hotel café and spent an hour window-shopping on Rodeo Drive, which was relatively busy. Perhaps the fans were out hunting for the stars given the events of the weekend. Only once she thought she saw someone who could be famous, hidden behind large sunglasses and a baseball cap, being ushered away by a heavy security minder from a boutique to a waiting car. Certainly the willowy frame of the girl was appropriate to the fashions of the profession. Somebody was snapping at her from behind a camera and the minder held up a warning hand. God! How nice it was to be reasonably successful, but fairly unrecognizable. What must it be like to have your fame quite literally written all over your face? Why did kids today feel such a desperate need to become famous quickly, be on TV—have the whole world know who you are and the context of your life, every time you step out onto the street? It was too trusting to assume that everyone who knew you would be a level-headed, sensible human being who would wish you well.

She had opted out of the walk-through rehearsal for the party; no one deemed it necessary for her to prepare her part; and there would be a quick soundcheck later instead. The rest of the afternoon was free to be spent with practice, lazing in the bath and quietly preening in front of the televised Oscar ceremony opening. Taking supper in her room, she watched the stars arriving on the red carpet, enjoying deciding whether she liked their outfits or not—too colorful, too ostentatious and so on. Funny to think she might see them later. Many looked astonishingly svelte and relaxed—difficult to achieve one would think. It would require unbelievable self-confidence—or presumably the ability to act!

The phone rang.

"Front desk, madam. Your car's here." After too much of this, she knew she would start to miss the independence of her own dear little car, tucked up in the driveway at home.

She tinkled the first few notes of "You Say Either" as she passed the piano, adjusted her hair as she passed the mirror and grabbing a clutch bag, she left.

CHAPTER FIVE

First—Night Fear. March.

The air was crackling, charged with a tension that lingered in the room, awaiting the arrival of the film world's elite.

Despite jet lag and the ridiculously ostentatious venue, Alex was feeling relieved to be here at last, the adrenaline of the occasion buoying her up, coursing through her veins, momentarily outweighing the burden of expectation.

The band was pouring out a dance number, still concerned with checking the balance and sound levels. *Impressive, tightly knit.*

The overwhelming dazzle of the room required some rapid deciphering. Various people were scurrying around, perfecting the finer details of the occasion, laying tables, tending to ice sculptures, while someone clung to a ladder adjusting the lighting, directed attentively from beneath by a woman with power-heels and a managerial air, who was repeatedly glancing at her bracelet watch and a clipboard.

The shoes and the healthy Californian legs caught her attention.

When she became aware of being watched, she hurried across, extending an effusive handshake, introducing herself confidently. "Hello, honey! I'm Deborah. Let's get you settled in."

She bustled up to the bandleader and gesticulated to him through the noise. He held up his hands, turning toward Alex with a disarming grin and hushed the band, which chose to wheeze down amusingly like an expiring accordion. The bass trombone blew a few rude notes and several wolf whistles trilled as he grasped her in a massive bear hug. It seemed appropriate to play along, so she fell into role, curtseying and batting her eyelids in Monroe-like pretense, apparently pleasing them if the ripple of appreciation was anything to go by.

"Take a break guys. Alex has to check the piano and warm up. Good luck, gal."

As the band slunk away, she plumped down at the piano. Dropping her bag habitually by the piano leg, she ran her fingers over the keys and without further ado launched into "It's Wonderful," her opening offering, while some disembodied controller somewhere appeared to experiment with the lighting effects, the spots darting and flickering around. The warm-toned piano was easy to acclimatize to.

So the sequined dress was a worthwhile decision. That part of her which accepted the necessity for these things noticed it sparkling, catching the lights out of the corner of her eye. To keep any dark tendrils from intruding themselves, she had tied her hair up high into a tight bun for the evening, vaguely attempting an elegant appearance.

Deborah effectively had abandoned her, disappearing back to other pressing matters.

Someone called out, "Great! Something soft and slow now!" She obliged with the beginning of "Misty."

The remote voice called: "You'll do. Wind it up when you're ready!" A brusque cue for her dismissal and after a few more flourishes to test out the instrument, it seemed appropriate for her to exit stage left without further fanfare.

There was no dressing room, just a communal area for the band in a side room where the haphazardly discarded instrument cases and several of the musicians were still loitering. She tucked her bag unobtrusively into a corner behind a curtain.

Kitchen staff hurried up and down a further corridor, juggling trays balanced with glasses and various delicacies. No one seemed to have a moment to spare or explain, contrary to the mollycoddling she was used to, so she hunted down a bathroom and then a flight of stairs, a route to the outside world to gasp a few last breaths of air. Unexpectedly, she stepped out into a semicircle of some of the band members who stood smoking in an intimidating-looking group in a small outside garden. They broke into encouraging smiles.

"Good gig!" one called with a warm, Californian lilt.

"Yes, amazing! Can't wait to see how it pans out. It's my first. Oscars, I mean." She petered out. It was social entrapment, but at least they were making an effort to be pleasant.

"They'll offer hospitality later. You'll see, they're just busy now," explained another. "We hear you're on with the Phil tomorrow?"

She nodded. "Yes. That's right. Something a bit different…"

"They're great—you'll love it. Anyway we'd better look lively, as they say on your side of the pond. See you on the ice."

"Thanks. I'm looking forward to hearing you all." She stepped hurriedly out of their circle, eager to escape, attempting to appear nonchalant even though there was no need: they had made the encounter pleasant enough. As they finished the remainder of their cigarettes, she experimented with a few pacing turns along the paths, an attempt to cover a lack of anything else to do and then headed for the stairs again.

Deborah, now without her clipboard, was fussing in the corridor.

"Oh, there you are. We're close to launch time. Let's make you at home. A glass of champagne?"

Launch time! Hah! Her stomach plunged over a cliff. "Just a half," she suggested. *Take the edge off, relax, but still feel the fingers.*

She smiled to herself at the familiar feeling of anxiety, relieved Deborah of the glass and settled at the piano, ready to play. People scuttled around finishing their tasks and assuming more formal positions. Her blood throbbed, just as much as at the opening tutti of a concerto, sending encouraging, pulsing warmth down to her fingertips.

It was always *the waiting* to play the first notes that became so full of dread and expectation. Something like waiting for the launch of the space shuttle, *probably, maybe, well, sort of.* Although considerably less expensive, or potentially life-threatening. Would the preparations work? Was she really this musical person? Once the initial liftoff was underway, then the technical detail could become all-consuming with a growing sense of relief that yes, actually she did know these notes intimately, that the careful preparation had paid off and her own skepticism would evaporate. That this instrument at her fingertips was her familiar, intimate friend. Something to be caressed and coaxed. She knew it would happen that way, it was just the waiting that grew excruciating. And an error would not cause loss of life, she reminded herself. She was *not* the surgeon with scalpel poised. There was no need to be a perfectionist about it. It was, after all, meant to be entertainment. She continued talking herself silently into it. She needed to feed off a sympathetic audience. If they were listening, onside, then she might be able to enjoy it. But they would probably be more occupied with their own concerns tonight, well, perhaps that would be more relaxing, just to be the wallpaper this time.

She could almost see the foyer from her position. Someone, who had been audibly notching down the minutes to curtain up, suddenly called "Positions! First car!"

Deborah gave a nod from her position in the welcoming committee; so Alex stowed the glass by the piano leg, flexed her fingers, took a deep breath and launched this performance. The press flashlights began to light the lobby entrance, producing a microclimate of an electrical storm as the first meteoric guests started to arrive. The lights swooped unsubtly over the keys, reflected by the many mirrors, potentially distracting and annoying. Concentrating a little harder to overcome this, playing by feel rather than sight, she sank gratefully into the music, unable to take time out to look away, feeling her erratic heartbeat settle; this opening, upbeat number was a demanding and complicated arrangement, modulating into remote keys. Peripherally, she noticed bodies filling the room, various colors and an increasing noise level, but it was her role to establish the mood, as if it had been there forever. It was not the time, or indeed at all possible, to break concentration at this point. She looked abstractly at the fingers flying over the keys. Briefly the thought crossed her mind that they must belong to someone else. Physical memory. What a wonderful thing! The notes had long ago become automatic. They seemed to be doing someone else's bidding of their own accord, instructed by some other external harddrive. *Focus.*

Toward the end of the number she became aware of a blonde girl, vaguely familiar, leaning gracefully in toward the piano.

"Love your dress, darling," the girl murmured above the background noise.

It took a second to realize that this svelte figure was addressing her and another second to find a moment to glance over.

"That's pretty amazing," the girl continued. Alex could see the gold of her dress, reflecting in the polished black of the grand. "Did you write it yourself?"

She hiccupped mid-arpeggio, but covered it and doodled for a moment to give herself time to answer: "Actually Gershwin, I had the great idea, he helped a little."

"Marvelous," the girl breathed, as she drifted away.

Alex glanced sideways and caught the bandleader smirking at her from the wings, so she sidled seamlessly into "You Say Either" to amuse him, causing him to send a conspiratorial wink over in her direction. There were vague glimpses of the gorgeous as they arrived, but the room was soon heaving, the volume increasing with the babble of voices and clinking of glasses being filled and toasted. It was hard to tell who might be there. Once or twice she thought she had glimpsed a legendary face from the corner of her eye, which threatened to be distracting, it being unavoidable to glance again, trying to catch a side view moving through the crowd. She wound up the piece, pausing to take a sip of the champagne from the hidden glass and stretch out. Some of them must have been listening, or at least aware of the sudden absence of the background atmosphere, as a ripple of polite applause rustled through the chattering and clinking. She smiled generally out at them, grateful for the acknowledgment, feeling the peculiar shocks of familiarity at some of the iconical faces.

Replacing the glass, she thought it seemed a suitable time to try the film music arrangement. After a flourishing introduction, it merged into a slightly disguised version of the main theme from *Disillusionment*, which had been up for the most nominations, coincidentally including the music, probably having won several awards. She had no way of knowing at this point. As recognition dawned on some of the listeners, an appreciative wave of applause swept through the room. Increasing the dynamic level, she modulated the music through some unexpected keys and started weaving in the love theme from *The Second Eclipse*, linking into dramatic moments from *Annie's Obsession*, alleviated later by lighter themes from the shorts and animations. The noise level in the room was increasing as some began to recognize the themes and played at placing them, others using it as an opportunity to break into conversation and network. This was the longest of the pieces and at the end, it was easy to slip into a disguised arrangement of "I Did It My Way," feeling it would be suitable for the jostling egos on such a night as this.

At the end of the set, there was an enthusiastic burst of applause. *Success enough*. She stood up and took a playful curtsey, mouthing *Thank you*. Perhaps it had not all been considered wallpaper.

The night's master of ceremonies professed his thanks and while he launched into the evenings proceeding's, further gratitude and congratulations, Alex was escorted out to the bar and through to the kitchen area for refreshments.

The glamorous Deborah indicated that it would be another hour or so before she would be on again, and a little wearily, realizing an encroaching headache was setting in, she pressed the cooling glass of champagne to her temple. In this position she was heading slowly out toward the band room, when she was knocked on the elbow and forced to spill some of the drink as someone bustled through.

Damn.

The rushing figure called a vague, dismissive "Sorry!" but disappeared at speed without further hesitation.

At least it wasn't red wine on a pale dress. She pulled up a chair, kicking off her shoes, and tried to peek through the curtain to people watch, still dabbing the drink from the front of her dress. Counting famous faces she could name, Robert, Keira, Johnny, Michael, Helen…she had reached sixteen when astonishingly she spotted…her! *Joanne.* That was her name, wasn't it? *Joanne Davison.* The face that had smiled so beguilingly from her screen at home. The very night Josh had rung with the news that she was being invited here. The sudden recognition prickled at her, sending a sympathetic shiver across her body. She was standing confidently in a group, elegantly dressed in a slim, silver gown, her hair cut into an unfamiliar, pixie style. Something of a mixture of Tilda Swinton's characterful quirkiness and Liv Tyler's grace, Alex thought. And yet very much herself too. She was listening to the announcements, laughing and clapping appropriately and from time to time ducking her head down to be whispered to by a variety of other guests. It was not the equally gorgeous men in the group that caught her attention she noticed vaguely, a subconscious thought she was used to making and generally ignoring. Something that simmered, but was best filed away. She rested her elbow on her knee, sighing like a teenager and settled in to watching her, drinking in the alluring body language, the strangely familiar expressions, the startling clear eyes, speculating on the size of the ego that would go with such adulation. *How peculiar to see someone so familiar and yet unfamiliar. So absolutely beautiful...*Aware that this was the sentiment that could only contribute to any inherent narcissism. From behind her curtain, Alex could watch her as if through the privacy of her own screen, admiring every nuance of expression and the finely chiseled figure, wondering whether she was conscious of the magnetic effect she had on people. It was a suitable distraction from her own throbbing head. *Of course, she must be. She must have heard it a thousand times. My own private showing.* She grinned to herself: it was not possible to interfere with the remote and put everything on slow playback here.

Then unexpectedly she looked over. Caught in the act of grinning and staring made Alex jump in surprise as she beamed the miraculous, full smile in her direction, held Alex's amazed gaze for a moment and laughed. She dropped the curtain in astonishment, paralyzed in the headlights, the privacy of her former viewing breached. Her heart pounded in momentary shock and embarrassment. Her screen at home had not looked back! When she dared to look again Joanne was moving on, turning away, her group melting into the crowded room. She looked quickly back over her shoulder, a serious expression flitting briefly across her face, but Alex couldn't be sure at what. Had she caused some offense? Wasn't it rude and terribly passé to stare at these people? Then the moment was gone and she twitched the curtain closed.

Unbelievable! That person, actually alive and moving, not just doing the pre-designated moves, carved, rehearsed to perfection. The band was starting its set. Her thudding head threatened to overwhelm the proceedings, so she closed her eyes to rest the embryonic migraine. For once jet lag was a bonus. Tonight it would be helpful to be kept awake into the early hours of the morning.

As the evening progressed into its comfortable zone, she was ushered onto the stage again. The party had changed its mood by now. Formalities were over and couples were slow dancing, so it seemed suitable to launch into a more mellifluous, mellow set including "Misty," "Someone to Watch Over Me," "The Street Where You Live," later rounding off with "A Foggy Day in London Town" and "A Nightingale Sang in Berkeley Square," which was often her signature for the end of the evening. As the tempo was much slower, she was able to indulge in occasional celebrity spotting along the way, when notes would permit, and ticked off a few well-known couples and less well known couplings.

And then she was finished. *It's done.*

Someone thanked her over the sound system and there was warm applause as the still-immaculate Deborah came up onto the stage with an Oscar replica, cut in crystal. A ripple of laughter murmured around as she was advised to be careful with its fragile quality and there was more applause as she was wished well on the rest of the tour, "which begins tomorrow night right here in LA."

Deborah nearly had to catch her as she stepped off the stage—not entirely an unpleasant possibility—as her legs were collapsing with tiredness. Alex politely excused herself from socializing and further refreshments, masking her exhaustion, almost unable to speak beyond the required civilities or through the smile professionally frozen into position on her face, claiming her commitments the following day as the excuse to go, asking for the car back.

Unbelievably weary when she reached the hotel, having passed unobtrusively, unwanted thankfully, through the minefield of autograph-hunters—they were not looking for her—with leaden legs and ominously aching fingers, she paced cautiously across the lobby, each step engendering a responsive throb of the head, feeling that the associated glamour of the evening was completely lost on her. *Her* life was so much more isolated, dull, disciplined than all that.

She pulled the grips out of her hair as she trudged, in an attempt to release the headache, massaging her hair back down into its usual vague shape.

What was she thinking! *No! Actually more real and less insane than all that! It must be tiredness. How could one possibly wish for this carousel?*

She felt the tension lighten slightly in her now released scalp.

In all honesty she wondered whether she could possibly recover the energy to manage the following day's concert, which was actually more important and enduring. Had it been a moment of stupidity, a whim to accept performing at this party? The evening had been fun, amusing, but so long, and it had the tinge of associated servitude. It was only the fee and the prestige that raised it above. That was the musician's lot at the end of the day: just being the entertainment.

And yet she felt strangely…flat that it was over. This must be the paradox that drenched this branch of the industry. A desire to succeed, proven by adulation, constantly offset by a need for privacy that without adulation becomes fear. It was something she felt a little, but probably to a lesser degree. Now a soft, cool pillow was the only goal.

The door of the lift was about to slide shut and enclose her in welcome solitude and peace, when someone pressed again outside and caught the doors before they closed.

Typical. She sighed quietly at the extra delay. They stepped inside, but because she was avoiding the effort of further human contact, and the painfully bright ceiling lights, and staring at her hands which were clutching her bag, it took her a moment to look up.

When she did, she was amazed as if caught in a movie still, alarmed even, to see it was her, Joanne, and she was staring with those remarkable, analytical eyes sparkling in some polite amusement, suddenly unexpectedly, uncomfortably close.

"Hullo," she said, grinning and holding out her hand. "I'm Jo. Fellow Brit."

"Yes. Alex." She took the hand, shaking it lightly, altering the astonished expression that she knew she must have been wearing into a faint smile. Apparently she was not in for a telling off.

Her hand fell to her side, tingling with unexpected sensitivity. Jo's hand disappeared behind her back and she leaned onto it against the mirrored wall of the capsule. She looked slightly disheveled now, as if she had run her hands through her hair a few times, the belt of her dress loosened, dangling limply at her sides. Strangely less intimidating.

"I know," she said.

It was peculiar to hear the crisp, London accent.

She was thinner, smaller than Alex had imagined, compact, but elegant, her features surprisingly defined in her face, presumably what helped to make it so...photogenic.

"You were great by the way. Great piano playing." She pulled the hand out again and emphasized this with a wiggle of her fingers. She looked a touch weary, the smile a little faded around the eyes now. *Like me.* Alex glanced in the mirror and tucked an unruly piece of hair behind her ear. The lift doors closed and their metallic cubicle began its upward glide.

"Thanks!" Alex replied, adding lamely with a shrug, "It's what I do."

"Yes, I had a feeling..."

"Oh. Of course."

Oh, conversation. Her thoughts threatened to domino unhelpfully and she felt the need to excuse her odd behavior. "I'm sorry, I'm a bit weary, I've only recently arrived and I'm on with the Phil tomorrow night, something a bit different, Tchaikovsky. That's why I had to escape immediately."

Jo appeared to be relieved to overcome the monosyllabic replies. "Me too. Arrived recently and an appointment in the afternoon. Not Tchaikovsky, obviously. More Fellini." She chuckled, consulting a delicate wristwatch. "This afternoon. I need some sleep. It shows if I don't have enough! Isn't jet lag a pain in the butt?"

Alex laughed too, immediately liking her more for the disarming honesty. "I know the feeling. Should I congratulate you, by the way?"

"Congratulations? Well I suppose. I didn't win it myself, but the film won a few."

"Oh. That's similar though, isn't it? You carry the film, even if you don't win best…" Her words tailed off, aware of treading on potentially sensitive subject matter. "Well done anyway. I was too tied up this afternoon to find out what was going on."

"I don't mind." She shrugged.

The lift stopped and opened on a middle floor, interrupting her awkwardness. Neither of them moved. The doors closed again and the lift continued up. It wasn't over yet.

"Looks like we both have suites then." Jo smiled.

"I hope I haven't been disturbing you with my playing. They told me the room was soundproofed."

"Haven't heard a thing. I'm only here tonight. But listen…I was just thinking," she began talking rapidly, as if anxious to fit it all in, "I don't know if it's an imposition to ask…and I've left it a bit late…just wondered…Spit it out Jo…" she ordered herself. Alex smirked, enjoying the unscripted, oh-so-human-struggle for the right words. "I'm having a bit of a party at the place we've rented for the next couple of weeks. I loved the atmosphere tonight when you played. What I'm trying to say is: who do I speak to, to find out if you're available to do private parties?"

Wow. A thrill went through Alex, the former sullenness and exhaustion evaporating. Josh's voice echoed intrusively: *Take every opportunity*…as if she needed *that* advice!

"Well, me actually." She bypassed Josh easily. "I'm on tour, so I do have some commitments. You mean you have one coming up?" She nodded. "When is it?"

"Tuesday night. Short notice, I'm afraid. I hadn't given it a thought until…"

She tailed off. But Alex was lost in her own rapid calculations. Tuesday night was free.

"I'm available. It depends what it involves." She attempted, perhaps unsuccessfully, to sound casual. "Why don't you finalize it tomorrow. Oh, I mean later today." She was laughing nervously again. "You know…after some sleep. I'm in the Ruby Suite."

"Great!" And with that, the lift doors opened again, Jo shook her hand once more, those alert eyes reading Alex closely, raising the other hand in a brief wave of acknowledgment while smiling part of that strangely familiar smile and they went their separate ways.

And finally I meet a real one when I'm almost speechless with exhaustion. Amazing, only in Hollywood could the truth be the same as fiction: that they really do exist—that you can bump into them in hotel lifts. And that you get asked to their parties. That's just not normal.

She would have expected these superstars to be at some glamorous, all-night party, not returning exhausted to their hotel rooms, like her. She re-ran the conversation as she walked away. Perhaps the LA glamour was not yet over. Her headache was fading. The anticlimactic feelings had lifted. She looked at her hand and flexed the still tingling, aching fingers again. Who was she kidding? Jo…she was gorgeous.

* * *

Alex was trapped. In the terrifying, escapeless way that dreams hold you, her feet weighed down. Trying every side door. It was some sort of cruise ship or was it a hotel? Or perhaps a weird, confused film set? There were too many people for the amount of available space and more were arriving, overcrowding, cramming themselves in, choking the enclosed area. There were cameras and lights everywhere. As if observed from every angle, each time she reached for a door handle she could hear a bolt snap shut above the background noise of the constant voices. Controlled externally. Her father and stepmother were sitting happily at a dinner table. They grinned as if everything was…ordinary. But the amount of people! Enough to drown in! They were pressing in, now trying to engage her in meaningless inaudible conversation, as if unaware of the impending disaster. They were becoming louder and more brightly colored, more

threatening and persistent and she was starting to panic…
claustrophobia setting in. One more door handle, surely this
would be the one. She tried it…

Suddenly a familiar sense of relief flooded through her as
she became able to step out of the dream…

CHAPTER SIX

But Truth is Stranger

Thankfully, she slept until very late, the blackouts cutting out any natural light. She stretched cautiously into action, rubbing the fading remnants of some bad dream or other from her face, beginning the day reluctantly, first calling for breakfast and then creeping tentatively to the shower to thaw the last of the night's sleep away. *So good to have a lie-in.*

Her body still ached. Last night, when she had felt *that* tired, it had not been possible to envisage launching into such a massive piece as the Tchaikovsky under concert conditions. At least now she felt refreshed, well almost, the headache fading. *How peculiar to be beneath the same roof as the film stars.* The lingering alarm of claustrophobia drifted somewhere. Perhaps that was how it felt to be *that* famous. To be harassed by the fans, who had let her pass through so easily? How peculiar to be watched, hunted. A shiver passed through her.

Under the shower she felt herself relaxing. It was mostly a relief, but also a vague feeling of disappointment that the Oscar party hype was over, although somewhere the excitement about something unknown yet to come still bubbled.

She was deeply thankful not to be needed until five p.m.

Vladimir, bless you! A change of mind-set was needed for tonight. And yet...there was another party to consider. The hand that had been shaken in the lift last night tingled with memory. *So strange, almost another dream.* She grinned again, enjoying the feeling of the soap over her skin and the warm water streaming soothingly through her hair.

* * *

It was late in England, too late to call Josh. Perhaps she would text him to give him a quick summary. He loved a little gossip. It might be best to abbreviate the details. She would just drift the afternoon away and begin exercising her fingers for the concert. Surely most of Hollywood would be dozing off the aftereffects as well.

The hotel sent up an American brunch and she tucked gratefully into the selection—bacon, waffles, eggs, fruit salad, orange juice—*A concerto needs stamina!* A respected teacher's orders from the past hung at the back of her mind somewhere.

It was no effort to laze the afternoon away, topping up with coffee and tea from the little kitchen and coaxing her fingers back into the required nimbleness. By three, it was time to prepare for the outside world and she packed a suit bag for the concert, stuffing in a wash-bag, makeup and more carefully, something to wear for the hospitality afterward. This was familiar territory, performed hundreds of times before.

The phone rang at ten to four to inform her that her car was waiting and it was time to depart for the concert hall.

* * *

Vladimir called her "our little Hollywood starlet" as she walked out onto the stage for rehearsal. She grinned sheepishly, to shuffles and matey cheers from the orchestra. The rehearsal was barely mediocre compared to the first thorough session earlier in the weekend, just a top-and-tail of the concerto to save energy for later, even for Vladimir. He did not appear to mind the slightly muted attempts, although he ticked the woodwind off for some intonation and balancing issues and asked them to shake the weekend out of their ears, much to the foot-shuffling appreciation of some of the string players.

* * *

Several hours later the house was packed and eager, perhaps with those looking for some alternative culture to the Oscar weekend. Viewed from the stage, the audience appeared to be one living sea of bobbing heads, mostly muted colors, highlighted occasionally by an adventurous flash of canary yellow or scarlet. The concerto, positioned at the end of the first half was received enthusiastically, the orchestra having recaptured its power and volume. Somehow accuracy and strength had returned, a surprising resurrection given Alex's earlier state of mind and the late night. Judging the audience to be serious about their music and not prepared for an Oscar-style joke, she chose a brief encore of an abridged, delectable Field Nocturne. Huge applause followed with a bouquet brought by Abi, the orchestral assistant, stunning in an evening dress, for the orchestra leader to deliver with a brief kiss signifying the end of her playing efforts, at least for *this* evening. The formalities tonight did not allow for a wolf whistle from the band, thankfully, but she curtsied gracefully to the orchestra and conductor acknowledging their gargantuan efforts.

* * *

Soon she was back in the comparative peace of the dressing room, with Abi flitting around, arranging several bouquets in vases.

"We might as well leave them here ready for Thursday night. Well played, Alex," she commented comfortingly, leaving her thankfully, albeit briefly alone, her heart rate returning to normal, her body feeling typically somewhat leeched of vitality.

She was her own worst critic. Already she was picking through the details of the performance.

There followed another knock on the door and Vladimir surged in, moistly embracing her with a damp kiss on each cheek.

The room was suddenly too small.

"Bravissimo, darling! You were towering. It was on fire, don't you think!" he gushed.

"Yes, yes. You were too—keeping that talented rabble together."

"Ah, they'd probably do it without me, but yes! I ignited the furnace. But I must fly, darling. I have a *Fourth Symphony* to prepare! I'll see you at the reception!"

"Yes! Absolutely!"

And with that he pivoted on the spot, beads of sweat flying off in all directions and was gone. The room was pleasantly empty again. She flicked the door lock, threw a grimace at her reflection and flopped into an armchair, happy to shut out the rest of the world and started to peel off her concert dress. Passages of the concerto still bubbled through her mind, niggling her with reminders of slight imperfections. The tiring weekend threatened to catch up. But it had been all right, despite the fatigue from the party, her performance had been acceptable, more than that.

A further knock at the door interrupted her musings.

"Blast." She pulled the shoulder strap up again halfheartedly, went to unlock. *Oh well, it's to be expected.* She was still thinking this thought when she gasped, astonished, grabbing her dress more fully into position.

It was Jo! Again! The familiar features in the flesh shocking once more.

"I wasn't expecting *you*!"

"No. Probably not. Good evening anyway. Hope you don't mind." She stood there gracefully, ignoring the exclamation, but not without a hint of nervousness, in the doorway, keeping a watch back down the corridor. There was something vulnerable, endearing about the unrehearsed chink in this perfect armor.

Alex sensed the implication for privacy. "I'm just a little surprised." Wanting badly to excuse her rudeness, cover her surprise. "Come in."

"Thanks. Bravo by the way." She stepped in, closing the door.

"Thanks," Alex replied and then performed an unintentionally comical double take as she said, "You were listening?"

Jo's eyes sparkled mischievously, she was enjoying the effect of her words. "Yep. Bit of a fan actually. I was in the balcony. Last-minute tickets."

"A fan of Tchaikovsky?"

"Mmm. He's…capacious," she replied thoughtfully, seeming to struggle for the right word, stroking an earring.

Something tingled unexpectedly. There was an awkward pause.

"So, I'm sorry I didn't make contact regarding that party?" she began hopefully.

"Oh don't think twice about it. It's been a busy day in a busy week. I slept really late."

"Me too." She paused again. "Listen, would you like to go for a drink in the upstairs bar now? We could hammer out the arrangements. I'm not bothered about seeing the second half."

Alex thought for a moment, taken a little off guard by this completely out-of-context appearance, attempting to suppress a little leap for joy.

"Erm…I think that'll be fine…but I'll see you there in a minute. I need to…shower and change." She petered out lamely, preferring not to explain the private moment. It made her defensive. "How did you get backstage by the way? I'm surprised they let you in."

As if instinctively sensing her unease, she concluded the conversation. "Ah, well, recognition has its bonuses sometimes. Right, see you up there?"

"Sure, give me a moment." She held the door for Jo. When it closed, she caught her slightly annoyed expression in the mirror, her face surrounded by the Medusa-like escaping strands of hair, realizing that it had probably showed plainly that she was touchy to be intruded upon in a disheveled state. *It's just too familiar coming in here. With no warning. Even if she is famous. Doesn't that just reek of assumption?* She was muttering all this to herself as she started slipping the dress off properly this time, trying to convince herself that any trembling was linked only to this annoyance.

* * *

Jo was perched gracefully at a barstool in the gallery bar with two glasses of pink champagne lined up. The place was conveniently deserted. She uncrossed her elegant legs to stand up as she glimpsed Alex approaching and indicated a more private armchair arrangement in an enclosed corner. She was casually dressed in evening slacks and a tailored shirt, glimpses of a slim, toned body pressing at the fabric. Refreshed by the shower, Alex felt an unexpected twinge, a dart of pleasure at seeing her, any irritation beginning to dissolve; pleased too that there was a special effort being made for her here. Starting to hope that they could be friends. *Let it be, Alex.*

The members of the audience were back in their seats for the symphony. There was a ripple of incidental applause from the intercom indicating that the leader had returned to the platform and then a louder surge, presumably as Vladimir took his position.

Jo threw a winning smile in her direction as they settled into the armchairs. "So this is a bit of a leap from the lift."

"Yes, and...unexpected." The first bars of the symphony drifted from the speakers, slightly distorted. She passed over a glass, clinking it gently with hers. As Alex sipped she realized how much she needed the cool, still bubbling liquid, sliding around her parched mouth and down her dry, and, she realized, slightly sore throat.

She thought her stiffness must have been obvious even though she was trying to contain it.

Jo cut the silence. "I *am* sorry to have intruded upon you suddenly."

It was a well-delivered line, taking the words unintentionally from Alex's thoughts, the air from her self-inflated sails. She no longer felt quite the stunned rabbit in the glow of Jo's headlights or quite so annoyed; the relief to have the first tour performance successfully completed was infusing itself through her body with the passage of the champagne.

"Yes, well…I'm not always at my best immediately afterward. I can be…moody. Or so my manager tells me. Thanks for the drink. I didn't realize how thirsty I was. Playing a concerto is so massive, exhausting, like running a marathon, I suppose. I'm no expert. Not at the running. Except that my arms are aching, instead of my legs. I think it makes you equally breathless." She felt herself babbling. Jo sat and watched, a smile growing on her lips, apparently amused at her performance. She was quietly observing her with those startling green eyes, her features easily, openly revealing the state of mind within. Those eyes had a very fine ring of brown and yellow around the edge of the iris, Alex noticed. She felt herself defrosting.

"Sorry if I was curt in the dressing room," she continued, hardly pausing for breath. "Despite the Oscar party, I didn't expect to be drinking with a…film star. Least of all have one knocking at my dressing room, when I was frankly feeling…a bit shagged—"

"Hah! Very funny!" Jo interjected. "It was a bit abrupt. I would have sent a message, but notes can be weird, unpredictable. I'm not keen on the paper trail." Alex's skin prickled at the idea. "And you might not have come."

"You send notes?" Alex inquired.

"No. It's generally considered bad form, isn't it? I have some peculiar ones sometimes."

Alex exhaled suddenly as if she had been unintentionally holding her breath. "I know what you mean."

Jo raised an eyebrow quizzically.

"Never mind," she added, seeking to change the subject. The bar was pleasantly desolate. "Good call coming up here."

"I'm a bit of a dab hand at avoiding the crowds when I can. As you can probably imagine…it's preferable."

"I should think so. Weren't you mobbed for autographs at the hotel last night?"

"Actually not. There's another way in. You?"

"They don't recognize me or at least they weren't looking for me…"

"Lucky you! That has its advantages, you know. So, as I was saying earlier…this party. You thought tomorrow night would be possible? Could you add a touch of your glamour to our gathering?"

"My glamour? Ha! My turn to laugh. My glamour pales into insignificance beside yours."

"Will we be getting over this 'film-star' thing soon?" she asked a little pointedly, frowning prettily, and after a moment's thought adding quietly, "I'm not exactly perfect…don't ever confuse what I do with what you see in front of you now. I'm under no illusions. It's mostly a marketing myth."

"Mm. I'll try…Are we talking professional piano playing here?" *You flirt, Alex.*

"Well, yes." Jo recovered her former bonhomie and in the style of an advertisement voice-over added, "However, all other forms of glamour are acceptable and gratefully received."

Alex giggled at her, now enjoying *her* performance. "That would be lovely. I'm a free agent tomorrow night, as opposed," she looked at her watch, "to tonight. Reception after the concert," she explained, but the orchestra was still on the long, intense first movement preamble of the symphony. It would be fun to string this particular Hollywood connection out a little longer. "You know it's strange to be talking to someone whose accent is so familiar and local to mine, here of all places."

She was sucking thoughtfully on a strawberry. She nodded. "It stands out doesn't it? Where did you grow up?"

"The Southeast. Sussex."

"The same. But Surrey. Same suites, same accents." Jo continued, not pressing for further details, replacing the strawberry stem and pulling a card out of her pocket to scribble an address on the back, "So tomorrow, come and do your stuff. People will be arriving about six for drinks. Come earlier to settle yourself in if you want."

"What's the venue like?"

"Venue?…Oh, coastal villa." Alex could sense an incomplete attempt to sound casual. "Rented for the duration. There's a… well I suppose it would have to be described as a ballroom or rehearsal room. Polished wooden floor, small low-raised stage, grand piano, white, a little bit bling perhaps…"

"Sounds great. Look, I'll have to go soon. Sponsors and conductors to please."

"The mysterious inner workings of the music industry."

She grinned at Jo. "Actually, the orchestral manager will be wondering where I've skipped off to."

Alex paused for thought, not wishing to imply that the world revolved around her. "By the way, how did your 'thing' go?" She asked.

"Oh, that. Not bad. Casting discussions. No conclusion just yet."

"Mmm. The mysterious inner workings of the Hollywood machine," Alex echoed deliberately, causing Jo to glance at her cheekily. "So," she made to stand up, a little reluctantly, "I'll see you before six or thereabouts."

"Thanks. I'm grateful. You can add a touch of elegance to the proceedings. We'll sort the fees out later through your agent?"

"Yes. Fine." *Business.* She dug in her handbag. "You'll need this then." She passed Josh's card across the table. "May I borrow your pen?"

She scribbled her mobile number on the back. "In case you need to contact me." She added a speculative fee to the back of the card. "Roughly. Are you sure you can afford it?" She passed the pen and Josh's card back to her.

Jo caught her hand briefly as she aimed for the card, catching her stare, then dropped her eyes to read the back of the card and feign at fanning her brow. "Just about…"

Alex grinned at her. She had…lingered. The pieces fell into place. Her heart thudded. Their secret codes exchanged. Strangely intimate.

"But I'm a little puzzled." She sat down again, covering her rapid thinking, perching temporarily on the arm of the chair. She took courage, playing with Jo's business card in her hand, studying the writing.

"Why do you come here? Surely you have *people* who do this for you? Why not use my agent?"

Jo twisted the card. "…Joshua Pembroke." She looked momentarily uncomfortable. The look was fleeting and her features melted professionally back into relaxation. She counted off on her fingers. "Actually I didn't know who he was. Too busy to do the research. A little disorganized over this. I know how it works with acting agents, but this…it was a lucky stroke to bump into you. Really lucky. They wished you well at the party for the concert tonight. You mentioned the Tchaikovsky. I loved your playing and tomorrow night's quite important, it could do with a little *je ne sais quoi*. I thought I should sample the product."

Alex had a feeling she was trying too hard to explain herself, some of her façade falling away. Jo seemed not to care. She sat forward suddenly, on the edge of her chair, her legs spread casually apart, one hand still toying with the card, dangling modestly between. "How often have you tried breaching the gap between the audience and the performer, either way? It isn't that easy to judge someone. I mean how many friends have you made, since becoming successful, who aren't colleagues or skilled social climbers or even, dare I say, gold-diggers?"

"Few." *Friends.*

"Exactly! I've received messages from strangers. But I don't answer them. I've had some pretty 'interesting' experiences along the way, believe me. One young man tracked my house down from a really annoying website that gives out too much information, when I was born, where my parents live now and so on." She had lapsed deliberately into a childish tale-telling voice, but returned to her own now. "He hung around until eventually spotting me in the area, tracked me down to the house, pestered me, sold a story to the tabloids, some fictitious rubbish. As if I would be interested in *him*. He was missing the mark in a number of ways. Barking completely up the wrong tree. And it went on and on. I had to get a banning order, move house in the end."

You're dropping hints. "Yes, I think I saw something in the papers…a couple of years ago."

"That was it! What is it that gives people the self-belief to go that far? Take my advice, don't talk to strangers!" She let the sober look go, fell back in the chair melodramatically, pulled her hands up onto the arms of the chair, leaving herself spread-eagled and added, smiling. "Or at least male ones…See?"

Alex's eyes had rested on the precious place that only a few layers of fabric kept from her. "I'm getting there…" She stopped fidgeting and looked up at her.

"It's okay, you know." She was staring intently, crystal clear green eyes that seemed to understand.

"I'm…getting there," Alex echoed.

Jo was suddenly more upbeat, pulling herself into a more respectable position. God, how easily that body moved! "Bring something to swim in tomorrow, if you like. If the party gets on your nerves there's a heated pool down toward the beach house."

She's pressing all the right buttons. "Now you're talking…" She laughed, "That's *my* kind of party!" She gesticulated with her hands in emphasis, one of which had moved suddenly close to Jo, who grasped it, looking over toward the barman briefly to be sure he was out of sight, and turned it over in hers.

"Graceful, clever hands." She shook it lightly in a faintly chivalrous gesture and, smiling beautifully, let it go. Alex shivered, surprised, her skin standing disobediently to attention. She had *wanted* to be touched by her again. It was a shock to admit it, as if she had already given something of herself away, subconsciously, too easily. The thought startled her briefly, as if she had lowered her defenses without knowing.

Jo grinned freely at her. Not being the actress, Alex felt she was probably doing a poor job of covering herself.

"Until tomorrow then."

They both stood, smiling encouragingly at each other and Alex turned to go, covering a certain wistfulness to be walking away and yet knowing fully it was a necessity, it was how this scene played out. Jo was gay. It was obvious now. She, who had always been rubbish at identifying it, she knew. But it was not generally known, was it? She couldn't think of anything reported about her. She could even think of men reportedly connected with her. Reportedly.

And something in her leaped for joy. It was a sudden unleashing of a something that she had kept at bay, not fully acknowledged since the age of eleven, when she had spoken tearfully to her mother.

Afraid. Knowing that her aunt who was openly lesbian had been rejected by the family, who she had been warned of as being "strange," who she rarely got to see. Afraid because she knew already she had what apparently seemed to be stronger than average feelings for her best friend. Confused, in tears, she had told her mother.

"Don't worry," she had tried to be reassuring, "You'll be perfectly normal and start liking boys soon. It's just a phase you're going through. And your father certainly wouldn't understand. Perhaps we should see a bit less of her."

Hurt that night, she had cried and nodded. Struggling to come to terms valiantly, trying to do the right thing, convinced only of a blip in her feelings, a regular "growing stage" in life, burying something so deep inside her because it simply wouldn't do. Unaware, so unaware, so innocent. A flash of the unfairness of it all surprised her. Oh! She had been so influenced. What would the result have been if her worries had been met with: "That's okay, love, some girls just like other girls best…that's allowed, it's perfectly fine."

What of that friend?

Oh my! The wasted years…the trying to be something else. And what of her aunt? Strange? Probably a woman who had done battle with her family, had been brave enough to acknowledge herself, to stand up for herself. Nature, *not* nurture. Nothing had been nurtured into Alex, for certain. Apparently there had been an attempt to nurture it into a cupboard, locked safely away. That was it! Lockdown. And now…meltdown.

Everything clicked into place, the domino effect tumbling rapidly into an instantly completed jigsaw. She had known and not known at the same time. Yes. She liked looking at women best. She had bottled it up, believed in the "phase" explanation. It explained why she felt awkward *with everybody*. She hadn't even known what was going on. That men unknowingly made her feel like she had to playact a role with them, that she found it easier to be close with women…up to the point that she had to hide something from them. Her particular type of obsession with romance…romantic films played again and again. It was the *romance* she was obsessed by, not the men. When she had looked so closely, frame by frame, she had been wanting…oh! *Not* to kiss the man, but to imagine what it was like to be kissing the *woman*. And she had dabbled with a few boys in her teens and earlier twenties, encouraged by what was expected of her, never settling, never finding the "'answer.'"

She had not thought of that suppressed memory for years.

All of this crowded in on her in seconds, a released valve, as if the floodgates had opened in an instant, bringing a sense of overwhelming relief. Perhaps it would not even have been possible to understand this if her mother had still been here, still exercising her influence, however well-intended she thought that had been.

And now she walked away…a little puzzled, greatly flattered, reminding herself sternly: *Booked to be the paid servant again. Keep it in perspective.*

But that moment of recognition, in that moment something inside her rejoiced. It was the sunshine forcing its way through the cloud on an overcast day. There were no tears now. Everything was lit up suddenly, spectacularly, in glorious color.

* * *

The champagne (and most of a liter bottle of water) had worked wonders on her by the time of the post-concert drinks reception. She threaded her way easily through the crowd, flattering the sponsors, flirting where necessary, cuddled by Vladimir and the orchestra leader, feeling more confident and fluid than usual, buoyed up by a sense of secrecy. She was introduced to a local Head of Keyboard, who wanted to talk shop for a while, needed Josh's card, and only toward the end was she briefly insulted by an unknown quantity, a male, who had had way too much to drink and asked her if she had slept her way to the top. *Bloody unbelievable.*

There was no way she was going to explain to him that she had not had time for a boyfriend in about three years and when she had, they had all too easily become jealous of the professional demands in her life. As someone else pushed past her, she accidentally knocked the contents of her glass all over the offensive man and apologized (in)sincerely. While he scrambled to clean himself, she slipped back to Vladimir's group and tucked affectionately under his arm, in sheer defiance, enjoying the deliberate ambiguity. She felt…unusually sure of herself. And she knew why. Everything made sense.

Exhausted, but glad to be seeing most of her colleagues again on Thursday for the next concert, she was seen back to her hotel. Delightful thoughts of the prospective party soon danced through her head as she lay dozing in her bed, the conversation with Jo running on a loop through her head; simultaneously reviewing snapshots of her life viewed through a sharper lens.

The edges of her world seemed a little more blurred than usual.

CHAPTER SEVEN

Ivory Towers

Recovering from the weekend's efforts, Alex found Tuesday passing easily. She had called Josh earlier in the morning, filling him in on the news: the first concert, the Oscars date, the pending gathering at Jo Davison's party. He had been suitably impressed, speculating playfully whether he could fly over in time for the party to help entertain any bored actresses, but on further consultations with his diary confirmed sadly that he was too tied up, almost literally, with Russian prima donnas at the moment to be there. Would she make sure that his details were passed on to all? She had laughed at him, then, gladly alone with her thoughts again, went to the hotel gym in a good mood.

Early in the afternoon Rodeo Drive cried out for a visit, and after browsing several glamorous boutiques she bought a deep purple wraparound top to go over a pair of slinky, clingy black evening trousers. Returning to her room, she made coffee and practiced the Rachmaninov for Thursday, going endlessly over the cadenzas. She was certain that her practicing often sounded dreadful, apparently unrelated difficult passages repeated and bent this way and that until they worked properly. It made her grateful, self-consciously, for the soundproofed room. *It's a good thing they can't hear me now.*

* * *

Late in the afternoon she took the hotel car to the address on the card, transplanted into another place by the strange exoticism of the palm trees and the balmy night. The security was impressive. It was necessary to negotiate her way in through an intercom and electronic gates, then once inside the high fences, trying not to feel intimidated, she trudged up a gravel driveway to the sizeable villa. It was about five thirty p.m. when she rang the bell.

There were footsteps across a reverberant hall. A slightly rotund, cheerful housekeeper opened the door with a congenial welcome and showed her through to the ballroom where a white piano stood at one end by partially opened French windows. She heard her disappearing and calling across the gardens.

It was pleasantly surprising not to feel the least bit nervous for a change, as if she were making herself at home. Settling down to play without further invitation, she dropped her bag and jacket casually on the floor and in a while heard running footsteps across the polished floor.

"Marvelous! You're here early." Jo slowed down, her floaty dress catching up with her, walked to the piano and bent down to plant a quick, unexpected kiss on Alex's cheek.

Startled, she backed off, blurting "Oh!...Hi!" to cover herself.

She hung close by, a wonderful smell and the sensation of soft skin lingering close in the air.

"So," she asked, "what do you want?"

"A leading question…"

"Piano playing!" Alex spoke playfully, hiding behind the words, "a little of this," trying a few bars of 'It's Wonderful,' "or this," Rachmaninov's *Variations on a Theme of Paganini Variation 18*, "this,"—'Misty'—"this," the opening bars of the Grieg concerto, "or maybe this," 'I Did It My Way.'

She was laughing. "Well…not the fourth or fifth, but yes to the first and third and maybe to the second, if they've had enough to drink and look like a cultured bunch."

Alex launched into the *Looney Tunes* theme tune.

"Very funny. Seriously though, well slightly seriously, not too seriously you understand, a suitable mishmash of your cocktail pieces would be most welcome."

"*Mishmash?*" Alex exclaimed, making a vague pretense at being offended.

Jo laughed again, a light, relaxed sound that was pleasing to the ears.

"Oh. If you insist." She doodled on the keyboard for a moment. "Nice piano by the way."

"Yeah, I thought so too."

"You mean you can tell?" She tried teasing her.

"It looks nice." Jo laughed, showing a pleasure, a willingness to be humbled, that made her instantly charming. "I play a bit. Grade five, if you must know. My parents made me, until the acting took over."

"Ha! Really? I knew it! A closet pianist. I, however…" as she continued to doodle on the piano, "…am a closet actress. Stage school, until the music took over."

"You joke!"

"Well, yes actually. Can't act to save my life, unless it's occasionally turning on some mild flirting with the right people at the right time."

"But that could come in handy…And the stage school?"

"Sad, but true. Could remember the lines, but never could deliver them convincingly. Died a death, several nights in a row, as Gretel in *The Sound of Music*, the drama teacher had his head in his hands at one point…" She was giggling now, embarrassed by the memory.

"Ha!"

"It's true!"

Jo was laughing at her.

"But seriously, well slightly seriously for a moment, not too seriously, you understand. Explain my role tonight." She added, mimicking her.

"Ah! Well! Play. Stop. Mingle if you like. Be glamorous. Eat. Drink. Play a little more. Feel free to 'skip off' as you so elegantly put it, anytime you like, when the shop talk gets tough. Millie's in the kitchen. She'll help you. Or I'll introduce you to Andy, my PA, if I can. He'll point you in the right direction. The pool, as I said is at your disposal, should you wish."

"Do I receive a crystal Oscar this time too?"

"Must make a mental note to order one…" She chuckled huskily to herself, walking over to a drinks table. "Drink?"

"Just a juice for now please."

The doorbell chimed. "Okay. I'm off. My apologies if I'm occupied. Couple of things to do. A bit of networking, I'm afraid. I'll catch you later."

She'll catch me later. The thought pleased her.

"There." She passed over a glass, her other hand holding Alex's receiving one briefly in place, which sent a shiver along her arm. She placed it next to the piano leg and settled down more comfortably to play, beginning with "My Way" and then stopping.

Jo laughed as she crossed the room, calling back "No… no thank you!" Alex smirked and started "The Way You Look Tonight." The evening had potential.

* * *

The party progressed peacefully and elegantly, tangibly more relaxed than the Oscars had been. She played happily as various guests came up to the piano and chatted, resting plates or glasses casually and a little worryingly on the top. She was almost used to seeing iconic figures in their off-duty state. It was as if some of the cast of *Lord of the Rings*, the Bond and Jane Austen films,

Harry Potter, *Mamma Mia* and *Love Actually*, to name but a few, had been shaken up in a cocktail and poured through Jo's front door. *They* were remarkably normal, quite capable of dropping a pastry on the floor. Several, but not all, had been at the Oscars party and congratulated her as if *she* had won an award. A couple of them, she presumed, could play the piano themselves; it was easy to tell from the accuracy, the correct posture even, in their films. As the doorbell rang, a constant stream of select actors, male and female, frequently British, sometimes with their partners and suitably placed presumably production-related people drifted in, until the large room was comfortably warm and chattering. A bubbly woman, introducing herself as Jo's American agent, Jilly, circulated among the guests, greeting her in passing in a gap between pieces.

After what seemed a suitable length of time, Alex opted for a break, feeling peculiarly autonomous, unchaperoned within the evening's unprogrammed criteria and strolled to the buffet table to take a plate. She found herself brushing shoulders with an actor whom she recognized by face but not by name, and he became complimentary about the choice of music and excellent execution. Overcoming her immediate embarrassment, surprised, she attempted to laugh, replying how strange it was to be meeting everyone, not quite of the same genre, but still "entertainment" and proceeded to recount the comment from the Woman's Hour presenter, for want of a better story.

"Ah, the BBC! Must look her up next time I'm over." He chuckled.

An arm slid around her shoulders with a friendly squeeze. "Isn't she something? I found her all by myself…"

It was Jo. It was an impossibility to ignore the empathetic wave that hit her as she caught her eyes with her cheeky glint.

"If only 'twere true. I was there the other night too you know," her buffet table companion teased in reply.

"Ah, how could I forget, the way you trod so elegantly on my foot while waltzing around. Blast, 'scuse me. How lovely 'twould be to linger, but I must just…" And with that she was gone again, leaving them momentarily at a loss for words.

"Mad as a hatter you know."

"Yes, I was starting to notice."

An attractive man, blond, tanned by the California sun, came over to nudge himself into the conversation and the actor drifted away, excusing himself gracefully.

"Hi. Andy, Jo's assistant." He shook her hand warmly, speaking with a hint of a Northern England accent.

"Hi, pleased to meet you."

"Jo asked me to be of use to you if you needed anything."

"That's kind. I'm fine at the moment, thanks." It was easy to warm to his disarming smile. "Just wondering though, if it's not an impertinent question…what that entails?"

"What assisting Jo or being of use to you?" He grinned.

"The former," she clarified, briefly worried about being too familiar.

"Mostly charging around," he continued smoothly, "paving the way for the next assignment. All sorts of things, really. Short notice changes, preparations, anything she doesn't have time to deal with, presumably the sort of things you need sometimes, clothes, cars, accommodation, planning, admin, reading and sorting the mail, both paper and computer, security and so on. It's interesting too, making contacts."

"Wow, I could do with one of you."

"Just the one of me, I'm afraid. But you can see how it helps."

"Absolutely. Well, I'll come and find you if I'm in need this evening. And if you have a friend in the same line of work who needs a job, let me know." She returned his cheeky grin, attempting to match him. *Fancy that…Jo's PA…What a dish.*

Floating for a while, she eavesdropped a little, aware of being an outsider and cautious not to overdo any drinking before playing again. She was never sure of the tone quality or the dynamic subtlety once a few glasses down. Then it was time to settle down to a couple more sets, one upbeat and as the event wore on, one slower paced set to relax the mood for the evening before finishing.

After this, it felt like an appropriate time to leave the hubbub and noise behind and as no one was paying any attention, with a quick glance at the hostess confirming she was busy and Andy clearly waylaid, taking her bag, she headed off to find Millie. She wasn't hard to locate. Once she had crossed the hall, the clank and bustle from the kitchen was obvious, and it was simple to find the way to a brightly lit, metallic kitchen, complete with central marble workstation where a formidable-looking Millie and a couple of others were working hard.

"Hi!" She attempted to call over the clatter.

Millie started in surprise at the sudden appearance and then recovering, in a businesslike way asked, "What can I do for you, honey? Oh, it's Alex, isn't it?"

"Yes, that's right. I've kind of finished now and I'm not really one of the crowd. Jo mentioned I could try the pool out, if nobody's around."

"Oh, sure, honey. Down the stairs," she indicated with a kitchen knife, "outside, down the long sloping path through the grove of trees and you'll be there. Towels are in the beach house. It's quieter down there. Want anything sent down?"

"Thanks, that would be great. Would a pot of tea be okay?"

"Give me a while to sort out the desserts and I'll be right on to it, honey. Enjoy." She whirled back into action, chopping and arranging fruit.

Following the directions Alex found herself walking through the trees, which parted suddenly to reveal the bluest, most inviting pool and a delectable little beach house nestling peacefully between the garden wall and the beach. The light was fading but solar lamps glowed softly, casting long shadows. The pool water was almost still, rippling a little in the breeze, catching the light and steaming invitingly. She went to the beach house and tried the door. It opened easily. The interior beckoned beguilingly; fluffy towels and robes draped across tempting, paisley-patterned armchairs that begged for someone to plump down into them. There was a discreet screen in the corner and a small bathroom off to one side. *Like a stage set, a film set...how appropriate.* Even an antique upright piano tucked against one wall. All that could be conveniently wished for. Everything breathed luxury. She wondered how much this entire venue would cost to rent for the duration, let alone the party tonight. Though blatantly out of her budget, how easily was it accommodated by Jo's? Or was it partly for show in the Oscar season? Speculating on film stars' fees, she thought the right answer was probably easily, especially when potential future deals would justify it and perhaps it was all about clever deception, setting the scene, implying your worth, as with the films themselves. She was herself a business, a company.

Perhaps she should be careful how far she ought to let herself be drawn into this magical world...but for now it was stupid to worry. She slipped out of her evening clothes, pouring herself into a pale bathing suit, pleased to have left the fuss of the party behind, smiling to find herself in this intriguing position, to be taking her own private dip into Jo Davison's swimming pool. It seemed strangely inappropriate to undress here, reckless too. She glanced around, afraid of being observed stripping off one role and stepping into another. Her body was stiff, particularly across the shoulders, from the constant playing. Perhaps tomorrow she would book a massage at the hotel in the morning, before the rehearsal. How blissful it would be to have one's own Andy on tour, doing the organizing. Presumably Josh would be an equivalent. But Andy was so very personable. She breathed a grateful, guilty sigh that Josh was far away. This freedom would not be possible with his constant fussing and watchfulness.

Outside the pool beckoned to her and the gently soothing, distant surge of the waves breathed a comforting background music. She dived into the water, slicing it possessively. *So luxurious. Hot and all mine.* She had swum a dozen lengths and was holding onto the side, relaxing back into the water, allowing her hair to float weightlessly out on the surface, when a noise startled her. A strangely familiar voice:

"Ah! I wondered what had happened to our lovely accompanist. The atmosphere has sagged a little without your music. Not spying, honestly. I was just exploring the gardens. The English Pianist! That would make a good title, wouldn't it?" The actor that matched the voice had stepped out from the grove walk.

She laughed politely, recognizing him instantly from the London stage, recovering from the surprise of being woken from her privacy. She pulled herself close into the side of the pool for the sake of modesty. "It's been done. But that was *The English Patient*! Can't compete with that, sorry!"

"Oh, I wouldn't say so…"

"You're too kind!"

"We Brits should stick together you know. Dangerous place, Hollywood. You never know what's lurking around the corner." He darted dramatically behind a bush and reappeared James Bond style.

"Funny, they never offered me that part…I wonder why?" He was laughing at himself, at his deliberate overacting.

Someone called distantly from the house.

"My cue," he chuckled, "better go. Good to meet you. Best of luck."

"You too," she called to the departing figure, smiling at the private show. The space was again hers alone. *The world is just a little peculiar this week.*

She returned to her reverie and swam again, finally hauling herself out and wrapping up in one of the robes. As she toweled her hair, a member of the staff appeared with a tray of tea and an assortment of the dessert items from the buffet.

"Millie thought you might like to eat down here."

"Tell her thanks. And you too."

"You're welcome." He nodded and departed discreetly, disappearing quickly back up the steps.

She poured the piping hot tea and placed it by the piano, preparing to play, utterly at home in the lap of this luxury. She could get used to this…she felt relaxed, her shoulders released, the subconscious tension of the past few days dissipated by exercise and warmth. She shook out her arms with satisfaction. The heat of the water made the blood flow to her fingers more easily. They felt nimble and ready to achieve. She sparkled over the keys, enjoying the effect:

I've got a crush on you, my sweetie pie…

It would be time to go soon. All over and back to…a little Rachmaninov. She delved into a few passages, busy with some of the more awkward moments. It seemed that half an hour or so had gone by. Time often tended to become lost when she was engrossed in this sort of work. But the ancient upright had its limits, restricting the tone control, and the Rachmaninov seemed strangely out of context here. She should save that for tomorrow. Something else perhaps…"Misty."

"Hear, hear."

She jumped a few inches off the stool.

Jo had been standing silently in the doorway. "Sorry, I didn't mean to startle you. It was a pity to stop you."

Alex's voice caught in her throat. The familiar voice connected somewhere beneath her skin. She felt naked, awkward. Suddenly aware that she had traveled far down the path of relaxing in Jo's home, half-dressed, she stood, leaning on the piano top for support.

"It's so lovely to hear the music drifting up through the trees. Thank you," she continued, apparently oblivious. "For your performance. Lots of compliments on my excellent taste in entertainment and your exquisite, as ever, playing. Mind if I come in?"

"Of course. It's your house after all isn't it? The guests?"

"They've gone. Jilly's just finishing a call, then she's on her way. When I said *we've* rented a place, I meant *she'd* rented a place for me. No one else is staying this week. Andy did a tactful job of winding it up and he's gone off to catch up with a friend in Beverly Hills. I've said my farewells for tonight."

The stage was set. "Oh. It's not that late, is it? I'd better be going soon. I hope you don't mind me helping myself as you suggested." She paused, pulling the robe up on her shoulder.

Jo appeared to be aware of her self-consciousness. "No, not at all. Glad you've helped yourself. There's no rush, either." She waved a hand airily at the surroundings, making it all seem terribly normal.

"It's gorgeous, thanks." Alex was unnerved, at a loss where to go next in the conversation and added lamely, "…Tea then?"

"Love some. Funny, how after a certain number of glasses of champagne or similar substances, one craves a cuppa to clear one's head!" She smiled. "I really do."

"Must be an English thing." She made herself busy, pouring, recovering some composure from the ease of her reply and the task at hand.

"Reckon so." Jo drawled a Southern accent, returning quickly to her own. "No, it's not that late, in answer to your question. They have commitments tomorrow. I only said six until ten or so. It was more of a 'work' party," she explained. "While you do that, mind if I have a quick dip too? Totally wiped after all that small talk."

"Be my guest. Hang on—that can't be right." Alex smiled at the conundrum and Jo's easy informality.

Jo went to the bathroom and reappeared after a brief interval, while Alex was still pouring tea and deliberating over a dessert. Suddenly she felt less vulnerable; Jo had equaled her in near-nakedness now and not daring to look up at first, almost afraid of being caught, she waited until she had passed to stare after her, fully appreciating the smooth, perfectly muscular back, the well-proportioned physique, the bikini, the oh-so-long, slender legs. She filed the mental snapshot away for future leisurely perusal.

It's worth being here just for that. She grinned and fell into a chair, tucking her legs up, listening to the rhythmic slicing of the water and the distant waves mixing together in an almost minimalist style, a peaceful, steady pulsing. How curious. The private bubble had been infiltrated. Indeed, it was faintly flattering that Jo seemed to have chosen to share the rest of the evening with her rather than do anything else more glamorous and exciting. *So strange to see her just…as herself.* Her thoughts drifted, but she shuttered them as the sound of the pool water and the wet footsteps reminded her she was returning, dripping to the chalet. Jo dried herself slowly and pulled on a similar robe, leaving it loosely tied. Alex looked into her tea, loathed again to be caught staring, particularly at the low, gaping V of the neckline where a string of bikini top barely held a delightful cleavage in place.

"Ah! Better," Jo sighed, flopping into the other chair, kicking out her bare feet and picking up a cup.

"Two Brits sharing a lift, I mean a drink, I mean a beach house. We've gone up in the world. Quite literally." She grinned.

Alex dared to look up, catching her expression and smiled back. "You're telling me."

There was a companionable silence.

"So you met Andy?"

"Certainly…he's quite something."

"Very handy. Handy Andy. We go as far back as drama school. Old friends. He was happy to take this on when things didn't take off as well for him. He gets to make some potentially useful contacts."

"Oh."

"Symbiotic really."

"Really?"

They gave each other a long look. "Now, now…he's gay…" And after a thoughtful pause, she added, "…too. He's one of the few people who know."

"Oh." Alex stopped to consider. Wrong-footed by the unexpected simplicity. "Er…How did the networking go?"

Her eyes sparkled…laughing. "They're fine. Well, the majority of them. One loony, one pompous twit and a few egotists, but par for the course really. I saw you having a brief word with Ken. He's so funny: intense, always something interesting to say."

"And someone familiar caught me taking to the water."

"Who was that then?"

She told her.

"I love him. He's one of my trusted friends out here. Actually, more like a guardian through the choppy waters. Ha! It's weird meeting them for the first time, isn't it? Some of them were famous when we were teenagers. They're our idols."

"Completely weird. Mind you, I have the same feeling meeting famous musicians. You know they know how to do it already. I watched their master classes and performances when I was still working it out. Well, I still am! It's a little intimidating, then you have to swallow the fear and think…perhaps we're just the next generation, injecting some new energy in or at least that's what one of them said to me once. Did you get what you wanted?"

"Well, it wasn't all work. Not quite done yet," she added cryptically, "still working on it. Some of it was simply thanks. You must have to do this too?"

"Yes, in a sense, at the concert or on tour. Rarely at my home though, thankfully. Most of it has been prearranged. It comes with the playing. I'd like to think that the performance stands on its own and speaks for itself, but there's always the rest to do too, concert talks and receptions, part of the package I suppose, like the other night."

"How was that one?"

"Oh, not bad." She paused to consider, wondering. "Until some drunken prick asked me if I'd slept my way to the top," she responded testily, remembering the insult.

"What? No! What an arse." Jo gave her a long studious look.

Alex burst out laughing at her response. She joined in. It took a moment for her to recover and continue: "I couldn't be bothered to list my CV or to tell him I've had no time for anybody since things became this high profile, and even before that they were competing for my time and they hated it. The success…it just puts distance between you and other people…" She ran out of steam. "Why am I telling you all this?"

"Don't know. Because I understand? Believe me it all rings a bell. Anybody creepy in your life?"

"Yes."

She noticed her shiver.

"More tea? Something stronger?"

"Am I going to need it?" She didn't need it really, it filled an awkward gap. She wished she were better at this. "Tea." She half-nodded, half-shrugged.

"So?" she encouraged.

"You know I haven't told anyone yet," Alex began tentatively. She wasn't just thinking about the letters.

"Well, feel free if you want to or not. It's not exactly unfamiliar territory."

"Mm, so…I've been sent these totally anonymous and unexplained notes and flowers. As if they know me or know where I am!" The words fell out quickly.

"Ah! Then you must be a member."

"A member?" She looked startled.

She continued, "A member of the TWYC. They Want You Club."

"Yes, that must be it! I must have been secretly initiated without my knowledge!" She paused, feeling a sudden chill behind the banter. "But it's a little ominous." She squirmed in her chair.

"It depends what they say. It's intrusive, but only on paper remember." Jo leaned forward intently, looking touchingly worried.

"But the thoughts…intentions…behind it. I don't like the thought of someone thinking that hard about it."

"That's only a problem if *you* think that hard about it. Andy deals with the mail most of the time. He can filter out the unwanted crap." She was attempting to relax her fears. "But if it ever becomes more…sinister, then you could take it to a higher authority. Perhaps you need someone to be more of a shield for you too."

She wasn't so alone with this. "Well, there's Josh in London. But he's busy with a number of clients. Anyway, you're okay," she continued, "You have ivory tower status."

"Ivory tower? The witch climbed the tower using Rapunzel's hair…"

"You're losing me…"

"Sorry, must be the champagne!" She smiled. "It doesn't matter, it just increases the odds. They seem to find you. Although the gates and walls do help. That's why you increase the security." She gestured toward the surroundings.

"Yes, that's what I meant…impressive."

"And all mine. Just for a few weeks anyway. It's weird slipping back into civvies in London, and because it's more pronounced here it makes it more commonplace, easier in some ways too. And yet, you can walk around London while people keep their heads down and barely notice you."

"But I haven't quite reached that stage yet."

"All the more reason to take care. You don't necessarily know when you reach 'that stage.' Suddenly you're being followed, photographed…and you're not entirely sure which story, which article, which event caused the leap in interest."

"Although certain publicity for you, a particular film build-up maybe, must set it off again."

"Of course, or a piece of meaningless gossip." She nodded. "No one was bothering with me until I worked on *One, Two, Four*. Then there was suddenly all this…speculation. New kid on the block, you know. Where had I come from? What was so special? Babble on the internet turning into a bit of a self-perpetuating frenzy. Picking the bones out of it all. It works both in your favor and against. The fans and the pessimists doing battle. That was the first summer I had to spend holed up; it was almost too dangerous to go out. It sounds ridiculous, but I couldn't go *anywhere* without being stopped. Sometimes a crowd gathered and grasped at my clothes if I strayed too close. I lost the freedom to walk down the street. People were looking for me. It sounds so paranoid!"

"It's peculiar, it feels so unexpected that it breeds a sense of ownership, though," Alex continued.

"Comes with the territory."

"Sadly."

"Ah, let's not be sad." She lightened the mood easily. "There are ways to keep that at bay. You don't respond. You keep your private life really private, make up a smoke screen story if it helps. They can become all stressed about something that is total fiction. Make up enough stories and no one can see the wood for the trees anymore. You can be protected by your hotel staff, the theatre staff or tonight my ivory tower! Be my guest, as a guest in someone else's house!" She chuckled. It was a sound Alex was starting to...love. "And the popularity has its uses. Start taking advantage of the bonuses that come with it—picking the work...who you want to work with, free gifts, bigger fees, bigger houses..." she waved a hand airily, "...jumping the reservation lists." She wasn't taking herself seriously. "I sank my teeth into some decent books that summer and tried to learn to play the guitar."

"Any success?"

"Not really..."

They laughed. Alex was intrigued.

"I'm sorry..."

"Don't be. It *is* alarming sometimes."

She attempted to change the subject. "So what do you like reading? I mean when you're not learning scripts, playing the guitar or whatever it is that you do..."

Jo grinned. "Oh, I think there's some Graham Greene, Forster, Wolfe and John Irving lying around here somewhere at the moment...and history...history seems so much more important as you get older...and I relax with Hill, it makes me feel I'm not alone..."

"Oh...that's good." She *was* unexpectedly pleased with her sophisticated taste, although she hadn't read the last author. She made a mental note of the name, determined to track some down and share the same pages. There was a lengthy pause. "This just seems a little surreal, sitting here. It's not what I had in my mind when the tour was planned..."

"Well...I'm sorry too...it's not without..." Jo paused considering her words, "some premeditation on my part..."

"Oh?" Alex experienced a fleeting twinge of...what was it? Fear, apprehension? Something else? It was the choice of word.

There was no response, just another silence.

"So no boyfriends, you said?" Jo inquired casually after a while, as if asking the time of day, the manner at odds with the leap in content.

Quietly, Alex registered the twist in subject matter. She weighed her response, suddenly feeling very awkward. "Not for a long time."

"Girlfriends?"

"Never…I mean…at least not yet. I'm only just realizing…" What had she been expecting? How should she respond? A little apprehensively of being bitten, she thought she would return the conversational serve with courage; after all, she realized that she *was* curious, so found herself asking quietly, "What about you?"

Jo did not flinch from the question. Perhaps she was getting better at this.

"No boyfriends, either. Not for a long time. Unless you count Andy," she teased. Alex cringed, and noticing, she added, "No. There's nothing *there*, of course. But he's such a good friend. And girlfriends?" She gave her a thoughtful look.

Alex frowned slightly at her, puzzled. She must be able to have her pick.

"Actually not for quite a while," she continued. "Actually a bit…what you might call…happy in my own company. Do you realize the implication, the expectation, particularly when you're relatively new to the scene?"

"What? The casting couch? I thought that was myth."

"You might think so. But you have to become rather adept at playing the game of will you or won't you, without *actually*… if you see what I mean. And I haven't been able to be myself completely. It wouldn't…exactly help in the roles I'm being offered at the moment." She frowned, apparently displeased with the thought. "I ought to be 'out' out there really, but it wouldn't help. I value my *actual* privacy highly. Where was I? Plenty of scripted…action one might say, you know. It's par for the course." She watched Alex's response closely, who hid by looking down into her cup. "Only digitally simulated, you understand. And of course, not hitting the right mark? An irrelevant exercise to me…shall we say?"

Alex managed a smirk. "History and work. We all come with it at this stage. But the media imply…" she began cautiously.

"Don't get me started on what the media imply," Jo interrupted testily, then caught herself, softening her voice again. "I know the media imply I'm playing my way through the equivalent of Wimbledon. As I said, it can be a very useful smoke screen. Half the time I'm being snapped with someone or other as we're on the way to a scheduled promotion or finishing a day's work with a friendly drink and the rest of the cast or crew. It's always assumed I'm laying whichever co-star I'm cast with. But it doesn't *actually* work that way. For a start they're not always as attractive in reality as they can appear on screen. Well, to me, at least. And it's a useful misunderstanding. Drown them in a fog of fiction. Sometimes I even ask my friends to leak some rubbish or other to get everyone off my back. That's the way to win a little privacy. The more rubbish that's out there, the less believable. They don't know as much as they'd like to think about me. For example: I actually like my own company, some solitude, and I have a depressed sister. I *do* like reading literature and world history in my spare time and there's more spare time than you might think, if nothing comes up for a while. It's not entirely back-to-back all the time. And I had a car crash, not my fault. That one was kept quiet. Believe me, I was pretty shocked for a while…but the rest of humanity doesn't need to know about any of that. *And*…they don't know they're barking up the wrong tree, do they?"

Cleary it had been a long time since she had to work so hard at it or had wanted to confess so much. As if all too often she had been the one *avoiding* the unwanted attention.

"And now, it's necessary to completely clear the decks, to try to make a window of opportunity, such as…" She stopped.

Alex could sense her deliberately laying herself bare, the innate offer of trust that it entailed. Perhaps she had overstepped the mark. Had she unintentionally implied that s*he* was guilty of sleeping her way up? She knew how bitter the remark had been to her yesterday. It was not possible to be entrusted with that much prestige or even pressure, without having the ability to go with it. People weren't that stupid. The acting world wouldn't open its arms to it, in the same way that a musician couldn't get away with fluffing their way through the professional world. It would be immediately apparent if you didn't have the memory or the technique to match it.

They rested from the flow of talk for a moment. Listening to the evening noises. The trees in the garden rustled restlessly, insects chirruped, ocean waves sounded faintly in the distance. The conversation had fallen into an easy rhythm and intimacy.

"You know, I was watching you at my cottage, in your recent Christmas film, the night I had the call that led me to the party, to bump into you."

"Intriguing…It must be the BBC. Let's not mention names."

Alex nodded briefly, smiling at the impossibility that she could be talking with her about it.

"That one was fun. Set in the rural Southeast, we were in places like Friday Street—like being inside an E.M. Forster novel you see, home territory. It made for a change."

"Not far from me then. I know that area, I'm near there—it makes me feel like I've entered the world of Tolkien—all those old trees, deep lanes and gnarled roots." She pondered, ignoring a brief twinge of homesickness. It was muted already by some other subcutaneous fire.

"Lucky you to live in that part of the world. Where exactly?"

"I have a cottage. In Thurslow. Near Godalming. Not so far from Guildford. It's quiet. Quite remote."

"I have a place in London. It makes it easy to get in for meetings and rehearsals, but not quite as private as I'd like sometimes. Although I suppose the city affords some anonymity. People stop looking at each other properly." Alex nodded. *She has a place in London. Of course.* The flames licked at her as she realized how close they had been.

Jo paused for a slow, measured breath. "Now—my turn. *I* saw *you*…playing a Mozart concerto while I killed time waiting for the light to fade enough on the South Bank for a night shoot. About a year ago."

"Oh!" Alex gasped, taken quite by surprise; she had vague memories of the season and the guests it had entailed. But no film stars. "I didn't know that."

She spoke softly. "Why would you? There are hundreds of faces out in an audience—I know that too. I had a good few years of treading the boards before all this. Still do sometimes, given half a chance. I was deliberately hiding at the back of a box anyway—not from you I hasten to add, just generally. You were at the Festival Hall with the LPO, wearing an emerald dress that was held up just on one side." She described it almost reverently.

Alex thought of it, hanging in the hotel wardrobe. Her attention to detail was causing that glimmer of recognition again, which she hardly dared to acknowledge.

"You played beautifully then too. Totally absorbed in the music. In you walked, this vision in the clinging, green dress," she illustrated, "like some Grecian goddess with dark hair falling across your shoulders and you settled yourself down to play, waiting quietly, while the orchestra plowed through a long introduction. I just sat, unexpectedly enraptured by this sparkling, crystal clear piano music dancing out and filling the whole of the massive hall to total silence. Not a single movement and only an occasional, stifled cough from the audience. It was a weird contrast. That much power coming from this...slender figure. I'd heard of you already, followed some of your reviews, that's why I bothered to go—you'd had a recording out— they were even playing it on the plane channels, it's a favorite download of mine," she said with what Alex thought was a hint of shyness, "and there was a radio interview that I caught back home, on the way to the airport."

She was staring at her silently. Surprised. Flushing red. Self-conscious from the careful attention.

"And then we're thrown together in LA. TWYC."

Alex's hair had dried into curls from the swimming and she turned to unraveling them.

"Ha! Is that the premeditation?" She breathed the laughter softly, subconsciously catching Jo's own expression. She was completely charming, bewitching. *Silver-tongued from the silver screen.* Should she listen to this cynical voice, a faint warning bell tinkling vaguely at the back of her mind? Sitting there, chatting, it all felt so...right. Perhaps the warning voice was a red herring itself, a preconceived idea.

"Actually, some luck involved too. As I mentioned, it wasn't that easy to cross the barriers."

Alex was startled momentarily, as if she had plucked the idea from her thoughts.

"Sometimes it feels like your every move is being watched, especially in the era of mobiles. I can't even walk to the corner shop at home without being snapped. Not possible to throw on an old T-shirt and jeans without some headline that something must be wrong with me, that I must have a hangover or a broken heart." She lightened up. "But not tonight. Tonight I get to choose. Come on!" She leaped up, throwing back the curtains to the beachward doors. "Let's look at the sea. It's a gloriously clear night."

Alex's heart pounded suddenly. She nodded, still bemused, feeling peculiarly detached, as if watching the scene unfold objectively. Jo offered her hand; she was *pleased* to touch her again. She realized she had been waiting to, hoping to. It sent an unexpected shudder through her. How could she not want to, knowing that only a bathrobe separated her from that tanned, almost bare body?

And they wandered out onto the beach, the lights of the house behind them.

The sand was cool now, a faint breeze stirring the night air. Their hands entwined, softly. Safely. Alex felt her touch throbbing with some kind of heightened sensitivity and wondered whether it was having the same effect on Jo. She cast a sideways glance at her and saw that she was away in her thoughts somewhere, looking out toward the surf, enjoying the fresh air, the freedom. So much of her existence was accounted for, watched, controlled and scripted to maximize the publicity and when away from all that, she was restricted by what was possible or would cause the least amount of fuss, attract the least attention, she was always aware of still being watched. To be out and wandering, with someone of her choosing, actually without the privacy of choice having been observed…even that was difficult to achieve…particularly the elongated *fuss* this choice would have caused. She dropped Alex's hand gently, altering her position to rest her arm lightly across her shoulders—a natural, comforting gesture—but so strange coming from her. Alex slipped her arm around her waist. It was so easy to do. Jo pulled her closer in, resting their heads briefly together.

The night sky stretched away out to the west. Mysterious lights dotted the distant horizon.

When the gentle roar of the waves came closer and the water started to lap silkily at their feet, they stopped to watch the last of the fading, distant light dissolving into the night sky.

"Isn't it beautiful…?" Alex began quietly, afraid of interfering with the atmosphere. Jo turned to her and ducked her head down quickly, in a fluid movement, kissing her lightly on the lips before Alex had even registered the motion. Suddenly. Unexpectedly. She had not quite arrived at the same place, still in some disbelief at their conversation, despite a certain anticipation which had been creeping up on her. Perhaps slightly removed by her tiredness, the jet lag. She looked at her, puzzled in the half-light, surprised.

"Jo?" The word did not seem to fit, to encompass this both familiar and relatively unknown person.

"Mm?" she murmured softly.

"But where did that come from?"

"It's been brewing for a while…"

Yes. Her consent must have been clear in her eyes. She moved, reaching up to kiss her back. Pulling her back with a sudden intensity.

Jo looked momentarily astonished. She, who should have known what to expect, should have covered the possibilities, professionally at least. This inquisitive awareness was welcome, a surprising confidence. She pulled Alex in toward her, her lips soft but urgent. Her first kiss with a woman. So soft, so beautiful, a sudden fire spreading from the nape of her neck down to the pit of her stomach.

When, after some time, they separated, Alex stared silently at her for a moment, then whispered, piqued by curiosity, "How did you know? I barely knew."

"I…I thought…I had hoped…I wasn't sure…but I knew you'd had broken engagements. Thinking that you were single. That your…history…might just suggest what I was hoping. It was a bit of a gut feeling, but I couldn't know for certain without meeting you."

Alex didn't mind. On the contrary. She smiled at her. "When you…kiss…you know, in a film, what does it feel like?"

She laughed at her playfully. "Well, rarely like this. No cameras, see?" She pirouetted prettily on the spot. "As you can imagine, *then* it's always acting for me."

Alex watched her closely, finding herself satisfied.

"What would you like? Dramatic reunion or intimate?"

"Dramatic reunion?" She wondered.

"Like this you mean," she gave a demonstration, sweeping her up, a theatrical kiss that made all the right moves, but left something out. Alex attempted to respond only limply, failing miserably, crumbling into giggles. Trying to be a little insubstantial, superficial, mechanical, lacking a soul. But she felt a tongue touch her lip as she pulled back and a wicked sparkle in Jo's eyes that showed she was teasing too.

"It's a weird kind of forced intimacy. After a day of that, you know the look of someone so well—can even anticipate their next move. It can be made to look really convincing, or so you would like to think," she spoke softly, reassuringly, "while you're trying to stay in character and are thinking about the technical detail of the performance—the director's had a cozy chat with you about keeping your head just at a certain angle, to make the most of the lighting,"—she showed her—"and they've made you retake it half a dozen times, which is actually causing you a neck-ache!" She laughed at her. "Plus there's a big, burly guy holding a prop two feet away from you and you might not be much in the mood…and don't want to give too much of yourself away…it's not exactly difficult for me not to be emotionally involved with a man." She smiled gently, ironing out the crick in her neck and whispered, "Whereas this…"

She searched her face, kissing her again, more intently, a tongue seeking hers, lifting Alex toward her until she was enveloped into her arms, sinking into the intensity, the electrical currents coursing down her spine as the front of her hips touched hers.

Jo leaned backed only slightly, keeping one hand in the small of her back so that their connection with each other was not broken and murmured softly, "The difference is choice. One is because you have to. You're being watched by a couple of dozen people, cameras and a lighting effects team, maybe even your colleagues. He might taste of makeup or hairspray or lunch. People don't smell the way you expect them to. It's all rather self-conscious." She laughed softly. "Whereas this is free choice. And no one tells you when to cut..."

Alex liked the answer and her easy verbosity. But she was losing any sense of perspective...and some of her self-control.

Relaxing into her, she drank in the moment, vaguely aware that it could not be enduring. In case she was in fact dreaming, she slid her arms inside Jo's robe just to be sure, feeling her shudder...*So this is what it's meant to feel like...*Her skin was deliciously soft, smooth, hot under the stroking of her inquisitive fingers, the bathing costume still slightly damp, her touch invoking her responses, swift, alert; a fire was spreading from the small of her back.

"Hairspray? I don't use it!"

Jo laughed, her voice husky, her face still submerged somewhere in Alex's hair. "Actually, no. You smell delicious."

It was so easy, so normal. Alex looked down to admire the beautiful body, her hand tracing the valley caused by her bikini top, unconsciously almost tracing the contents, feeling the tremor through her.

"I'm cold." She realized it suddenly, although inside she was burning and filled with a sense of urgency.

"Yes," she agreed, "it's flaming cold! Let's go!" Releasing each other they ran back across the sand like children, directed by the beach house lights. It gave Alex a moment to catch her thoughts.

"We can warm up in the pool." Jo fastened the beachward doors with deliberation.

Discarding their robes, she dived in first, Alex stepped in more carefully, loathe to soak her hair again and when Jo had surfaced, they settled together on the pool steps. Jo sat on the step behind, wrapping her arms around Alex's shoulders as they thawed themselves in the warmth of the water, steam rising around them.

An unspoken rule had been stepped over.

"You knew." Jo said it quietly.

"Yes. That was easy. But only at the LA Phil concert. Something clicked for me that night. I had been…in denial."

"Oh joy," she said with genuine feeling. "I clicked something for you…?"

"You could say that." Alex reached her arms behind her, around her, finding the back of the bikini top and unfastening it.

Jo sighed, a pleased breeze of a noise. Alex turned herself to look, brushing Jo's lips with her fingers and then tracing water droplets down to where they dripped at the most prominent point. Her lips automatically followed the same path. Jo shivered and then grinned, pulled away from her, diving out into the pool from the steps and swimming across its width. She beckoned her over. Alex followed and straddled her legs playfully around her against the far side while Jo dangled against the pool wall, supported by her arms.

"So what do the weeks ahead hold for you?" She asked the question quietly, brushing a piece of wet hair from her cheek, unexpectedly serious, as if it was suddenly only natural to want to know her diary.

A different reality reared itself for Alex as she started reeling off the schedule on her fingers, pulling away, "Ah… tomorrow rehearsal, Thursday LA concert…fly to Vancouver, two concerts—boat to Victoria, one recital—back to Vancouver, lecture recital. Fly to Seattle, two concerts—fly to San Francisco, two more concerts—back to LA, final LA concert, San Diego, one concert, possible recital class in LA to finish. Not much then. You?"

"That's packed." Jo went on in a similar tone to hers: "Two more weeks here, finalizing some casting. Script readings etcetera. Two possible film leads in the pipeline. One shooting starting in a couple of weeks. A bit of touching up on a pre-release in a week or two, depending when they need it. Interviews for a launch and so on. Then I leave for Italy."

"Not exactly free agents, are we?" The thought brought Alex achingly back to the present. "I need to go back to the hotel now. They'll wonder where I am if I don't return soon. I think the staff are instructed to keep an eye out when I'm touring—single girl—security, you know. And I have to be out in the morning."

Jo pulled them back together, until, feeling the length of their bodies touching at various points, it became completely essential for Alex to find her mouth again. She separated herself reluctantly, forcing herself to think practically, momentarily afraid of being swallowed up by this new identity, hauling herself out, a prickling awareness of Jo's eyes following her as she dried off, then disappeared behind the screen to change.

Jo clearly didn't want the evening to end, wasn't entirely sure how to prolong it at this stage, apparently not having been vastly experienced with rapid seductions—aware too of pitching it badly, rushing and ruining this one opportunity and the chance would be gone, finished. Not knowing that Alex was there too, her mind racing ahead, working out the potential obstacles. She came in and caught her hand in an easy movement as Alex reached for her top, tracing her long fingers carefully to the top of Alex's fingertips and then intertwining them with hers. Alex felt...self-conscious. Had anyone else received this treatment? And yet, she shouldn't just assume it.

"How are you getting back, have you booked a car?"

"Not yet."

"I'll drive you. If you like. We can talk a little more." She held her gaze, reassuringly, Alex found it hard to look away, unable to ignore a smoldering sensation in the pit of her stomach, Jo's sincerity dispelling her misgivings. "I can't let go of you that easily."

Alex's breath caught. She considered the offer for only a fleeting moment: equally reluctant to end the possibilities so abruptly.

"That would be lovely." Smiling back, she stroked the angular line of Jo's jaw with the back of one finger.

Jo went to the bathroom to change and by the time Alex had finished making herself presentable, she had reappeared, her dress now informally and loosely thrown on, looking both gorgeous and approachable, more of a perfect cleavage showing than before. A healthy shiver coursed through Alex...she so wanted to linger there again.

Jo grinned as Alex gathered her bag together, suspicion hovering that she must be caught up in some secret film. Promoted from employee to companion in the course of an evening.

"This way." She closed the beach house door and scampered up the steps. Alex followed as nimbly as she could and stood waiting while Jo fetched the car.

The night sky and the emerging constellations seemed an appropriate backdrop to the strangeness of this particular night, mirrored and yet shrunk into insignificance by the unfathomable, unpredictable worlds and distances out there. Unlikely, even. Her world was going supernova in the space of just a few days. It served only to focus and concentrate her thoughts. *Flirtation, fling, whatever it is, it's not very feasible, not even practical.* But that had not stopped others from trying. What can be achieved without stepping off the edge sometimes?

After only moments of this speculation, she arrived, the Mercedes skidding a little on the gravel as it braked. She leaned across to open the door and Alex hopped in lightly.

"Tinted windows," she pointed out. "Useful. Oh I don't mean that I have much to hide...just that the ravens are always out there."

Alex nodded vaguely, yet to understand fully. "This is a peculiar week. Do you ever have those times when all the boundaries seem to have moved—a little bit *X-Files* or *Matrix*, even John Cage maybe? As if your take on the world has changed perspective?" She wondered out loud.

"I think I know what you mean. Hollywood typically tends to do that. Anything seems a possibility here. After all, they can create or re-create just about anything."

"But this…!" She brushed the back of Jo's hand on the steering wheel, trying to make her point. Jo grinned. They fell silent as the lights passed by. Lost in thought.

Not talking.

She pulled up close to the hotel, but not right outside. It was relatively quiet. No media hoards or loitering anxious fans tonight. Alex gave her a long look. She looked so right. It felt natural. *Is that it? There might not be another time. Such a thing had happened before. A missed opportunity. It might just finish here.*

"Thank you…" Alex waited a moment, thinking, struggling. Hoping Jo would take the lead. But what could she do now? She couldn't very well invite herself at this point. She switched off the engine, watching.

She continued, "…for a lovely evening and for driving…"

"Well thanks for your playing and company." There was a lengthy pause between them. "I don't want this to be the end." Jo spoke more distantly, embarrassed even by a sudden anxiety, struggling too. "I know I'll want to see you again. It's been hard enough to have this chance." She tailed off.

"Oh." Alex couldn't hold back anymore. Her hand went to the delicious glimpse of bare thigh where her dress had ridden up while driving.

"Look…would you…I mean, do you *want* to come up… just for a while?" She suggested tentatively, aware of the almost audible thudding of her heart and the conversational vacuum. "I can't believe the predictability of that question. It's not the best line ever, is it?"

Jo was wearing a thoughtful expression, controlling the flicker of a smile, pausing, aware that it was a moment in time that affected more than their immediate freedom of choice. A dark flame had ignited in her eyes as she stared back. Her hand closed over Alex's, holding it in place. Neither of them could ignore the unspoken excitement.

"Well, I could, quite possibly. I don't know when else I'll get the chance to see you again. But I don't want to compromise your position."

"Good. You're not." It came out in a murmur as Alex watched her lips while she talked.

"You go first. I'll park. I'll say I've popped in for a drink, if I'm asked at all."

Alex nodded. What did it matter? Who would suspect it?

"And I need to make a quick call. I won't be long."

"Sure." The cloak-and-dagger. The forethought was curious, verging on being unnervingly well-prepared, but then the realization dawned that there were staff to instruct, other duties to consider. She must be used to having to think ahead. It sent a pleased shudder through Alex…and the memory of her words returned…*it's not without some premeditation on my part.* She had employees and employers who wanted to know where she was, or at the very least when she would be back. Hopefully she would not be too specific. Alex was fully aware that it was only Josh's distance across the ocean that kept her from being tied down. She left her to it and went into the hotel. *Just a drink and a chat.* They both knew that was surely a pretense and not all that was wished for. Either way she just wanted to know her better, for longer.

Perhaps she would be delayed. Perhaps something would come up in the phone calls that would inexplicably alter everything.

Inside her room Alex had peeled off her jacket and started to make coffee, her hands shaking slightly, her thoughts attempting to decipher this relatively unknown person beyond the mask of the actress, when there was a knock on the door. She peered through the spy-hole and grinning, let her in.

"Hi! Again!" Jo was wearing unnecessarily large, dark glasses. She removed them as she stepped over the threshold and brushed her lips on Alex's in an easy, relaxed manner as she passed her to enter the room, her dress drifting against her leg. It breathed familiarity. Then she remembered that only nights ago Jo had been in a no doubt similar suite of her own. She closed the door. Jo's every move exuded a natural, physical confidence, and yet there was something instinctively reassuring too, a feeling that Alex was prepared to go with, subtly somewhere, that she was not completely at her ease. That she was risking something of herself.

"Wow, they didn't give me one of these!" She ran her fingernails gently up the piano keys. Alex shivered. "I even suspect you have the better suite."

"They reserve the best for the most sophisticated, you know," Alex joked. Jo grinned, taking it in good humor. She continued, "But seriously, I doubt that..." and went to pour the coffee. Jo came over to the kitchen area to watch and run her fingers gently up Alex's back. She stopped, momentarily surprised, in the middle of her pouring, unable to trust her steadiness, replacing the coffeepot, in danger of spilling its contents.

Jo watched for a moment, placed her lips lightly to her ear, then pulled her toward her and kissed her again gently, pushing her softly against the counter, drinking her in, murmuring, "Oh Alex..." And oh how she *wanted* her to, needed her to, her sweet smell filling all her senses, melting her consciousness as she breathed into her ear, "Alex? I could only have dreamed that we would have this chance. And I *have* dreamed it. Believe me."

She gasped for a breath, thrilled by the information.

"Do you trust in me? That I will only ever do my best *for you*."

"Yes, I believe I do. I feel like I've only seen the top few layers though..."

"Yes, it's all rather faster than I would have liked to pace it, but it's like...there's such a small window of opportunity, it hasn't been easy to coincide and now, suddenly, in your hotel room, I didn't mean to put you in an awkward position..." She spoke huskily, her eloquence falling away. "Trust me not to overstep what you want..."

But Alex was already there, she did believe her, in her consideration, in the explanations she had given and it wasn't just madness; the coffee ignored, the decision halfway made.

"There's no compromise...I asked you too...I want you here..."

Already feeling dislocated from the world at home: it had been a long time since such a moment of privacy or such feelings had woken in her...who could pass up such an offer? The electrical thrills were firing tendrils from somewhere deep inside... Her hands were already around Jo feeling the mold of her, following the natural shape from the small of her back downward.

"I do want to know more about the next few layers," Alex whispered, the almost transparent layers barely covering the offerings beneath, and this time she led Jo over to the bedroom and pushed her gently down on to the bed, sending her backward and pinning her playfully by spreading out the fabric of her dress, laughing at her surprised expression, hoping to have shattered her premeditated images, kissing her with more intensity and the knowledge born of instinct. And everything felt so right, so unthreatening. She could see she was caught up in that moment, her eyes sparkling, struggling to free herself from the dress and trying to roll her over, the outside world and its intrusiveness receding into worthless obscurity.

CHAPTER EIGHT

Jo

In the morning, Alex was woken blearily by a tapping on the door. For a moment she couldn't remember where she was, that is until a tidal wave of elation hit her. She looked at the clock, nine a.m. and turning, saw that she was still there. *Not a dream.* She was on her back, her dark hair tousled, one arm outstretched on the pillows. The sheets not quite covering her beautiful body. Roughened by the night. Stirring a little. She shook her gently.

"Wake up!" She kissed her cheek softly. "Wake up! Piano tuner. I forgot!"

Jo roused herself as she went to the door, slipping on the hotel robe.

Alex opened it a fraction, checking over her shoulder that the bedroom door was closed.

"Hi! I'm sorry. I completely forgot. Please excuse me. I had a late night. Help yourself, while I sort myself out."

A sweet-looking, middle-aged man entered the room, nodding appreciatively at the furnishings of the suite, and settled himself with his kit bag at the piano, already starting to test out the notes. She glanced across the room for evidence of their evening and, satisfied, retired to the bedroom, closing the door.

Jo was just awake, but chuckling softly to herself.

"Not your usual wakeup call is it? I suppose the piano in the room has its down side," she whispered.

"You wait until you hear my warm-ups." Alex laughed softly. "Breakfast?"

"Oh yeah! Full on, please. We can share it."

Alex made the call.

Jo pulled her over toward her, as silently as she could manage. "So it's official. Beautiful all over! Outside and in."

"Cheeky! Ha-ha! I thought that was you!"

"You didn't get all the way round!"

"Didn't I?" She laughed.

"Come on you…shower!" She put her finger to Jo's lips, hushing her, dragged her upright and pushed her toward the bathroom by her gorgeous rear.

Once inside, she closed the door.

"Two doors between us, better than one, you see…" she turned on the shower and kissed her intently, slipping off the robe.

It didn't seem unsuitable to climb in together, barriers were down.

The water was reviving. So was what followed.

"So, what next?" Jo asked, deliberately ambiguously, after kissing her neck, keeping her voice low.

"I have a Rachmaninov rehearsal. Car at ten thirty." Alex took the practical route.

"It looks like your hands are tied even more than mine, over these few weeks." She lifted Alex's hands above her head, jokingly tying them upward, so she could kiss the rivulets of water running down her arms, hungrily wherever she wanted. Alex stifled a giggle.

"Listen. I have a plan." Jo pulled her in by the small of the back, against her stomach. "Sketchy as yet, but we'll see what we can do. Let's swap details, phone numbers, e-mail addresses, let me know your hotels. I'll see if I can catch up with you somewhere. I have gaps."

"Me too. A few…Well, small ones," Alex added hopefully.

"I have the car or I can fly. Perhaps we can drive down from San Francisco. It's a great route along the coast," Jo added optimistically, releasing her.

"Tonight. I have to dine with Vladimir." Alex feigned seriousness.

"Vladimir?"

"Conductor," she explained.

"Ah, networking."

"Mm…But afterward I'm clear."

"Clear to say…meet at mine?" she offered.

"If you like?"

"Like? I like. You could dine light or skip dessert, we can have something on the terrace."

"Sounds perfect. I could let you know if I'm held up at all," Alex murmured through the sound of the shower while she admired Jo's breasts. *Heavenly*. They heard the breakfast arrive.

"Okay. Let's go. Things to do. If we keep quiet and breakfast in the bedroom, he'll be gone soon. It's hardly out of tune. It'll only take about fifteen to twenty minutes." She stepped out of the shower, dried and dressed.

"It's been a watery start," Jo laughed softly, "waves, pool, shower, champagne, tea and coffee…"

Alex brought the trolley through to the bedroom, being careful that the door covered her.

Hearing the clatter, Jo emerged, in her crumpled dress. "Look at this! Do me a favor will you?" she asked softly. "Can you lend me something? If I go out in this…it's going to look so obvious…May I leave my dress with you to bring later?"

Alex nodded, giggling, and rummaged around, pulling out slacks and a top, holding them up against her.

"It's just, if I stroll out with that dress on, I'll definitely look like the woman on the town who has been out all night."

Alex told her about the fleeting private show from her guest doing 007 last night as she tossed her the clothes.

"Will that do?"

There was a knock at the door.

She nearly dropped her coffee cup and hurried to slip out of the room, with care.

She returned quickly. "He's gone. You can stop whispering." She picked up a delicate watch. Like a bracelet, with a minuscule face. "Gosh. Time's getting on. Do you mind if I...? Spare me for a moment." She slipped out of the room, taking her cup with her.

She went to the piano to begin a few rapidly flowing scales and arpeggios, easing her fingers into the day.

"Best be off then...work to do," Jo said, catching her as she reached the bottom of a scale and kissing her lingeringly, apparently deliberately leaving her with a sense of unfinished business. "See you later?"

"Time?"

She went to the telephone table and scribbled on a piece of paper, tearing it off and handing it to Alex, retrieving her dark glasses as she did so. "My mobile number...Call me when you're on the way. I'm tied up this afternoon too." She paused. "You're not going to get cold feet on me?"

"Does it look like it?"

Jo shook her head and caught her face in her hands for a second, staring intently. "It's been amazing. Sudden, and amazing."

Alex put her hand on hers, pinning it there momentarily. "Yes. I'd go with that." She apologized, a little distractedly, "Rachmaninov calls...Sorry. I'll let you out. Like the disguise by the way." She stroked the angle of her jaw before opening the door, breathing in a last gasp of her smell as Jo leaned to kiss her neck. "Very incognito." She smiled at her.

"Yes," Jo answered, "*did they do it?*" she mimicked. "Privacy, see...It will be worth it."

And she was gone.

Alex closed the door and had to return to Rachmaninov. The center of her very being throbbed, a long-hidden fundamental drumbeat reawakened. Sudden and amazing. Exactly.

* * *

Josh called while she was in the car on the way to the rehearsal, stuck in the morning LA traffic, cars snailing their way along.

"How's it going?" he asked.

"Great!" She answered trivally. She wasn't telling him the best bits. "You'd have loved the party." She reeled off a few names.

"My girl, we have crossover of a different variety!" He was laughing.

You don't know the half of it.

"And I'm really chuffed with you and for you." He continued, "The phone has been going over here. Johnson wants you, after Smiley—and would you play a little classical too! This is the stuff you like, right? Crossover—popularizing? LA has confirmed the recital class at the end of the tour, the Beeb have booked you for another of the Prom series, someone's pulled out, and this one you will not believe...Your hands are needed to star briefly in a film!"

"What? You must be joking!" She remembered passing Josh's card around a few times, when asked.

"Yes, my golden girl. *Global* has a crucial pianist scene and needs it to look realistic and as you're there and...quote... *your hands are so beautiful*...would you be hand stand-in on the piano for the actress? Actually you wouldn't believe the fee he's mentioned, just for that."

"When?"

"It can fit in before San Diego. And you won't mind if I drop by to witness this and make a few more contacts?"

She swallowed a sigh and satisfied herself with rolling her eyes. "Of course. Can you send through the details?" She paused. "What's the Prom?"

"Mozart B-flat. Must fly now. Places to meet, people to go. More later, darling. Bye."

She toyed with the phone in her hand. California was truly unexpected.

* * *

The Rachmaninov rehearsal was perfectly efficient. They had needed to work only on matching the phrasing ideas between wind and piano and in a distracted moment she had modulated incorrectly at the recapitulation in the first movement; but realizing her error, had covered it quickly, laughing up at the orchestra, who sent out some appreciative shuffles. It was a moment of blues. *Sorry Rach. Actually he probably wouldn't have minded…I'll blame it on last night.* She gave Vladimir a grin and he raised his eyes at her, laughing, overdoing an expressive, pianistic impression.

* * *

She drizzled away the afternoon in the vicinity of the concert hall, while the orchestra worked on the *Symphonic Dances.* Across the massive parking lot, there was a California sports bar where she grabbed a Caesar salad and watched football bemusedly on one of the many screens. Afterward at an enormous mall, she browsed for souvenirs to buy for friends and family and a bottle of something for later. How pleasantly mundane life could be at one end of the spectrum while being unrealistically glamorous at the other. It was all an illusion. Jo's and her professions counted on creating an illusion, another world to be lost in. Thank God the extremes balanced each other out. But perhaps it wasn't so easy for Jo to create that balance. Not so easy to wander to a mall—although perhaps easier in LA than England. She wondered vaguely what was occupying her this afternoon and strolled back to the venue with bags in tow to turn a few corners in the concerto, revise the memory blip on the piano in her dressing room and generally crash out in the corner for a while. Leanne, her best friend, sent a text through confirming her Vancouver visit. *My best friend.* Goodness, she'd have to find a way to tell her. Would she cope? Would she still be her friend? Hell, perhaps she knew her better than she knew herself. But it wouldn't be possible to tell her everything. There was a huge issue of secret identity here. And what to tell? A fling? An affair? And now she was out. To herself at least. Was she in danger of fancying her old friend? She searched her feelings anxiously, but no tremors responded. On second thought it would have reared itself as an issue already had it been ever likely. That was something of a relief anyway.

These thoughts trawled through her while waiting for Vladimir to be free. She called the hotel and booked the full massage that her creaking frame was demanding for the following morning, attempting to distract herself from these potential complications.

Vladimir appeared promptly at the end of the rehearsal and escorted her to his car, which whisked them away to a restaurant near to his hotel.

They talked shop and speculated on the possibilities of crossing over between popular and classical fields and how to attract the audience. She spent some time describing the Oscar party to him, the conflicting glamour and servitude of the date, the extremes between the genres. He agreed, sounding intellectually mystical in his thick Russian accent—"One is subservient to and dependent upon the audience, the composer, the performer and in the peak of the moment the music itself after all. At our concert the music should be the most important. At that party," he said it almost distastefully, "presumably the actors were the most important." She ordered lightly, looking discreetly at her watch, wondering how long she needed to persevere. She still ached pleasurably from the previous night and longed to escape some of his monologuing to pursue a more diverting evening. As they finished up the main course, she opted immediately for coffee, begging an early night and a little preparation for tomorrow as her excuse.

He agreed it was a wise move for both of them, given the extent and intensity of the concert and offered her a lift back to her hotel. This she accepted gladly, knowing she would be changing cars and departing again, the excited anticipation coursing through her confirming that, tonight the actor *was* the most important.

They embraced politely in the car and her obligation was over.

* * *

By seven, the hotel car had dropped her off on the next block from Jo's house. She was amused by the secrecy and waited for the car to depart before walking around the corner, Jo's dress in a bag dangling from her arm. Her blood raced at the memory of slipping it off her and the abandon with which she had kicked it onto the floor, the small silk panties that the act had exposed.

She called the intercom at the gates. Her heart skipped unsteadily as she waited, hoping that nothing had changed. Aware that everything had changed for her. This was unfamiliar territory. She felt like a call girl at the gate, a lesbian call girl. The thought made her laugh out loud. She was buzzed in immediately and Jo was there, framed in the doorway. She closed the door behind them, held her shoulders and kissed Alex's ear, while they breathed each other in.

"Hi." She spoke softly. "Come through. What's the joke?"

Alex explained.

A wicked chuckle escaped quietly from her.

"Exactly! See!"

On the terrace, facing the evening sun, a couple of lounges and a small table laid with an ice bucket, beer, white wine and a selection of the previous evening's leftovers welcomed them.

"Millie's out. I gave her the night off," she explained. "How was Vlad? The impaler?"

Alex placed her contribution into the ice bucket. "Fine. Well, a bit interminable actually, but well-meaning, I think. Escaped from any impaling, anyway."

"Ha! You look weary. Come on. Put your feet up." She patted one of the chairs and settled herself in the other, pushing aside a pile of paperwork, kicking off Birkenstocks and shrugging her arms into a cardigan. It was a far cry from the red carpet. It looked strangely familiar and relaxed. She took a beer from the bucket and swigged from the bottle. "Want one?"

"Lovely." She passed one over. Alex toed off her shoes and queried herself. "Weary? Yes. I suppose so. It's been nonstop this week. And I ache from the playing. I've booked a massage tomorrow. I'll have to go back tonight. Tomorrow's really tough."

"Mmm."

"I ache from last night too…in a good way, I mean…"

"God, I'm glad you said that! That means I don't have to!" She smiled.

"How was yours? Your day?"

"All right. The makeup artist didn't notice, or at least didn't comment on my raw lips…" She chuckled wistfully, touching her fingers to them. "This pile of paperwork comes as a result of today's efforts. More work! But for now—to business." She put on a pair of reading glasses, looking unexpectedly academic and pulled some blank sheets and a pencil from the pile. "Your schedule, my schedule, let's see how they compare."

Alex liked the efficiency and pulled her BlackBerry from her bag. As she filled her in with the details and contact numbers, Jo scribbled busily—drawing up a tabulated arrangement for the two of them.

"And this is me…" She handed Alex a copy from her pile of papers, then added her details to the table to see where they tallied. She thought for a while, chewing on the end of the pencil. "Okay. This is how it might work…" She leaned over the dividing table to point a few things out. "This weekend's a write-off. And next week I'm busy, you're in Vancouver, Victoria and Seattle. But…and this is where it starts to look good…"

Alex put her hand on Jo's arm, pulling herself up to face her, cross-legged. "Wait. Hang on a minute."

"What you don't like my planning? I'm sorry it's a bit of a fault…looking ahead."

"No it's not that." She spoke quietly, "I love your planning. It's so sweet. It's…keen. But why keen? You could be with any one of a number of beautiful actresses. I suppose I'm asking… Why me? Why now?"

"Look, I haven't been totally straight here." She took off the glasses, dangling them from one hand and then giggled at her unintentional ambiguity. She gazed intently at Alex. "I didn't want to sound…scary…certifiable even…but I was…what's the best word…enchanted that first time I saw you and it kept playing through my mind. I tracked you down in the Proms guide and found myself free on the day of the concert. Guessing you'd be in your rehearsal, and able to linger in Knightsbridge…so near to the Albert Hall…the two things coinciding so easily…I walked along to the place, heart pounding at the impetuosity, and smiled sweetly at the house steward, telling them a bit of a tale about researching a part and…they let me go in. I went up and up to the top boxes in that massive place, you know, near the top balconies, with snippets of some crazy piece…"

"Stockhausen, probably…" she murmured, entranced.

"Thanks, yes. Glimpses of this crazy piece drifting through open doors on the way and sat there, hidden, watching you hammering out the piece with…"

"The BBC Symphony Orchestra…"

"In this massive place, echoing all around, with no one to hear but me, apparently. And it occurred to me that I wanted to see you closer and found my way down a maze of staircases and corridors to the backstage area where I could watch you from the choir wings and the intensity and sometimes laughter in the rehearsal…"

"You should see the counting in that thing…"

"And you were funny and beautiful too, as well as being blindingly talented in this inaccessible, amazing way. And it occurred to me that I would probably never find a way to meet you and say hello, because you're a musician and I'm an actor and we'd never be in the same place, not without creating a whole heap of unwanted attention. And then my time called me away and I left before you finished and that was it…It's a bit TWYC, isn't it?" She smiled a little sheepishly this time, dropping her gaze, and shrugged.

Alex was mystified at the thought of being watched in such a manner by such a glamorous female. "And then…"

"We coincided at the Oscar party and that was pure coincidence; and the lift…that was good luck."

She tilted Jo's face toward her and gave her a gentle kiss. "It's not TWYC. There were no weird notes…"

"I was tempted…"

Alex smiled at her. "You were just doing what I was doing when I couldn't take my eyes off you and watched you in slow motion, frame-by-frame on my television…and from behind a curtain at the party."

"You did, didn't you?"

"Oh, yes. Shocking, isn't it?"

"I have to admit I did see you peering out from behind the curtain. And…"

"You were absolutely gorgeous and it made me want to kiss those lips…" She leaned across and did, again, delighted by the warm response.

"I could just as easily ask—why me?"

"I'm still working on that one…but I'm very pleased to say I've discovered that there seem to be a few little gray cells on the other side of that pretty face…"

"Very funny, Poirot. Okay. So, where was I…"

She pointed to the schedule. "You were saying this is where it starts to look good…?" Alex let her hand go. Jo put the glasses back on and returned to the papers, her chain of thought recovering from the disruption.

"Yes…Wednesday week…I'm off for three days. I could fly to San Francisco, pick up a hire car, take in your concert, meet you—stay the night?"

Alex nodded encouragingly.

"Aha!" She smiled, pleased to be on the right track. "Then my drive back to LA down the coast road. It's gorgeous… breakfast in Monterey…Pebble Beach…seals on the rocks… Then, having called your hotel to expect you on Tuesday and your fixer that you'll be on your mobile as you've met up with a friend, you stay a long weekend here, we can work from here. Experimentally. I'll give Millie some time off. What do you reckon?"

Alex lay back on the lounger and stretched out her legs. "Here? Quick moving...but sounds...heavenly."

"Perfect." Jo slapped the paperwork down on the bed with an air of finality and removed her glasses.

"As long as you don't mind me having to practice?"

"Work's work. Of course. I don't mean to be so prescriptive. It's just the only way I can see of coordinating some time together. How about a relaxing swim?" She stood up decisively.

"I didn't bring anything."

"No matter...one of those advantages of the ivory tower." She grinned and pulled Alex up from the lounger by the hand.

They strolled down the garden, arms linked, through the grove of trees. When they reached the secluded pool they let their clothes fall to the ground without bothering with the beach house and slid into the water.

* * *

Later, their appetites for the pool sated, feeling languorous, they threw their clothes on halfheartedly and strolled back to the house.

"So, if you're coming to stay, wouldn't you like the full tour?" She led Alex inside, going from room to room until she was familiar with the interior of the house: studio, gym, bathrooms and bedrooms. They stretched out lazily on the bed, chatting together, until Jo admitted, "I've had this on my mind all day," and Alex's whole being surged with grateful agreement.

As if a match had been applied, the mood smoldered, they were staring quietly at each other, different now, sharing privileged knowledge, memories of the previous night. How hungry Alex was to feel the silk of her skin again! Her lower abdomen flooded with anticipation. Jo's brilliant eyes seemed to be searching hers for answers, waiting, unmoving. The perfect receptacle. Alex's hands felt up her arms, sensing the firmness, the latent strength just beneath the fine fabric of her shirt. She drew her hand over Jo's face, tracing eyebrows, cheekbones. Jo remained still, watching, amused, then unable to resist, drew

Alex to her by the waist, so that Alex could take in her curves, surprising lightness and fragility, feeling upward to the warmth of breasts that were begging her to...Jo pulled the front of her dress down, beating her to it, placing her mouth over one nipple, hungrily tracing her tongue. Soft noises escaped each of them and Alex drew her in toward her again, working her way up her neck to her mouth, finding her lips parted, welcoming. Jo started, seemingly surprised to find that while she had been otherwise distracted other hands had already loosened her clothing and taken hold of her, sinking into her, and she flopped backward onto the safe welcome of the mattress, gladly becoming overwhelmed by the immediate purpose, Alex's hands feeling their way hungrily up her legs, gathering her skirt on her arms...

Reluctantly, when the waves of excitement had settled and breathing had returned to a relatively normal speed, Alex swung herself slowly, thoughtfully, off the bed. She retrieved clothing on the way, explaining herself quietly: "Sorry, I'll have to go. This concerto tomorrow is massive and I nearly slipped off the rails thinking about last night during today's rehearsal."

"Apologies for the distraction," Jo responded huskily, propping herself up onto one elbow.

"No, distract away...I'm a pro...I can cope." Alex laughed. "Oh, you look gorgeous. I can hardly bear to move away from you. But it's really hard, even without feeling exhausted. What would the equivalent be? Maybe a tough day's shooting or some chunky Shakespeare? I don't know."

"Hang on. I'll drive you. Just drop you off. Come on. Shakespeare? Haven't been asked to do any for a while."

"Isn't that a bit hackneyed for you?"

"You're kidding. It's all the rage. Just to prove you still have what it takes."

"Oh, you'd make a great Catherine. You wouldn't have to speak. The French army would just swoon at the sight of you!"

"Ha! Ha! Let's go. You're right about a tough day's shooting...I should warn you, sometimes I'm fit for nothing. That's the bit they don't mention in the publicity. They like to think you can walk off like the elegant heroine and dance all night."

Alex liked the thought that she might need to be warned, that there would be a future. She collected her belongings and Jo drove her back, kissing her reluctantly goodbye in the car.

"I hadn't wanted to rush any of this, you know. It's just the pressure of the moment…availability somehow."

"I know too."

"We can make this work if we want to…" She looked at Alex hopefully.

She nodded. "See you in San Francisco." It sounded distant, unlikely.

Despite the twinge of disappointment to see her drive off, Alex was grateful too to be alone, to be able to fall into a cool bed without expending further energy. This beautiful woman was so much of a distraction. Beautiful was not a sufficiently accurate term. She dazzled her. Everything about her demanded her full attention. And it was not just that, there was still more to discover, more beneath the façade, but the pace was simply too much. It would be an impossible tour if she burned herself out so early. And already it was hard to find the space. The events of the past week were overwhelming, an unbelievably surreal work of art, painted in huge, sweeping strokes and striking colors that stood out in contrast against the usual scenery: different worlds colliding and sparking off each other. Their actions, her personal revelation, all had happened so quickly that she hadn't had the thinking time to catch up with herself. Encroaching into such a totally alien area of the entertainment world was bizarre. There was an insubstantial, temporary feeling to the whole thing and this brief fling felt like a holiday romance, sure to evaporate with the vapor trail on the plane as she left for another city. And yet…it was privileged—a moment of intimacy. It was almost absurd to think that it could have any staying power, when Jo was surrounded by beauty and temptation at work and Alex was, well basically, having a simultaneous love affair with an inanimate object, which only came to life if she gave herself to it absolutely. And frequently on opposite sides of the globe, let alone country. And yet…could such a thing be possible? It was not abstract digital images of Jo which she took to her dreams, but rather more specific and personal knowledge that made her smile as she drifted into sleep. *I don't suppose many people know about those glasses or that scar…*

CHAPTER NINE

Back to Reality

I saw you at the party. You looked fabulous.

The card lay open and her hands rested limply in her lap. *What the bloody hell?*

She'd been distracted enough to forget about all this and now...*No. Hell no, as they say over here. I will not be affected.*

She tore it up and threw the pieces in a trash receptacle as she walked through the hotel for her massage.

...Bliss. The masseuse ran her hands expertly over Alex's aching muscles and all thoughts of that intrusion and the tension from her playing dissolved, drowned by the aromatic oils and the sympathetic touch.

Back at her room she spent a peaceful hour working through some yoga, aware that she shouldn't push too hard with her muscles artificially relaxed. It was a practice she'd taken up at college when the going had become tough at one point. *That bloody pianist...No!* she commanded herself. It was pointless going over that again, and irrelevant. Emotional turmoil had not helped her then. It had not come up in her mind for ages; she must be…stirred up. She made a conscious effort to change the direction of her thoughts. She found she was looking forward to Leanne's arrival. Her best friend. They'd been through some highs and lows together and if it was half as much fun as when she had joined her in Hong Kong it would be fantastic. She rang ahead to the hotels in Vancouver, Victoria and Seattle to check that there could be a spare bed or sofa bed made up in the suites and asked the Victoria and Seattle hotels to arrange a rental car. One of them would be sure to use it. Would she tell her everything? She wondered. She would have to move on from here, not dwell on or pine for the events of the past few days.

* * *

The Rachmaninov was a resounding success. Afterward she said a sad goodbye to the LA Philharmonic and Vlad the Impaler at a brief drinks gathering. The orchestra and its conductor had become strangely warm and familiar in this absorbing opening week, although there was one more date still to complete with them on the return leg of the tour. Vladimir, who was departing at this point, assured her they would be meeting again and she kissed the good-looking leader on the cheek as she said goodbye. *An actor's kiss*, she smiled to herself.

Her bed seemed empty that night and she thought again how grateful she would be to see Leanne, otherwise she would be dwelling on *her* too much. She placed a hand gently over the warm areas where Jo had touched her, protectively covering the secret memories of the week…and slept.

* * *

On the plane to Vancouver the next day Alex leafed through a selection of magazines bought in the airport shops. She had not slept well. There had been a dream, an uncomfortable scenario where she was approaching a flight of steps to some occasion or other, arm in arm with Jo. She had been grinning confidently, but she could still feel now, even in retrospect, the anxiety as they approached together. Suddenly a murder of crows with huge black wings had flown down at them, changing imperceptibly into cloaked photographers with flashing cameras. The blinding, epileptic lights had convulsed her, she was falling onto the floor, thrashing around beneath their feet, being trodden on, stepped over, she could hear Jo calling for her, anxious, defensive, but she could no longer see her, she was drowning in the cloaks and feet...

She returned her attention to the magazine's Oscar issue and flicked through, looking critically at the article on her, managing to raise a chuckle. She searched a little greedily for a picture of Jo and found it, captured in the group in which she had first seen her, from a different angle, holding drinks up to the camera in salute. In the light of recent experience her face appeared different. A reminiscent twinge prodded from somewhere within. One of the actors was draped possessively on her shoulder. She smiled. She really didn't mind. *I have secret knowledge.* It was a private badge to wear. One of the trashier magazines was publishing an interview with the actor in the film that she had savored at home..."*I loved her amazing kisses,*" the icon enthused, as if dropping some unsubtle hint. *I really don't mind,* Alex reminded herself, *it's acting, it's publicity...it's what they do...and if they're doing it well, then it will be convincing.* And the article? Marketing. She surprised herself with her lack of possessiveness.

What if that were it for them? What was to be done about it if she never heard from her again? It wasn't worth the worry. She would not be a wallflower, a hanger-on, a stage-door johnny.

She chuckled out loud at the expression. There were other issues to be getting on with. The concerts...a career. In itself... it had been a treat. But it was smaller than the whole. Her real kisses seemed to linger over her even now. They were hers to keep, even if only in memory. A pleasure, an honest compliment. Even if never to be repeated. A gift. An LA souvenir. San Francisco seemed unlikely. She scanned an article on a reality

TV show, which made her laugh to herself again and turned her attention to the more professionally pressing matter of going over the finger patterns of the Rachmaninov for later.

* * *

The flight was not interminable. After glimpses of the mountains and the wilder spaces of the west coast, the plane put down at Vancouver. Following baggage claim, she was welcomed by another orchestral manager and the roller coaster continued. All was smoothly organized—*thanks at least for that, Josh!* The procedures already seemed routine. They stopped off at the hotel first and Alex fell in love immediately with the new harbor-view room. The orchestral representative went for a coffee in the hotel café, while she settled herself in and whizzed over the piano keys a few times, familiarizing herself with the new piano; then she was escorted to the concert hall, where the orchestra, already in rehearsal, welcomed her warmly, her reputation now preceding her on the tour. A new chapter; LA was fading already into a dreamlike state.

* * *

It was a delight to be alone again in the hotel room later, anticipating the arrival of her friend. The place seemed pleasantly quiet, as if she had stepped off the Hollywood carousel, somehow more parochial. The hotel was so much closer to the hall. She could walk there if she wanted.

How would it be with Leanne, in the light of her new self-knowledge? She wondered, afraid that she might have to put on an act.

When the knock at the door came and she opened it, it was at first to a huge bouquet of flowers. Fear-motivated adrenaline skipped a heartbeat for her. But then:

"Hi, love it's me! I'm in here somewhere!" Leanne's refreshingly familiar voice emerged from somewhere in among the blooms. "Here take these, the foyer said would I mind taking them up. Just arrived for you!"

She took them, a little warily, and Leanne came in, followed by a bellman hauling her suitcases.

Alex quickly read the card. *Just me, wishing you luck up north. Kisses, J.* She wondered briefly: *Josh or Jo?*

Her heart lunged for another reason, then not wishing to appear distracted she launched herself into Leanne's warm embrace and they fell about giggling. Everything felt...normal. She set about making some coffee.

"So good to see you," Alex said. "How was the flight?"

"Long, sleepless. What about you? How's it going?"

"Yep. All fine. A bit tired already."

"I bet. Poor you. We'll be exhausted together then. Any joy with those concert tickets for later?"

"Your own box. Both nights. I think the boxes come with champagne, etcetera."

"Fabulous. You're a darling. Sounds great." As she kicked off her shoes, Leanne asked, "So who are the flowers from?"

"Just the previous conductor. He calls himself Jock. A right joker..." She lied quite easily. "I'll make you coffee."

"Great. Let me help...Any funny business with Jock then?"

"God no. Not him." The implication hung in the air.

"Hello? Action elsewhere, sweetheart?"

"A little. I'll tell you later." Leanne looked intrigued, but apparently could sense some reticence. Alex distracted her, "You?"

"Oh! Glad to get away. I heard they're having a baby." She shrugged. An ex-boyfriend she had loved, probably still did.

"Oh, Leanne. He was never right for you. Too selfish. Come on. Let's not dwell on any of it. It's us for a week. This is you, by the way..." Alex indicated the second bedroom. "Two bedrooms. Settle yourself in. And we have a car, not here, don't really need it here, but Victoria and Seattle. Both. You can have it to explore, as long as you drop me off and pick me up."

"This is sounding better and better."

"You must be tired too."

"Not yet. A bit excited. But do you mind if we relax and just eat up here before we go out tonight?"

"Sure. That suits me too. I'll need to do some practice in a bit. After the coffee, how about a swim? The indoor pool looks good…bubble pool, too."

"Absolutely. Cheers, love." Leanne raised her coffee cup and they clinked, laughing.

"It's so good to have you here, a dose of familiarity in a seething sea of egotism."

* * *

They mooched their week away in affable friendship. Only once were Alex's waters ruffled when she woke, crying out from the frightening manacles of a dream from which she was struggling to free herself and unable to wake. When she did and finally went to the small kitchen area to drink water and attempt to revive herself, Leanne called out to her. She went through to sit on her friend's bed, confessing all about the creepy letters and flowers. Unable to shake off the unsettling dream, she climbed in with Leanne, who vehemently insisted that she start to keep the offending articles in case the police could be of help back home and, finally pacified, warmed by the sisterly vicinity of her friend, she slept more soundly.

Alex had to work, of course, which interfered with a potential holiday with Leanne. They both enjoyed standing on the ferry deck to Victoria watching the dark waters and scattered islands pass by, but Alex missed the whale-watching trip in Victoria, a little jealous as she slaved at another Tchaikovsky rehearsal, not least when she found out the tour had intercepted a whole pod of orcas with youngsters and a large male. They managed the Seattle Tower and waterfront together, as well as a couple of decent meals out and a tearful, girly evening in with *Sleepless in Seattle* following the waterfront tour. Leanne entertained herself independently, which worked rather well while Alex had rehearsals and practice, and her friend thought she had almost hit it off with one of the bar staff at the Fairmont…

but, too late unfortunately, on her last night, with no chance of expanding upon the possible opportunity. The friends parted wistfully, putting a date in their diaries for Alex's return, assuring themselves of the next meeting and Leanne took the hire car to the airport, leaving Alex behind to head on to San Francisco alone. Having said nothing to her about Jo Davison.

CHAPTER TEN

The Convertible and the Villa

The brief time in San Francisco was enlivened by messages from Jo in preparation for meeting and by managing to squeeze in some sightseeing trips to the giant redwoods and the harbor tour. She had not let go. It was not just fleeting…not yet…

After the second concert, as she left the stage door, a little wearily and thankful not to have a reception tonight, a dark convertible with the roof up flashed its headlights at her. She wandered over expectantly, lugging her concert bags. The window descended smoothly.

"You made it."

It was Jo.

"You betcha. As they say over here." She pushed the passenger door open. "Jump in. I'll throw the stuff in the back."

Alex ducked into the car while she loaded the trunk. She got back in the car and leaned over, taking Alex's face in her hands and they spent a few minutes kissing thoroughly inside the privacy of the car. "God. That feels good." Alex rubbed her nose gently against Jo.

"The Ritz-Carlton, you said?"

"Precisely."

"Yep. Know it. Let's get out of here then." She pulled the car away. "How was the concert? Sounded well received, what I heard."

"You caught some of it?"

"Just the last part, the flight was later than I'd hoped for. Sounds so exhausting—all that octave stuff at the end."

"Exactly. I could do with an unwind in the Jacuzzi."

"Jacuzzi? Mmm, delightful…Room enough for two?"

"Oh, I should think so," she teased. "If you buy the champagne?"

"Think I could stretch to that. Worth a celebration," Jo echoed.

They pulled up at the hotel. Alex jumped out more lightly and happily now. "I'll find out where you park. Like the car, by the way." She disappeared inside the hotel and returned moments later, "Round the back. Here's the pass. See you in a minute, I mentioned a 'guest.'"

She hurried on ahead to the room with her bags, tidied it quickly and started filling the huge corner bath. The champagne bucket she had ordered at reception was the first to arrive, and she only just had time to pour and sip before Jo appeared. She kicked the door gently shut behind her, plumping bags down on the floor and came over to hug Alex.

"I missed you."

"And I you."

"Been busy?"

"I imagine you know what it's like…"

Jo helped her out of her evening dress, slipping off the straps and undoing the tight zip at the back. Her hands ran down Alex's back as it became freed.

"No reception tonight?" she murmured into her ear.

"Thankfully no. Last night." Alex helped her with her T-shirt and chinos, sliding them sensuously from her body. "Oh my…"

"Good timing then." Jo kissed her neck and shoulders and went on down her body as the corset of the bodice loosened.

"I received flowers. They were from you?"

"Uh-huh."

"Then I need to say thanks, but I think we need another code name for you, rather than '*J*'—my delayed thanks is because I wondered whether it was Josh, my agent, for a while."

"How about Betty? BB as in Betty Boop."

She caught on. "Betty? She's a naughty girl!"

"So?…" She kissed her more intimately. Then explored a mental leap. "So…where's the naughtiest place you've made love?"

Alex paused to consider whether to tell her, enjoying her playful mood. "Okay. Bearing in mind this was some time ago: swimming pool changing rooms, field of cows at night, well I presume they were cows, I couldn't see them, I could just hear the snorting, might have been a human audience with sinus trouble—who knows; organ loft; by myself on a plateau of rock at a remote cove and in a field of high wheat…if that counts."

"Adventurous. What an array! By yourself, I like that image too. To yourself. It has to happen sometimes."

"Mmm," Alex sighed, recovering from the exposure. She should make her suffer in return, "You?"

"Mmm." She paused to consider. "In a private beach villa, about a week and a half ago."

"Ha! But that's not fair—I gave away more…" Her embarrassment prickled her skin to the roots of her hair.

"No you didn't. I've just given away rather a lot." She paused for thought. "It all sounded…delightful. Perhaps you'd like to expand upon the 'by yourself' bit…"

Alex gave her a light slap on the rear and led her away to the luxurious bathroom, taking the glasses with them.

"Oh, bliss!" She sank into the bubbles and turned off the taps.

"What does this do?" She flicked a button. "Let's see, ah! More bubbles."

"The perfect antidote. Oh, that was hard work!"

Jo rubbed her shoulders, neck and softly down her arms.

"How do you do that actually?"

"What? The playing?"

"Mmm."

"You must know. It's basically the same as you. Years of practice. Mind-numbing repetition! Actually it's not mind-numbing, you need to be exhaustively alert. How do you learn the lines to a film or a play?"

"Read it, memorize it, analyze it. You just know what's coming. It seems to stick somehow."

"Photographic memory?"

"Maybe. Wouldn't want to boast…"

"Exactly. Do you have to act it all out in front of a mirror?"

"Occasionally…" She grinned.

"That I'd like to see."

"You know, it fascinates me." Jo put down her glass and dived under the bubbles, finding other places to kiss.

"This fascinates *me*," Alex murmured, mostly to herself.

* * *

The next day, after an early alarm, Alex caressed the beautiful Bösendorfer piano with a reluctant goodbye and they checked out, leaving messages of thanks to the hotel staff and San Francisco Symphony. Jo brought the car round and loaded the cases; then they leaped in enjoying the freedom of it all. Fewer people would care about either of them in San Francisco and the car afforded a certain anonymity that an airport would not.

They drove quickly out of the city and headed for the Route 1 coast road, stopping at Monterey Bay for a late breakfast, watching the surf rolling in. After Monterey, Jo lowered the roof on the car and they flew along beside the coast, weaving through scenically spectacular Big Sur, with the surf and seals far below them on one side, rugged mountains on the other, the wind ruffling through their hair and LA far ahead. The noise was such that there was little room for conversation—the exhilaration of the fresh air and speed were enough.

When they hit the outskirts of LA the lights were coming on as evening drew in. Jo flicked a switch and the roof went up again.

"I'm a bit knackered now. That's a hell of a long way. I remember now, it's always easier in thought than in deed! I'm just double-checking, you are staying with me, right? You've fixed it?"

"Absolutely."

She grinned, but said no more and steered the car nimbly back to the beach villa.

Over the next few days the imaginary drawbridge was drawn up against the outside world, lowered only for unavoidable engagements. Free time was eked out together undisturbed, by the pool and on the beach, where a minute lasted forever, even though the days threatened to fly by. The housekeeper had disappeared as conveniently arranged, but not without surreptitiously stocking up the kitchen. Andy had returned to the UK. They popped in and out of the house for various appointments. Alex had work, socializing and practice and went out for the final rehearsal and concert using Jo's house as her base. It was odd to feel so at home in LA.

"I'm sorry I can't come," Jo apologized the day of her concert. "I'll be too easily spotted at this one. It's the location of the hall. And I have some prep to do."

"It's fine. I need to concentrate anyway, you'd just be a distraction!"

"I can live with that."

Tuesday arrived all too soon. Jo had to pack for Rome. Alex had to leave to convince Josh of her part of the story; she had to be at the hotel when he arrived to pick her up.

They parted lingeringly and reluctantly. Jo drove her to the hotel.

"When do I see you again then?"

Alex felt anxious, suddenly in danger of being bereft, an exposed child with her favorite toy taken away. "How does this work, your huge career and profile, my schedule?"

"I thought that was you…We'll make it, if we have to." Jo kissed her, still within the safe confines of the car. "And I think I have to…We have contact details don't we? There'll be plenty of time when we're not on different continents. Hopefully."

"Of course. See you then, darling. You've made this tour extra-special. Thank you." Alex tried to sound more frivolous than she felt.

Jo left and blew her a kiss as she looked back, while the bellman manhandled Alex's luggage into the hotel. She could just see her grin that grin that she knew so well.

* * *

Josh arrived as expected on the stroke of midday. "Darling!" he gushed as he embraced her. "Come for lunch. The shoot's at two, nearby, not far, time for a sandwich and catch up."

Already, she felt a little irritated with him, that he assumed possession of her so easily.

They ate briskly in the hotel café and she filled him in with the professional, not the personal, parts of the tour. "You've done brilliantly then," he cooed. "Now for your hands...let's have a look at them. Are they looking all moisturized and beautiful?"

The remark was cringe-worthy. "I manicured them last night, especially for the camera, you know."

"Let's go then."

They paid up and called a hotel car to go to the studios. The MGM lot was abuzz with activity when they arrived. Costumed actors and actresses milled around and technicians scurried to and fro, but they were quickly ushered into a small, quiet back studio, where the piano keyboard on a beautiful old walnut grand had been carefully lit. Alex was hastily dressed in a period costume, her distinctive hair pinned high out of the way, her face powdered, and then she was instructed to make herself at home, to "take a seat." A disembodied voice from behind the bright lights and camera called out: "Okay. About five minutes of the Mozart, plenty of elegant movement and fire. We're focusing on your hands here. This is a high-class girl, frustrated in love, taking her emotions out on the instrument...you're familiar with *A Room With A View?*"

Alex nodded helpfully. "That sort of thing. In the style of Lucy Honeychurch!" she exclaimed, referring to a main character.

Alex obliged, having to play the piece several times before the director yelled, "Cut and print!" The costume was peeled off again. Then they were steered via a staff coffee bar on the way out.

"Many thanks, Alex." The director squeezed her familiarly on the shoulder.

Josh butted in, reaching out to shake hands. "Josh. Alex's agent. Hello."

The director continued to speak to Alex, politely rebuffing Josh with a nod of acknowledgment and a cursory handshake. "We're in the middle of setting up a ballroom scene, but let me just introduce you to the co-leads, before you go." He led them to a small group, clustered around coffee cups.

"Alex Palmer and Josh Pembroke," the director introduced, "meet our female lead, whose hands you have just doubled for, Jo and our co-star Rob..."

Jo turned around at the first words of the introduction, open-mouthed in surprise. They had not discussed this one— *how could that have happened?* She reverted immediately to looking more mundane and intoning, "Oh, hi," as she shook hands politely with each of them. "Still here?"

She caught Alex's faintest glimmer of a mischievous smile. "About three weeks in all."

"Very nice. The compliments keep rolling in about your performances."

"Of course!" Josh butted in. "Alex did your party!"

"That's right." Jo confirmed laconically, toying with her coffee cup.

"Josh! I spoke with your PA on the phone."

"Pleased to meet you," she replied automatically, eyes twinkling, raising one eyebrow a fraction.

"A pleasant surprise." Alex smiled. "We'd best be going. Other commitments."

"Thanks for filling in for my musical inadequacies!" Jo added charmingly.

"Well, goodbye," Josh bubbled in. "Excellent to meet you both. If you need any quality entertainment again, just give me a call and we can book you up with Alex."

Alex raised *her* eyebrows a little, annoyed to be a commodity, as Josh dished out business cards to all within reach.

"Goodbye," she said firmly, aching a little at the word, not knowing when she would see her again, or even if. She looked briefly, wistfully back as she steered Josh away and Jo caught her eye, smiling a brief smile at her as she talked to her colleagues.

"Amazing, meeting these stars isn't it?" Josh babbled.

She remained silent, only nodding, as they walked away.

Josh had to return to England before her, after various meetings with contacts in the vicinity. *Fortunately*, thought Alex, not wishing to be stuck with his persistent small talk and fearing giving herself away with the anticlimactic feelings of leaving America behind her, afraid that it would be the end of more than one adventure.

Her final commitment, the class at the LA Academy, was stimulating enough to be distracting, incorporating some refined, well-prepared playing of the Beethoven sonatas and a rewarding exchange of ideas. A couple of the pianists were particularly talented; she had even picked up ideas for different fingerings in discussions during the tricky adagio of *Opus 111*; and she had enjoyed expounding upon her jazz ideas in the piece.

Jo seemed like a distant memory already, stolen moments, the images threatening to drain away again, like the desert sand through her fingers, until she surprised her with a text message and a photo while she was waiting at the airport: *Arrived Rome. That was an amusing moment at the studio! Stunning location and hotel. See! Call me when you're back. X*

The thrill from receiving the message reminded her again that she had changed, a door had opened in her, exposing her vulnerability, but making everything so real, so alive.

Perhaps it wasn't just the holiday romance she dreaded it might be.

CHAPTER ELEVEN

Nightingale's End

"Josh! Hi, come in!"

Josh stepped over the lip of the threshold, grinning cheerfully and clutching a bottle of champagne.

"You're drenched! Here, I'll fetch a towel." It had been pouring with rain all day. Floodwater was standing inches deep on parts of the country roads.

"I rushed from the office. Held up by Natalia. Quite literally."

"How is she?"

"As opinionated as ever. Telling me how to do my job."

He followed her through to the kitchen, toweling his hair as he continued, "How're you doing, love? Still in recovery from the trip?"

"Absolutely. Shattered—even the few days off were filled up with the P's—preparation, practice, perspiration and quite a lot of post-concert socializing. Tiring. But strangely, a little flat to be back and without it all. And somehow the rain isn't helping. However, thanks for all your organizing."

"Aah! No problem. Let me cheer you up. I have good news. Drink?" He waved the bottle, adding, "Chilled already."

"Perfect...News?"

He popped the cork. The champagne crackled as it slipped into fluted glasses.

"Here, love. You'll like this. Bravo!" He handed her the glass. "The phone's been going for you all the time, Proms, Oscars want you back next year. I hadn't mentioned that yet, had I? Does that cheer you up? Thought so. So many compliments: second installment of the Sonata series, Grammys details. I'll fill you in. I need to thank the West Coast brigade. You're the best." They clinked glasses. "Cheers!"

Alex was gaping slightly at him. "They want me back? That's...brilliant news. And...complimentary. I'll look forward to that. Yes. I will. That is cheering." She allowed her thoughts to drift there again. Then realizing she had been staring into space too long, added, "What about the film medley? Want to hear it?"

"Sure. Private performance, you might say."

She grinned obligingly at him.

They carried their glasses, settling themselves comfortably into the living room and she played, her thoughts refilling with warm California memories. Josh lay back in the sofa, listening and watching intently. At the end, as she gulped at the champagne, he stood, applauded enthusiastically and clinked her glass again. Taking both glasses carefully he placed them on the mats on the side of the piano.

"Superb! The way you tangled them in together. I recognized at least half a dozen. Not bad for me. Shame you can't record that, what with the copyright issues." He pulled her up to her feet as he continued, "And I've been meaning to tell you what a star you are for breaking in across the Atlantic." He danced with her playfully. "Come here." He kissed her gently on the cheek and twirled her around confidently.

She laughed at him, backing away a step. "Oh, Josh, you've said so already. You've been so sweet and helpful..."

"So they all tell me…" He pulled her back, leaned down and kissed her again, more persistently, "just one more…" Reaching around to her lips this time.

A snake of fear uncoiled unexpectedly, deep within her intestines. She pulled back, more firmly, "Josh, you're sweet… but there's something I've been meaning…"

"Ssh…don't talk…I've been waiting for this moment."

He pulled her shoulders toward him and kissed her more fervently, coming up only briefly for breath. "It's been a long time coming…"

She stood unresisting, but also not participating, her arms loose by her sides, waiting for him to finish.

But it was taking too long. She leaned away from him, trying to hint heavily. He stopped for another breath.

"Josh…hang on…" he was resistant to her efforts at pushing him away.

"You said it's been so long."

"Yes, but I hadn't meant, I wanted to tell you, let me speak for a moment—"

"Later. You know how I feel."

"Josh, I don't really—" she began to protest, but he placed his fingers on her mouth and held her more insistently, kissing the side of her mouth and feeling downward with the other hand. Transgressing the barriers where sacred recent memories lay. The serpent inside her struck suddenly, painfully at the walls of her gut. She felt unspeakably afraid, cold, everything caught momentarily in slow-motion. He was much stronger than her. She had no way of regaining her ground. He moved his hands to hold her arms, too tightly. This closely, she could see his over-excited, dilated eyes. He was committed, unable to go back without a considerable loss of face. Possibly unable to stop himself. Fear was climbing in her throat.

"Josh! No! Wait." She tried to calm her voice. "It doesn't have to be…You shouldn't." This was not what was meant to happen.

She saw fury rise in him. He lashed out, spinning her around. The glasses crashed to the floor.

"No! You're right. I shouldn't...I shouldn't wait any longer. I've *been* patient!"

"What?" She gasped, the air knocked out of her lungs, tears stinging her eyes. Unintentionally, she had said the wrong thing.

"The teasing, the looks—the kiss you gave me at that party."

"I didn't tease...that was ages ago. You..." Horror-struck.

"I know what you've wanted. You've been too busy to know it yourself, I *have waited*." His voice and eyes were hard, his hands gripped her arms tightly.

"Josh! Stop! I don't know what you mean. What are you doing? We're friends."

"Yes, friends," he hissed the word bitterly, "but we could be much more...should be..."

"Wait!"

But he would not wait and she screamed in terror as he forced her back against the wall, fumbling clumsily at her legs and his trousers, pushing hard against her. "You mustn't do this..."

"Don't tell me what I can or can't do. I've helped to create you." He spat the words at her.

She managed to scream again, but he stopped her mouth with his hand and she bit him hard, connecting, tearing at him with her fingernails. She wanted to knee him somewhere painful, but her movement was too restricted by his proximity, and she forced her knee upward between their bodies. With a violent shudder she realized he was anticipating her struggle.

He slapped her hard across the face, spinning her senses. "Josh!" Hoping his name might bring him back to reality. She started to cry and kicked out at him hard, connecting briefly with his shin, drawing only a brief grunt from him; but he was too strong for her and had freed himself from his clothes, fumbling and pushing her backward toward the wall and forcing her downward. He was overpowering her.

She sobbed, tasting blood on her lips. "People will know Josh, don't."

"I didn't tell anyone I was coming here? Did you?"

Her flash of fear must have been in her eyes and confirmed his suspicions because he muttered, "See? And I had surprises for you. The videos, the letters, you could have come to me for friendship and comfort—you should be grateful!" He barked the last words at her.

"But...we're meant to be friends..." It was a plea. This close he smelled foul, of bitter cigarettes, tainted alcohol, sweat, something else... She yelled, "Stop! Now Josh!" He hit her again and she tried in vain to scratch him again and push him away. It was insanity. It couldn't be happening. He was destroying everything. She couldn't free herself to speak, feeling herself suffocating. Briefly he slipped from her face and she managed a yell. He forced her head back viciously, grasping her neck with his free hand.

"Stop! Now!"

And it was then, miraculously, that her neighbor broke in upon the scene. The French windows had been slightly open despite the rain and Pauline was pushing through them, darkly silhouetted in the doorframe.

"Young man, what on earth do you think you are doing?" She spoke in a fearsome tone which was way beyond any negotiation, her hands on her hips, the apron of authority and testosterone-quenching domesticity hanging officially at her waist.

He turned, shocked by the intrusion, his blatant intention standing out of his half-mast trousers. Alex gasped for air, sobbing, bleeding, clasping her stomach, continuing to slide down the wall, her clothes torn in several places.

Her valiant neighbor stepped forward slowly, calmly. "Now then—"

"Fuck..." he gasped, wiping blood from his mouth, grappling at his trousers to pull them up and in a moment of sudden decision he fled from the room.

But he did not go far. As he wrenched the front door open still struggling with his clothing, he was confronted by Pauline's husband. Josh made a dash for it, but tripped over his sagging trousers and the slippery threshold lip and fell heavily onto the stone steps, hitting his head with a resounding crack on the corner of the bottom step.

Alex had watched the unfolding scene astonished. Josh lay motionless. Silent. His clothing still in a state of semi-disarray; a pool of dark blood began to spread from beneath his upturned, mechanically blinking face, the blood dissolving at the edges in the falling rain.

Pauline's husband stepped past and hurried inside. "Alex? Pauline?"

"Here, Bill. We're okay," Pauline called from the back room.

"Phone! Quick!" he yelled.

"Hallway, Bill!"

He ran to the phone and dialed 999.

Pauline had her arms gently around Alex's flinching shoulders. She had vomited against the wall. "There, dear, come here..." She coaxed her to her feet and helped her round to sit on the sofa, childlike. She went to the drinks cupboard and poured a couple of whiskies, taking one to Alex and putting it in her hand.

Alex was breathing in uncontrollable shudders, her head in one hand, the glass trembling in the other.

Pauline sat down beside her, taking off her cardigan and placing it around her trembling shoulders, pulling out another clean handkerchief from the pocket to offer her. Silence haunted the room.

"Alex," Pauline prompted gently, "what happened?"

"He...we...he's my agent," she began, "I invited him. He came to congratulate me...us...on the success. Hear the music. He's never been like this..."

"We knew something must be wrong. Bill went up the garden to pull a cabbage and your patio windows were still open in the pouring rain. You never leave them open like that in the rain, because of your piano, you said. And he heard a strange noise. Listen, Alex, the police are coming. I want you to come with me. Stay in our guest room. Right now, I insist. Come on. I'll help you."

Her stream of words were vaguely comforting, bringing Alex's swimming head back to reality for the briefest of moments. Pauline helped her up and guided her from the room around the broken glass, through the French windows, away from the appalling view at the front of the house, picking up Alex's handbag as they left and headed out into the back garden.

Alex was muttering to herself, the incessant rain streaming down her face, "I can't believe he could do that..."

The emergency services were pulling up. Pauline led her away.

* * *

As the evening wore on, Pauline Waldren, unexpected heroine, showed the police through to her kitchen to find Alex, still shivering in the borrowed voluminous cardigan, both hands around a mug at the kitchen table.

She made to stand, wobbling, her knees without strength, already beginning to ache all over.

"Don't get up, love," the sergeant said kindly. "Mind if we sit with you for a moment?"

"Okay," she whispered.

"Tea? Coffee?" Mrs. Waldren fussed, starting to pull out her best cups.

"Yes, please. Er, one strong tea, one coffee thanks. Alex, I need to ask you what happened."

"Yes...of course," she answered very quietly, "it was so sudden...so appallingly unexpected..." She recounted what had happened, seeking the comfort of the cardigan sleeve at times, prompted sensitively by a female case officer, while the police constable scribbled his notes.

"...and then Pauline was at the French windows, my savior. You were brilliant," she gulped, "and he ran...and Mrs. Waldren said...fell."

"Alex," the sergeant said and leaned seriously across the table. "Listen. I'm sorry to have to tell you this, there's no easy way, if you can prepare yourself...because it's about Mr. Pembroke. The thing is, he didn't survive the journey to the hospital, he passed away. The ambulance crew had to attempt to resuscitate him and it proved to be…impossible. It looks like he was under the influence of some narcotic substance as well, making it all harder to control."

Mrs. Waldren who had slammed a mug down at the first piece of news now put her hand to her mouth, "Oh! My Bill, he had nothing to do with it—"

"It's all right Mrs. Waldren. Mr. Metcalfe across the road was putting out his milk bottles. He heard the disturbance and saw the last part. Alex, this is a bit shocking—can you bear with me? We've had to search the house and forensics are there now. But we've already found two webcams set up. One in your bedroom and one in the hallway, monitoring the front door. We're presuming these aren't yours?"

Alex managed a shake of her head, staring at the officer.

"They've been cleverly wired up, discreetly wired up. We can't say for certain why they're there, but once we've uncovered the footage we'll understand everything better. This may not have been without some forward planning."

"Webcams…how the hell? He said the teasing, the looks…I didn't tease. Video cameras! That's disgusting." She felt invaded further. "The notes…"

"Notes?"

Alex recounted her worries about the anonymous letters and her friend's advice to start saving them.

"That's important. You have them?"

"In my room. Back of the wardrobe, small suitcase, inside a plastic wallet."

"Thank you. We'll need those. "Now for you. You need to rest. You've had a shock. Do you want any help at the moment?"

Alex shook her head. "No. I'm all right. My doctor came round earlier. J…Joshua…He didn't get…far. I just need a… whisky and…a bath? Can I bathe? Forensics don't have to…?"

"No. It's fine. This is pretty clear cut, but we'll have to go over it again with you, search his office, car, home. You're free to do what you want, as long as we can contact you. We'll need you to give and sign a statement. And if you don't mind, there will need to be some photographs for our records. That can wait until the morning."

"Th-thank you." Alex shivered uncontrollably.

"Come on, love," Pauline Waldren interjected. "A nice hot bath. Let's sort you out and then—bed. There's a portable TV in there. You go and try to relax."

She took her upstairs and ran the bath, found her softest, fluffiest towel and a spare dressing gown and returned downstairs to the police, carrying some of her damaged clothes to give them as evidence.

* * *

Alex lay back in the bath surrounded by bubbles popping similarly to her belief in the real world. She mentally reviewed all her contacts with Josh, seeing them in a new tainted, despicable light.

Webcam in the bedroom? Where? She would find out later. *How long had it been there? What might he have seen?* She shuddered as she recollected the possibilities. He would have known more about her than she wanted. She gasped. Would she have given something away recently that might have set this off? *The letters...the flowers! It was...poisonous...insidious. Double-crossing bastard! What to do? He was her agent and her...friend? Was. She'd be needing to transfer her work.* She sobbed at the ridiculous practicality. *It's all unbelievable.* She held her hands out in front of her, fingers outstretched but trembling and then suddenly sank her head under the water, attempting to drown out the disturbing visions. She rubbed her face vigorously, suddenly finding it was agonizingly painful, and afraid of soaking off the surgical glue on her split lip, she surfaced and patted it carefully with the nearest towel. She reached blindly for the soap and rubbed every inch of the rest of her body until the skin was tingling and blanching at her touch.

There were times when it had seemed that he had known her every move. *Oh God. That's exactly what he had known.*

Right. Out of the tub now. I can do this.

She dried herself carefully, patting her face dry, put on the spare robe and went to the bedroom, her legs feeling weak, her head spinning from either the whisky or the shock, or a combination of the two.

Pauline had left her handbag on the bed and a fresh tray, with whisky and another pot of tea.

Bless her.

She sat on the bed and picked up her mobile, and wrote numbly: *Josh attacked me. He's dead.* She sent it to Leanne, her Dad and Jo. *The moment of truth.* Had she teased him? She thought back. *No! It was only repartee—bantering—it was or should have been…normal.*

Throwing the phone on the bed, she downed the whisky in one gulp and fell back on the pillows.

CHAPTER TWELVE

The Knight

The phone beeped persistently in Alex's dream, several times, until she was woken drowsily. She scrabbled around for it. Her head was aching and a dull realization was pressing in on her.

3 messages received. She scrolled through: *Dad—you missed a call at...; Leanne—Bloody hell. The evil git. Will call again tomorrow.*

She read Jo's too: *My God! You okay? Possibly tied up here until tomorrow lunchtime, then I'm on my way home. I'll come straight to you. Hang in there.*

She felt a stream of relief running through her. Perhaps her friends would rally her. She stood up shakily. Her face was hurting. She popped a tablet from her handbag and looked in the mirror. She was puffy around her mouth and swollen across her right cheekbone. Her whole body ached, her stomach jabbed at her painfully.

Hell. And she had concerts coming up. *Concerts coming up?* What was she thinking? She shook the thought from her head and went cautiously down the stairs, treading carefully so as not to jar her aching body or wake the household.

There was a note on the kitchen table: *If you can't sleep, help yourself to anything. The police have finished. Everything's tidied up.*

She made herself a mug of tea and some soft bread and butter and ate cautiously, feeding the body automatically rather than the soul. The clock said 1:05a.m.

Too late to call? No! Surely if anything falls into the category of emergency, this does.

She dialed Leanne.

Leanne sounded drowsy. "Alex. What's happened?"

She explained, talking a little painfully, her mouth smarting. Tears springing threateningly to her eyes.

"But what the hell? It came out of the blue?"

"Do you remember? The dream, the letters, all him! And worse, webcams set up in my house, secretly. How the hell? I don't know…yet."

"What do you want to do?"

"I don't know. I'm at Pauline's."

"Look, I'm stuck in Nottingham at the moment, but I'm home by Friday. Come here. You don't want to be there for a while. As long as the police don't need you."

"Okay. Thanks. That sounds good. I'm going now. Will you…call me in the morning still…please?"

The brief memory of Josh's frustrated rage flashed through her.

She didn't want to respond to Jo's message. She felt dirtied and unclear of her thoughts. She went to the living room and flicked on the TV, searching through the channels, unable to focus on anything, the bright screen making her head ache even more. She switched it off, and then, borrowing a coat from the hooks, unlocked the back door and went barefoot out into the garden, the damp ground, the unsullied night air. *Better. Clarifying.* The weather had improved. Clouds scudded quickly across the backlit sky. Her house huddled, an ominous hulk in the shadows. She had never seen it in that way before. She felt faint…she would sleep again. *Think in the morning, not now.* She heard the owl screech and a fox yelp, as if in reply. The cold bit into her bare ankles. And yet…the fire of the West Coast tour still burned somewhere. *I bloody well can do this.* She told herself, *It's not my fault.* Her thoughts rambled uncontrollably as she wiped the grass from her feet on the back doormat and returned to her room, lowering herself protectively into the bed. She knew she must be in shock. She felt empty, detached, her brain working separately from her body.

*The world is full of betrayals. My world has been…*Her thoughts drifted into a dream.

* * *

Early on, my best friend at the age of ten betrays me, gossiping to another girl, who is only too glad to relay the spiteful information back to me. I can see her now. The secret nobody should have known. She has been such a lovely friend, we have done so much together, been on family holidays. Jealousy? Who knows. Betrayal? Yes. End of friendship.

So I have no intention of trusting anyone in quite the same way again. And yet…another girl comes along, we're close, perhaps too close…verging on the intimate…the parents weigh in to separate us, fending off their fears.

So I become part of a group this time. A gang, dispersed intensity perhaps. But this is even more complicated. The channels of communications and emotions crisscrossing, confusing the signals. And anyway when I start doing well in school, better than the rest of them, they dislike me, calling me names and piling on the emotional bullying. I am a relationship retard. I am starting to think I am better off on my own. Nobody lets you down when you are on your own. You can do what you want, when you want, when you are on your own. And I start to enjoy this. I can fly away into another world on my own.

I can walk for miles and miles, through town, onto the beach and stare at the waves for hours on end, the pebbles clattering in their wake, and nobody else is complaining that they are bored and want to move on. I can play the piano for a thousand hours and become really good at it, because nobody else tells me I should stop and it is like a friend, the way it plays with me, the way it responds. Without complications.

A boy takes a shine to me. We arrange to meet under a tree in the park. But his open, wet kiss engulfs my whole face and I run as fast as I can. I feel his saliva on my face. Another girl says I stole him, but I did not. I did not know there was anybody to steal him from. He asked me. And I don't much care for him anyway. I just think I ought to, I've been told I should.

Then I go to music school and have a few friends and we laugh together, but it is probably only skin-deep because they say spiteful things when I am successful and really they are all showing off, drinking too much. It is the thing to do to join them at the pubs and nightclubs on a Friday or Saturday night, when really I cannot wait to get away and be home and quiet again, my ears still ringing from the noise, a feeling of overexposure lingering. And the tales of their exploits that they enjoy shouting so noisily on the commuter train that they make the ears of the businessmen throb.

But then I kiss a boy in one of the practice rooms and this is really something else. Actually, I ask him to kiss me, because I don't know how it's done. He's gentle. I bury my feelings deeply, thinking this must be what I want. I do not need those superficial friends who are waiting to watch me fall over. This goes a lot deeper. I find out some things I never even knew about before, nobody has told me before what touch can achieve. The friends hate me for going off and leaving them. Now I am starting to wonder whether perhaps I am selfish. Perhaps the emotional scars have hardened me. Or perhaps no one has ever been particularly kind to me before. Or perhaps they just wish it was them. Or perhaps I'm just playing at this, because I've stopped listening to my true feelings… Anyway, this boy is amazing. Beautiful. Muscular. Physical. But God, can he talk. About himself. I do not mind much when he goes off to university and writes to me saying he has met someone else. I go back to my friend, the piano, and play better than before, now that I know something I had never known before.

* * *

At music college, it is perfect. I can wall myself up in a practice room claiming to be working. But I'm still so naïve. The strange young man who comes to my room to listen to music and talk, leaps on me and does something I am not prepared for and was never expecting. I am pinned down, I cannot move. I do not tell anyone. I probably should. I don't have anyone to tell. There ought to be someone, but there isn't. And when I find out that he does the same to others, I am shocked, horrified. I hide in my room and don't answer the door the next time he comes calling. He stamps outside in the corridor shouting at me. And that's the end of it. I can bury myself in the music again. I am better off on my own.

Back to the music. The birds singing, the warmth of the sunshine, the sound of the rain, all become even more piercingly beautiful, thrown into relief by the human betrayals.

I think of the work again and am taken pleasantly by surprise this time when things really take off. I have to travel to do this. I'm pretty good at it. They like me. It's a surprise to be likeable. The audiences, the newspaper critics. Radio. Television. Recordings. The colleagues are talented too and they are never jealous, they don't have to be. This is good. The lonely bit inside me can be walled up. I am wily. I will bury myself in this forever.

I start to remember why it is easier to be alone and uninvolved.

And people come knocking at my door. And I can't trust them? Or one I can, one I can't?

Nothing has been as it seems. Is this just a lesson in life? Have I been particularly unlucky? Is this totally normal? Perhaps I am a hopeless judge of character. Perhaps I was...because I had hidden myself too deeply.

Perhaps there is this one, true, loyal person and everything will make sense again. Perhaps I have just been looking at everything from the wrong angle, through the wrong filter. A sense of perspective on this mad, askew world will return. Perhaps I have met her. But I'm such a poor judge. How will I know?

* * *

She woke suddenly realizing she was hypothermically cold, the bedcovers now a twisted heap on the floor. The dream, part truth, part uncomfortable fiction, prickled at the back of her consciousness. *A bad judge...*

Her thoughts spun incessantly.

She pulled the blankets back over herself and fell back into a fretful sleep, startled awake, between dozes, by stabs of pain and sudden flashes that something was hideously wrong.

* * *

The phone woke her again at 6:45 a.m. Her head was still thudding, whisky or bruises, she wasn't sure anymore. A dull ache of misery lay in the pit of her stomach. She groped around for the handset and answered, "Hello?" Her voice croaked unexpectedly.

"Hello." That musical, longed-for voice.

"Jo!" It came out in a whisper.

"How *are* you?"

"I've been better." Still croaking.

"What the hell happened?"

She spoke cautiously. "I'm sorry I really can't bear to go over it all again. It's been going around in my head all night. Basically he came socially, he was friendly and then turned into this hideous animal. My lovely neighbors prevented him. They heard me. Thank heavens for them. He fell on the way out, hitting his head and they couldn't revive him on the way to the hospital. Drugs in his system too."

"Bloody hell. And you?"

"All right I suppose, just about. Shocked. Bruised. Mainly my face: he hit me, but beyond that he didn't get far…"

"The total bastard. I might have killed him myself, if he hadn't done it to himself already…"

Alex was silent, fighting tears again.

"I'm not bad you know…training in several martial arts…"

Alex would have smiled under other circumstances, but now the words were suddenly overwhelming. "I wish I had." She suppressed a gulp.

"Alex? Listen. They've cleared me for the morning. I'm out on an early flight. Actually, I'm at the airport now, about to board. Can I come?"

"I'm a mess." She struggled to speak.

"I'm coming. Late morning, you're not that far from Gatwick are you? Thurslow, right?"

"Yes, that's right. We're the cottages after the hill, there's a dip in the road. You can see them from the pub. Mine's plain brickwork, not whitewashed. It has a name. Nightingale's End." A huge sob escaped.

"Okay. Pack a bag. I'll take you away from there."

"Oh!"

"You don't want to be there if the media get hold of the story."

"I hadn't thought..."

"Hang in there. I'll see you later."

And with that she was gone.

She wasn't sure she wanted to see her. She looked in the mirror, she was tousled from a rough night's sleep...and the bruises! Even more swelling was coming out, distorting her face. She felt suddenly panicky. *I can't see her. I don't know her well enough. She could be another. Not now.* Aware of the fallacy in her thoughts, she sent a hurried text anyway: *Don't come. I can't see you.* She felt ungrateful. But it would surely burst the magical bubble of LA, which stood out as a beacon of hope and truth somewhere before all this...muddle.

There was a knock at the door. "You okay, dear?"

She wiped her eyes.

Pauline brought in clothes draped over her arm and another tray, this time laden with a selection of toast, bacon, more fresh tea. She sat companionably on the edge of the bed and poured the tea.

"What shall we do, love?"

"What do the police say?"

"They're popping round quite early for you to sort a few things out, check and sign the statement and so on. They're going to investigate his business activities. They'll probably be needing to speak to you again, but I don't think there are exactly charges to be pressed...Well, he's not with us anymore. The family might have a few things to say about it, but I've a feeling they'll be wanting to keep it quiet, when they've heard the half of it."

Alex shivered.

"Sorry, love. You've been very brave."

"I don't feel brave. Can I go to the cottage? It isn't cordoned off is it, a scene of…crime?"

"No. It's been dealt with. You can go. If you want. I fetched you these." She indicated the slacks and sweater. "I hope you don't mind. Do you want me to keep you company?"

"Yes. Please. That would be nice. After some breakfast. Have some toast?"

They ate silently for a while.

"Where's Bill?"

"Gone to tend his vegetables to clear his head."

"Him too. I'm so sorry for putting you all through it."

"It wasn't you. Don't think twice about it, love. I'm just glad we were there to stop it."

"Oh my God. Me too. What if…"

"Don't what if."

"It keeps creeping back though."

"It will, love."

"Pauline? How do I look? A friend wants to see me."

"A little bashed, but better than last night. I think you should see them. Friends are necessary at times like this, aren't they?"

"Oh! I think I've put her off."

"You can always call her again."

"My judgment seems to have gone a bit wobbly."

"I'm sure it might feel like that, but it hasn't really."

She picked up her phone and texted two words. *Please come.* She felt the tears threatening again.

Pauline put her arm around her shoulders. "Let it out dear. You'll feel better."

* * *

After the breakfast, they walked quietly round to the cottage. Pauline went first, letting Alex in. She drifted around the house looking at it with fresh eyes. There was a greasy stain on the front path. The police had taken away the lamp fitment in the hallway telephone table. She limped up to the bedroom.

Everything was tidy, apart from the lampshade having been removed from the standard lamp in the corner of the room. She shuddered. What had he seen? She pulled the small case from the back of the wardrobe. It was empty, the anonymous letters gone forever.

She started to feel peculiarly cleansed, contrary to her initial nervousness. Josh's presence had been scientifically expunged from her house. There were no dirty secrets here. She went back down to the living room, entering this room more cautiously, but there was no sign of the struggle, only a repulsive lingering smell. Pauline was in the kitchen, making tea again.

Alex threw open the French windows and let the new air stream in, attempting to release any remaining evil. She sat down at the piano. The last time she had sat there... She took a deep breath and started her usual warm-ups; but tears threatened to engulf her again, the bile rising in her throat. She hurried to the downstairs bathroom and vomited.

Pauline came through from the kitchen in time to see her wobbling back, wringing her hands. "Oh, love. It will start to feel better. It'll just take some time."

"But what was he thinking? He's been so kind in the past..."

"Who can tell? He lost control of himself, that's certain."

"I mean, I suppose I always thought he was a bit odd, but it was just how he was. Oh, Mrs. Waldren..."

"Pauline."

"Pauline. Thank you, for everything. For being there at the right time." She put her arms around Pauline's shoulders and hugged her.

"This friend who is coming, she wants to take me away from here. I think she's right. I can't face seeing this place right now, and there might be press arriving if the story gets out. Do you mind? Will you keep an eye on things?"

"Don't worry, love. I think that's a good idea too. I'll take care of everything."

"You are an angel. A guardian angel. Would you come to the concert on Saturday? I might find it easier to play, knowing there are friends rooting me on. I can get tickets for both of you, they keep some back for the soloist."

"Oh, that would be lovely." Her broad face flushed; she looked genuinely pleased.

Alex realized that concert tickets were probably well beyond what she and her husband could afford. "I'll treat you to dinner at the restaurant beforehand—" Even the mention of food made her gulp. "—just to say thank you."

"You don't have to, dear."

"I know, but I want to…please."

"Thank you. That would be lovely."

"Will you stay for a bit, while I play?"

"Fine, love." And she settled herself down on the couch with a cup of tea, helpfully burying the image that hung in Alex's mind, of Josh being its previous occupant.

* * *

During the morning her dad rang apologizing for phone signal difficulties on their cruise. And after hearing the story, he was anxious to hurry home, but Alex urged him to finish the holiday with her stepmother. They would be back next week anyway and Pauline and her friends were organizing her. She could do without any parental or faux-parental fussing, even her father's genuine concern. The police dropped by at Pauline's house to complete Alex's statement and assented to her plan to escape, as long as they could contact her by mobile as necessary. Photographs of her injuries were also necessary for the file. Necessary, but humiliating, despite the sympathetic woman police constable. They confirmed that they were searching Josh's home and office. Alex imagined the shock for Jenny. *Oh! And all the other clients…and his family…*

"I hope they don't hold me responsible for it all."

"You mustn't think that." The policewoman said, helpfully, "Victims of an assault all experience a variety of guilt feelings, it's natural, but it doesn't mean it's true. You mustn't worry. We have a specialist to help with this if you like."

Alex had cringed at the words "victim" and "assault." But she shook her head. "Not at the moment."

"Anyway, the family is pretty appalled."

* * *

So she returned to the house alone, showered, cleaned her teeth thoroughly, changed and packed a case, including an evening dress for the weekend and all the music for the next couple of weeks. She was just fastening the case when the doorbell went, causing her to flinch, hesitating to answer it. She looked from the upstairs window and saw a gleaming dark blue BMW parked in the driveway. Only one person she could think of would be likely to be driving such a car. She scampered down the stairs and threw open the front door. "Jo!" Her heart skipped a nervous beat.

Jo stepped in, her body language looking a little weary, but casual, dressed in jeans and a loose T-shirt, her hair swept back. She closed the door behind her, propped her sunglasses on the top of her head and held Alex gently in her arms, quietly stroking her hair. She felt the tears coming again and gulped. Jo took face in her hands, tilting it upward, letting her hair fall back from her face. She shied away, turning slightly to one side.

"Oh, Alex." She kissed her very gently on the uninjured cheek, brushing the tears from her eyelashes. "Come on. We're going. Shall I fetch your bags?"

"Upstairs."

She jogged lightly upstairs and came down moments later carrying the case and garment bag.

"Nice house. These?"

Alex nodded.

"I'd give you the guided tour and offer you refreshments, but..." She attempted to make her tone light.

"Not today. Another time maybe. Come on."

"I must just tell my neighbor that we're off."

"Fine. I'll see you in the car." And within minutes they had joined each other in the car, hiding gratefully behind the tinted windows and were flying down the country lanes, leaving it all behind.

"So, what do you have to do next?" Jo asked quietly, as she pulled into a wide out to let a couple of horse riders pass by.

"Beethoven Third. Saturday. Festival Hall. God knows if I'll be able to…"

"But free till then?"

"Yes. The rehearsal's in the afternoon."

"And the arrangements will all work out, still in place, even with…"

"For this one. I think so." Then after a moment, her thoughts spilled out. "Thanks for coming. I'm sorry about the messages. I wasn't sure I could see you. I felt weird…I don't know…ashamed." She paused for breath, adding quietly, "Like I must have brought it on in some way. As if I was…stupid for not seeing it coming…"

"No!" Jo said, alarmingly vehement. She caught herself. "You mustn't let his obscene obsession continue to affect you. He probably would have wanted that. It's all finished. He's finished. And how could you have seen it coming?"

Alex was holding back a hard, tight feeling in her throat. "Yes. I suppose."

"Definitely."

"I just thought, I should have listened to my instincts more carefully. He…always had a strange edge to him."

"And lots of people have a strange edge to them in our business. Instinctively you have to end up tolerating it to a certain extent. Hindsight makes it too easy to persecute yourself."

"He had cameras wired up in the house."

"Oh God, that's beyond obscene."

"Yes."

"Invasive."

"Yes."

"The whole thing is."

She noticed Jo tensing over the wheel. She gathered herself, deliberately trying to change the subject, asking cautiously, "So where are we going?"

"Your choice." She sensed the reticence and saw Jo visibly force herself to relax. She sighed. "There is a choice. Originally, I was planning to go to my parents. I haven't seen them for a while. Or back to my place. Hampstead. It depends on how you're feeling."

"If…we went to your parents, as you planned…How would we explain me…this…Do they know about?"

"They wouldn't ask awkward questions. I've called them, told them I might be bringing company, they only know it's a friend who's just had a lucky escape and needs to get away. I haven't been more specific than that. But they do know I'm gay, you don't need to stand on eggshells."

"Some way to meet your folks!" Alex almost managed a laugh. "Ouch!"

Jo stretched an arm out as she drove and stroked her jawline. "Or I could drop you at my place. See you later. I have to go back there afterward anyway."

"No. Let's do it…if I'm on my own I'll just brood about it. Jo?"

"Yep?"

"I feel a bit panicky."

"Yes. I know. Take things slowly. Nobody's going to expect anything of you."

"Okay. Thank you…thanks for coming."

"I wouldn't be anywhere else."

"They've given me tranquilizers. But I haven't dared touch them yet."

"That's okay too. They're there if you feel you need them. By the way, that's my lawyer's card in the tray there. Thought you might like to try them, later on. They could handle everything. They were excellent, when I had…that incident."

"Oh yes. I'd forgotten." Alex picked it up, remembering Jo's brush with a crazed fan. "Yeah, well. It wasn't exactly a moment of glory."

After some time of passing hedgerows, fields, through villages and light-dappled alleyways of trees, the car pulled up into the paved driveway of a not insubstantial house. Jo appeared to sense her tensing up as they pulled up in front.

"It'll be fine. No one will hassle you. They've been through some highs and lows with me, too." She pressed her thigh. Alex flinched. "Sorry."

"No, it's not you. It's just me, a bit sore."

Jo hopped out lightly and went around to open her door, helping her, holding her by the arm to steady her, whispering reassurances. She led her to the door and when her mother opened it in a wide welcome, Jo hugged and kissed her and then turned to Alex, all introductions and attention, doing her best to smooth the social pathway, as they shook hands.

"Mum, this is Alex. We met in LA and she's just had a bit of trauma, as I said on the phone. She needed to get away. Please can I swear you to secrecy? You don't mind…"

Alex had dropped her head at the mention of it all, finding the ground suddenly required her attention. Jo lifted her chin gently and put her arm around her shoulders, giving her a gently encouraging squeeze. She took Alex's hand and led the way inside.

"Of course, of course. I'm Jackie. To you. Alex, come through here, the conservatory is beautiful today. Your father's down the garden at the moment, Jo. He'll be up in a minute. Have a seat, Alex. What would you like to drink, we have everything from G and T to coffee?"

"Anything. G and T sounds good. Thank you." Alex answered quietly.

"Jo?" Her mother beckoned her to help in the kitchen.

They soon returned and Jackie said, "There you are, dear. You make yourself at home with us today." She passed her a glass tumbler, smiling encouragingly. "I've realized who you are now. I'm sorry I was a bit slow off the mark. I think we may have seen you on my birthday at the Proms, a Beethoven concerto, someone famous conducting, I think?"

"Vladimir Ashkenazy."

"Oh. Yes. I loved it. The last movement was so…happy."

"I'm glad you liked it. It was pretty incredible playing for Ashkenazy. A little daunting too. He can do it better than I can."

"If you've had enough of us all at any time, you can play. We have a lovely piano in the dining room. You can close the door, feel peaceful, shut us all out. I understand you've had something of an ordeal."

"Mmm. Yes. I thought this man…he was supposed to be a friend. What is it that makes someone flip like that?" She spoke as if to herself.

"He must have lost control. Been brooding on it for a while. Jealous, who knows? Whatever you do, don't pin it on yourself. It may have been an unlucky coincidence that it was you. If it hadn't been you, it might have been someone else who had to face him. You may have done someone else a favor."

"I hadn't thought of it that way."

"At least he didn't hurt your hands."

"I hadn't thought of that either." She flexed her fingers and smiled apologetically. "Thanks. It's not my preferred way to descend on people. It's kind of you to have me."

"You're most welcome. A friend of Jo's is a friend of ours."

"What's Jo up to?"

"I've got her making a salad, make these daughters useful, you know. We don't want her thinking all that's below her, do we?" She smiled, a friendly, disarming smile reminiscent of Jo's, although the face was much more care-worn and her hair was longer, curly, the highlights camouflaging her age. She wore the years gracefully, linen trousers and a silk shirt hanging informally on her trim frame.

"You must be very proud of her. She's achieved a lot."

"Quite. But then it's been a lot of hard work along the way, ferrying her places in the early days, a lot of expense, the arguments and emotional drama that goes with it all, especially at the beginning and so on. In fact the ups and downs just get more dramatic the further into it one gets."

"She's my knight in shining armor today."

"So I gather." She patted her hand gently. "Oh, look. Here's Alan."

Jo's father appeared, loping up the lawn, the family similarity immediately apparent in the loping long stride, elegant frame and even that distinctive jawline. Introductions ensued and he gave her a little old-fashioned bow, charming her instantly, reminding her of Jo back at the concert hall bar.

Jo appeared from the kitchen. "Chores done. Hi Dad." She pecked him on the cheek and they hugged.

"Want a tour of the garden, Alex?"

She took a glass from the tray and they excused themselves, wandering outside. She led her past a tennis court to a small pool by a summerhouse bordered with hedges. Alex linked her free hand through Jo's arm.

"You okay? Not too awkward meeting them?" she inquired gently.

"Fine. They're easy to like. This place is amazing."

"Well, they've only had it a few years. Once I'd accumulated some Hollywood salaries I helped them buy this. Back payment, you see."

"That's good of you."

"Appropriate, I'd say."

"So, how was the filming?" Alex attempted to steer her thoughts away from herself.

"Oh, beautiful locations, apart from some grimy back streets." She talked airily. "An annoying, clingy young actor, but one or two good friends too. Dan's especially reliable, helped me to get away this morning."

Alex smiled at the inside information.

"Does Andy go on these trips too?"

"Sometimes, but he's been overseeing some work at home." She flinched.

"He'll be gone by now."

There was a comfortable-looking window seat in the summer house, piled with cushions. It looked so inviting that Alex slipped her arm and went to try it.

"Oh yes. This is it. This is the life. Just leave me here for a bit."

"Seriously?"

"Semi-seriously. I don't want to appear rude."

"I tell you what. You do that—I'll go back to the house, keep them company, do a bit of catching up. I'll fetch you when lunch is ready." Jo shook out a blanket and laid it over her. Alex managed a weak grin. She dropped a light kiss on her forehead, away from the injuries, and strolled off, sauntering elegantly. Alex lay back in the increasing warmth of the sun, and closed her eyes, feeling a sense of peace for the first time in the past eighteen hours.

After about an hour Alex reappeared sleepily in the doorway of the main house. "Sorry. I must have dozed off."

"How are you feeling?"

She nodded vaguely in reply.

"Your mobile's been going Alex and it was on the news," Jo remarked. Jackie went to dish up the meal.

Alex looked worried. "What did they say?"

"Pretty discreet, actually." She continued, "They've parked a traffic car on your driveway and your neighbor covered for you. They're calling it accidental and not suspicious."

"Well, some blessing there then. Although *his* behavior seemed pretty suspicious to me."

"I'd screen the incoming calls, if I were you."

"Mind if I check before we sit down to eat?"

She went out of the room and returned in a few minutes.

"Several messages. Leanne, that's my best friend, checking up on me; Pauline, my neighbor," she explained, "saying not to worry, they have it all in hand and nobody's pointing the finger at me."

"Should think not!"

"And the police to say that Camden-Waterhouse Associates of Mayfair have been instructed to take over his portfolio for the time being."

"Good. Sounds like the long arm of the law is reaching out and doing its bit," Alan suggested.

"There were a couple of hang-ups too and a message from a reporter. How he found my number so quickly, I don't know. A bit creepy actually."

"Mmm. It happens. Silence is the best policy for now."

"Food's on the table!"

They went to sit down for a relaxed meal in the conservatory, the doors to the garden open wide, a fan stirring a breeze above their heads and large-leaved plants bobbing in the moving air currents. The others tucked in, but she ate only a little, finding her appetite limited by the rigid knot in her stomach and the continuing facial discomfort which proved to be painful with each bite. She felt embarrassed.

"So, what do the next few weeks hold for you, love?" Jackie asked her daughter.

"Week off this week. Shooting starts in Cornwall next week, just a few scenes. That's why I need to look over this revised script."

After Alex had toyed with her plate and hidden in the background of the conversation for a little longer, she apologized. "I'm terribly sorry. I just can't seem to eat much today."

"Oh, it's perfectly understandable, dear."

"You mentioned earlier that I might be able to play. You see I have this Beethoven coming up on Saturday...would that be convenient?"

"Please do. Just through the hall on the other side. Help yourself. Would you like a coffee in a minute?"

"That would be lovely. Thank you."

She removed herself from the group and crossed the cool hallway with some relief to be away from the possibility of awkward questions, closing doors on the way. Her fragility was so near the surface as to leave her pale and vulnerable; it would be too easy to burst into tears at any moment and not the best place for such a display. It was flattering to be here, at her parents' home. Significant. And it would have made her incredibly nervous anyway, without the weight of other anxieties bearing down. Perhaps it was a distraction. It was one way to break the ice, she supposed.

The room with the piano was the more formal dining room, with a large, polished table that would seat about twelve and bookcases around some of the walls. A grand, but currently unused fireplace occupied most of one wall and at the far side stood a baby grand piano. She walked over and lifted the lid, a Yamaha. She put the lid up on the long stick and played a few notes. *Somebody must play. It's in tune. It's rather lovely. Funny, to have a piano here. It must be something instinctive that I like people who like pianos!*

She pottered through a few scales, exploring the instrument, enjoying the privacy, the change of environment, increasing in complexity, contrary melodics and dominant seventh inversions and was soon utterly absorbed and temporarily carried away from her weariness.

She had paused briefly and was about to start the slow movement, when a hard feeling in her throat suddenly made it impossible to swallow. The bile threatened to rise from her stomach with increasing panic and an image of Josh's angry, violent face swam through her mind. She pulled her hands away, blinking tears away from her eyes and shook her head, trying to rid herself of the image. At about the same moment, Jo came in carrying the coffee.

"You okay? Present from my mother." She took a coaster and put the coffee cup down on one side of the piano, looking at her intensely.

"Yes…I think so. I was just playing and then I could see his furious face…"

Jo went behind her and massaged her shoulders gently, bending down to kiss the top of her head. It felt…surprisingly good.

"You will be okay, you know. I suppose it will happen a bit." She said this quietly. "I'd give him a punch for you if I could. Hey! How about that? When you get that picture in your mind, think of me landing him a punch and knocking him over backward, feet up in the air like some sort of Laurel and Hardy slapstick. That might rid you of it! Or if that doesn't work, you could imagine I'd delegated the task to Andy. He's pretty fit."

"I remember." Alex found herself smiling weakly through the passing tears, resorting to her sleeve in lieu of a tissue. "That might have worked…except that Josh is already…" She dissolved and Jo hugged her close; she could feel her hands running gently through her hair.

As the tears subsided her words came in gulps. "I'm wondering if I can play on Saturday. The slow movement is so...wistful. It'll set me off. And once I start, I can't think. I asked my neighbors to come. I'm getting them tickets and a meal beforehand. I thought it might help, if I knew there was friendly support in the audience. And I owe them. They stopped it all. I can't believe he's..."

"Don't. Do you want me to come?"

"Can you?"

"Absolutely. I'll get a front row seat, right under your right arm."

"How? I mean everyone will recognize you, you won't have a moment's peace."

"Not necessarily," she said mysteriously. "I'll show you later. But for now have a swig of this..."

She reached over and passed the coffee cup and Alex found she could swallow after all and that the searing liquid revived her spirits.

"There might not be any seats available."

"Don't worry. I'll see what I can do."

* * *

The rest of the afternoon passed pleasantly in the garden, chatting and reading and then Jo made polite excuses, giving their thanks, with fond farewells from Jo and politely rebuffed apologies from Alex they were driving quickly away from the place.

"So, all right?" Jo asked.

"Reasonably." She nodded and scrabbled in her bag to put on a pair of dark glasses. "Incognito?"

"Very good." She chuckled.

"So, do you mind coming to my place?" she continued. "Pretty good place to hide out for a while. No one would know. I have a piano..."

"You do?"

"Almost grade six ability, have you forgotten to whom you speak?"

"Oh yes! I'm lucky…everyone seems to have a piano."

"It's the quality of the friends you pick. We can drive right in. No one will see. I've even had the foresight to order a delivery of groceries."

"Impressively domesticated."

"One tries. Do you need to call anyone?"

"Not right now." Alex thought for a moment. "The thing is…"

"Uh-huh?" she inquired as she negotiated a cyclist and a row of parked cars on the North Circular Road.

"I live…like to live…a fairly quiet life when I'm not working."

She waited for her to continue.

"Your house, is there…are there a lot of people coming and going? It's just that I'm not sure I'm…"

"I think you'll be surprised. It isn't one continuous party, despite what the media like to imply. I can't. You have to allow them to perpetuate the myth, so to speak. Actually it's not without its uses to have that image, but really, I can't work at the level I'm supposed to if I'm living the way they'd like to imagine. It's nowhere near as exciting as they'd like to believe. Sometimes it's incredibly dull. There can be lengthy gaps between projects with early nights. Or there might be vast amounts of reading and preparation. If there's nothing in the pipeline, I have to admit I'm quite capable of being utterly boring and not a little miserable." She shrugged sheepishly.

"Strangely, I'd pictured relentless activity."

"You've seen me during a busy patch."

At that moment, her phone began to ring.

"Quiet life?" Jo chuckled. "Are you sure?"

Alex found it and answered without thinking. Jo put her hand on her knee, trying to remind her.

She flicked it to the hands-free speaker. "Hullo?" she asked cautiously.

A cool, deep, efficient voice spoke: "Alex Palmer? Peter Camden of Camden-Waterhouse Associates. We've been instructed to act for you until further notice, regarding your forthcoming engagements."

"Oh, yes. I'm Alex. Thank you."

Jo's knuckles on the steering wheel relaxed visibly.

"Well, we've been checking the arrangements for this weekend and they're all in place, if you still wish. There's more information about the Grammy Award, which appears to have been lying in your file, a proposal for an East Coast and LA tour to the States and contract details regarding a second series of sonatas with EMI that I need you to view. The diary looks busy, but…Would you be able to come into our Mayfair offices over the next few days?"

"Yes. Of course. Just give me a couple of days and I'll call you back. I just need a little time to…to gather myself. Would you mind going through the diary…canceling anything that's not urgent, low-key appearances or interviews, just for a few days, maybe the next week or so? Apart from Saturday, of course. I need to let that one stand. But anything else, that won't attract too much fuss, if I don't…"

"I understand, Miss Palmer. Of course. I think you will find our business arrangements professional and acceptable. We'll run the decisions past you."

"Thank you. I'll call you. Goodbye then."

"Goodbye. We shall hope to see you soon."

"Designated, temporary agent," she explained to Jo, once the call had finished. "Sounded efficient."

"Good. You need someone reliable doing the organizing. You were saying…the quiet life?"

"Yes, who am I kidding. Where are we going to exactly, by the way?"

"Well…I'm not sure I should tell you. I don't let any old Tom, Dick or Harry know. and I haven't known you for very long. Perhaps I should blindfold you—"

"Don't!"

"Sorry. That was a bit of an insensitive joke. I'm so sorry. I wasn't thinking. I have a rather splendid place just off Hampstead Lane, walking distance to the Heath."

"I know that area. I had an attic room for a while as a student in Highgate. That's millionaire's row."

She smiled modestly. Alex gave her a grin. "You must have won the lottery or something."

"Ha! Ha! Very funny. Okay, I deserved that for the blindfold thing. We're even."

They drove in companionable silence for a while. Alex gave her knee a squeeze.

"Ah! Don't do that! You'll have me involuntarily slipping the clutch!"

"Thanks," she said, "for making something reasonably normal out of a totally abnormal day."

CHAPTER THIRTEEN

Ivory Towers 2

Soon the car pulled away from the busy lights of Finchley Road and climbed up a leafy street toward Hampstead. Jo pulled off into a quieter side road and partway along turned into a driveway enclosed by security gates. She slid her window down and punched a code into an enclosed keypad. The gates glided open. They drove through, the gates closing firmly behind them, safely shutting out the intrusions of the outside world. They continued on up a driveway, turning a corner into a courtyard with a small, presently still fountain and an imposing house looming in the encroaching darkness.

Jo hopped out and started to unload the trunk. Alex followed, more cautiously, feeling unreasonably anxious, suddenly together alone, the evening opening up vacantly before her. *But it's Jo*, she reminded herself and her curiosity about the house and her London lifestyle was sufficiently preoccupying. They carried their bags up to the door.

"You're limping," Alex noticed.

"Yes. Pulled a muscle in a chase scene in Italy. It seems to tighten up in the evening."

"Painful?"

"Not really."

A light flicked on automatically. She punched in another security code and fumbled with some keys. "Extra security," she explained, "I had more installed when I moved here after...that incident at the previous place..."

"Yes, of course." *No wonder she's so sympathetic.*

She disappeared briefly to silence the beeping alarm warning and flick on the lights, illuminating a warm, spacious hallway with an elegant staircase, curling up to the higher levels.

"Home," she announced and gestured welcomingly. She stepped forward, closing the front door, relieving Alex of the bags and taking her in her arms; feeling her tense, she gave her a gentle squeeze and quickly released her.

She knows.

"Welcome. Make yourself at home. Let me give you a tour." She pushed open the first door, off to the left, flicking on lights as she went and drawing curtains. "Ballroom stroke rehearsal room stroke piano room, through to studio, or at the moment small cinema, through to spacious open-plan living area and doors onto the garden." The grandeur was lightened with surprisingly homey touches, pictures and exotic ornaments, apparently souvenirs from various parts of the world. She was imitating an estate agent, gesticulating with her hands as she went and she flicked a switch to illuminate a patio area, the covered end of which held a hot tub with gardens beyond that disappeared into the night.

"You approve?"

"Of course. How could I not?"

"The hot tub was already here, by the way. I don't bring gangs of girlies back just in case you were wondering. There's a pool down the other side too, heated and covered and you can slide the ceiling open in the better weather."

"Fabulous. I packed appropriately, it seems..."

The door buzzer went making Alex jump.

"Food," she explained. "Hungry?"

"Actually, yes. I am now. Not so much earlier, sorry."

"Not exactly the most relaxing way to meet parents. Hang on a minute. Kitchen's through there. I'll see you in a sec."

She disappeared and Alex heard her murmur into the intercom, the front door open and the crunch of the gravel.

Alex went through to a kitchen, partly opening out onto the end of the living room, in which one could happily park a car or two, with a more formal dining room off to the other side. She refilled the kettle and flicked it on. *Yep. This would do very nicely for a few days.* She smiled at her ridiculously good fortune and drifted back through the living area to try the piano. It was good, a black, full-size Steinway. *Someone has taste.*

Jo was back in the kitchen when she returned, sorting through bags.

"I asked them to leave it at the gate. It was all paid for anyway. Don't you just love the net?" Then rethinking, added, "Well, some of the time…?"

"Well, I know what you mean. Very nice piano by the way."

"I can't claim credit for it. They sold it with the house. Presumably wealthy enough to buy another, rather than have the hassle of moving this one."

"They can't have been that musical then. No one in their right minds would part easily with one like that. It's very responsive."

"Good, good. Help yourself to it. So, what do you want to eat?"

"Do you have anything comforting? Pizza maybe?"

"Yup!" She dug around and held out a pizza.

"And salad?"

She nodded.

"Wine?"

She rummaged again and brought out something white.

"Perfect."

She popped the pizza in the oven, the wine and some beers in the fridge and searched the cupboards for plates and glasses. "Cutlery's there." She gestured toward a drawer, finishing the unpacking and then started opening a pile of mail, the first of which was a large, fat manila envelope.

"I need these. Scene changes for next week. I'll have to have a look at them in the morning. Would you mind wiping a cloth over the table on the terrace while I finish opening these and we can eat out there, take advantage of the mild night?"

Alex obliged, happy to help, to be given something to do, then she fetched her handbag. A few reassuring phone calls were necessary, so she rang Leanne and left a message about meeting on Friday. Perhaps Leanne would accompany her to the new agents' offices in exchange for lunch out? She felt disproportionately nervous about meeting the assigned agents and what if word had leaked out and reporters were lurking around? It could have felt weird to be so isolated, not even the police knowing exactly where she was, especially after what had happened. But listening to her feelings for a moment, she searched for their response. *Nothing unsettling.* They could track her phone if they needed to. But nothing was going to happen. This was Jo, not... She'd proved her loyalty already. She had too much at stake anyway—her public life, her career and this precious blossoming connection between them.

She had set the phone to beep only, after the agent's call, so was surprised to find there were still more messages from anxious friends, some of whom hadn't been in touch for a while. She sent a brief, group reply back, then went back into the kitchen. Jo had gone, but a couple of trays were laid with everything except the pizza. Peering into the oven, she could see it was obviously time to remove them, so she did just that and placed them on the plates, then carried hers out to the terrace. Jo appeared shortly afterward carrying the second.

"I just went to check on the pool and flick a few switches. Looks fine, if you fancy it later." She looked at Alex tentatively. The last time they had swum together had been in Los Angeles and it was loaded with associations.

Alex smiled at her a little uncomfortably. "Okay."

The food demanded their attention for a while.

"Jo," she ventured after a while, trying to take her mind away from where it kept involuntarily wandering.

"Mmm?"

"Tell me your story. When did you know...you know, that you liked women over men?"

Jo raised an eyebrow at her.

"How do you *do* that? Raise *one* eyebrow?"

"Don't tell anyone, but it took some time practicing in the bathroom mirror when I was a teenager."

She had actually achieved the near-impossible and managed to make Alex laugh.

She continued smoothly, "Now let me see. I think it's fair to say that it crept up on me gradually...I was a bit of a late-developer, incredibly skinny. They used to call me the purple matchstick due to the fact that I wore a purple scarf wrapped around my head in the depths of winter."

Jo made her chuckle again at the thought of her being anything other than supremely glamorous.

"I was already getting into acting, roles in school productions, a brief spell at stage-school had landed me a couple of bit parts in adverts."

"Really? You mean I may have been watching you on the telly?"

"Only if you paid attention to toothpaste and cereal commercials. So I'd had a couple of fumbles with boys and couldn't really see the point behind it, but actually I had this *massive* crush on a girl in my class at school. I would spend lessons staring at the back of her head, trying to answer a teacher's question in a totally smart or witty way to get the whole class and especially her to turn around and look at me."

"I can see how this ties in with being on the stage."

"Yes, perhaps you're right. When the penny finally dropped, I think in actual fact my jaw dropped during a sex education lesson, I plucked up courage and faced my mother over it one evening. And she was magnificent. She listened and explained and said that was what happened sometimes. That I would have to decide what it meant for me, but that it wasn't uncommon even if it wasn't much talked about, especially at school and being a cultured woman she shoved a few books my way, Sappho's poetry, something about the Isle of Lesbos and getting to know yourself. She said it made me special, unique. But as you know, although I've been open enough to myself, my family and a few sworn secret close friends, I've kept it from my work."

A tear had sprung from Alex and trickled down her cheek. An envious tear.

"What did I say?" Jo put down the fork that she had been using for emphasis and leaned across the table to tuck a piece of hair behind Alex's ear and catch the tear, stroking her cheek in the process.

"It's a good story. My mother was different."

"Tell me."

"I'd had this best friend, we'd known each other for years and gradually it was developing into something else. I don't know whether it was from her or from me, or both of us simultaneously, at such a young age…"

"How young?"

"Eleven or twelve, about then."

"Okay…"

"At that age, you don't have a perspective…so I asked my mother. I remember having to pluck up an enormous amount of courage, lying in my bed one evening. I can still visualize it. She would come and tuck me in and we'd often share some important moments then, sort the world out and so on. I told her what was starting to happen, what I was feeling, how I was afraid because I thought I'd become like my ostracized aunt."

"And?"

"I was told not to worry…it was just a growing stage. I'd start to like boys soon. That I should put it far at the back of my mind and in no way mention it to anyone else, nobody would understand, it would lead to a lifetime of difficulty and my father especially would be furious. So I did. I pushed it so far down that I buried it almost completely, other than an uneasy feeling that

I couldn't quite put my finger on. No pun intended." She was feeling stronger, telling the story to Jo.

She smirked. "I get it. But really…that's so harsh to a child."

"She didn't see it that way. I think she was trying to protect me."

"They have a habit of doing that, parents."

"But now, I get it. I see the damage it has caused. Years of uncertainty, being awkward with other people…"

"You're not awkward with me."

"You're *particularly* special."

Jo grasped her hand across the table.

"But the mixed messages I was sending to myself, let alone other people. What if Josh was misreading me because I was so crap at showing anything? I feel guilty. He did ensnare me in a kiss one awful Christmas party."

"And?"

"It was nothing. He was doing it to everyone in sight."

"Exactly. Everyone has to take a path into adulthood and it's not an easy one. There are mistakes and experiments along the way. It's just that we…everyone perhaps has to make a different voyage."

"You are a gem."

"And your mother, she's not here now. Of course."

"Exactly that. Perhaps I'm free from her judgment. Okay. Time to stop. We're going too far down the Freudian path for me this evening now."

Jo nodded and squeezed her hand. "What about the ostracized aunt?"

"She's still around. Lives in the Lake District."

"Then we should pay her a visit…"

There was silence for a while as they pondered each other's information.

"So what are you working on?" Alex asked in a break between mouthfuls, sipping carefully at the wine, trying to lighten herself up.

"Would you believe it? When we sign the contracts for these things there's a confidentiality clause where we're not supposed to discuss it…with anyone. I suppose it's because everything's subject to alteration and they don't want the great idea getting out, so someone else beats them to it. It would put you in a difficult position in fact if I told you. Suffice to say, it's a bit of a spy thriller, where I get the guy halfway through, but it turns out he's on the wrong side. That sort of thing. Decent script and director—Georges Salangal. I've worked with him before. He's excellent, but a hard taskmaster; he won't stop until it's absolutely perfect."

"You mystery woman."

"Ha! I need to work out a bit though. There are some stripped down scenes over the next few weeks. Wouldn't hurt to tone up."

"You have a gym here?"

"Oh, yeah. I haven't shown you the rest yet, have I? The gym's near the pool. I'll show you after this. Feel free. You know you should treat this place like your home. Do you want to stay all week?" she suggested, catching herself at the end of the question, as if allowing rather too much cat out of the bag.

"That's a tempting offer. But I don't know. I feel like the wind's been knocked right out of me, like my legs have been kicked from underneath me."

Jo watched her patiently while she struggled to formulate her thoughts, not interrupting the process.

"I'm not at my best, as you can see. Leanne's back by Friday and I'd like her to accompany me when I visit this new agent. There are some contracts to sign, various details, music for this new commission for the Proms, which could be a bit wacky, a second series at EMI and a Grammy nomination. Josh should have been dealing with it all…"

"Yeah. Exactly. Should have been, instead of…But, anyway… Look, I don't mind if you're not at your best. Let's get real here. This isn't the award ceremony for the most in control, the most normal…"

Alex managed a giggle.

"Have a think about it. I'd like to think I was…taking care of you. Let the dust settle. Talking of awards…EMI? Grammy? Well done. I didn't know about that."

Alex felt a surge of affection for her, for her consideration, for her negotiation of the awkwardness of today, the awareness of practicalities, for her ability to steer in and away from the sensitive subjects. "I think it's for the classical sonata series, there's a proposed East Coast US tour too."

"East Coast tour? That reminds me…tickets. I'm just going to take a look at the Festival Hall website. Excuse me a moment." She slipped out of her chair and disappeared inside.

Alex sat peacefully finishing her meal, smiling at Jo's subconscious restless energy, listening to the night rustling in the garden. A town fox emerged from some trees to one side and ambled across the grass, breaking into a scamper when he caught sight of her and disappearing into the darkness. It felt, thankfully, a million miles away from the incident of the previous night. *Josh dead? Lying cold somewhere. It's so unfathomable. There'll have to be a funeral.*

Jo reappeared, breaking her distracted state of mind. "Fine, that's sorted. There were a couple of spare seats on the front row, so I nabbed one. Not cheap are they?"

"You have to pay for quality," Alex teased her. "But you said you had a plan?"

"Ah…Let me show you. Hang on a minute." She disappeared into the house again and Alex finished off her salad while she was gone.

After some time, the person who returned wore glasses, a shawl and a shabby wig, she hobbled a little and said, "Ah! Aleeex. Zere you are. I 'ave bin looking for you. Let me introduze myzelf, Petra Rahmanoff. I 'ave not zeen you zince ze mazterclazz of '98."

"You are joking!" She nearly fell off her chair in astonishment. "You're kidding. You'll never carry it off…"

Jo stood more upright. "Are you questioning my acting ability, madam?" In mock sincerity.

"Oh, no of course not. But you'll definitely win the Oscar for best female lead if you pull that off. No whizz-bang special lighting or anything."

Jo returned to normality, peeling off the wig, "It works best with suitable makeup of course."

"Okay. I dare you. If anything will stop me from falling apart on Saturday, it will be knowing who the old dear sitting just under my right armpit really is. I might have a problem not giggling."

"Madam, I accept your gauntlet, and laugh in the face of danger. I shall practice my part more during the week. I'm afraid it's your turn now. You have to pass an audition."

She really fell off the chair this time. "No! What? I don't have to, do I?"

"Uh-huh!" she insisted, amused. She was being deliberately distracting.

"Oh, no. Humiliating."

Alex sat herself down on the doorstep to the terrace, not taking herself seriously, attempting to relive a moment of the school show many years previously and curled a lock of hair around one finger, as she tried to sing for a minute.

"Okay! Stop! Enough! Thank you. We'll call you. Well, we might…"

"Hah! Now you have to play the piano. Fair's fair."

"Oh, you're kidding…it's been ages."

"Uh-huh!" She shook her head.

"Oh, help!"

They went through to the other room, arm in arm and giggling. Alex reopened the piano. "There you are. Off you go!"

She fished in the piano stool and hoisted out a piece of music, making a meal of theatrically sitting down at the piano, flicking back imaginary coattails and pushing her Petra glasses down her nose, squinting comically at the music. She played shakily through the first page or so of *Für Elise*.

"Actually not bad, you know. Just a few more lessons should have it…"

"Ha! Now your turn. Then we're quits."

"Oh, okay. What do you want?"

"You choose."

They swapped. Jo leaned gracefully in the curve of the grand piano, while Alex adjusted the piano stool and settled herself, then launched into one of her favorites while Jo daydreamed, listening.

"That's just gorgeous," she said, quietly, when it had finished. "Like you. That's like one of the first things I heard you perform live, back at the South Bank. I didn't imagine I'd have you here."

Alex smiled humbly. "Are we done now?"

"Come on. Let's go for that swim. I'm not far enough down my glass of wine to drown yet and I could do with stretching this wretched leg." She led her out of the room, via the hallway and Alex scooped her costume from her luggage as they went.

The telephone started to ring.

"I'm not in," Jo said simply. She shrugged.

"Bathroom?" Alex asked.

"This way by the pool and gym." She pushed a door open on the other side of the kitchen, leading to a hallway and indicated a room off to one side.

Alex went in to find an immaculately presented shower and changing room. Slipping off her dress and changing into the costume, she felt tears sting her eyes again as she paused to examine her bruised face and body. Her cheek was changing to blue over the cheekbone, but the split lip was looking slightly better and without her realizing, it had hurt less during supper, she had talked with Jo almost normally. But the act of piling her hair up revealed sinister emerging marks on her arms and throat. Bathing naked seemed wholly inappropriate. It was only just possible to bring herself to peel her clothes off at all.

She found her way past the modest gym to the pool, surrounded by potted plants, a waterfall pattering at one end and fanned steps at the other.

"Impressive," she exclaimed quietly to herself in surprise.

Jo was already in the middle of a powerful length, one of several from the look of the disturbed water and rebounding waves. She had changed into an unrevealing Speedo costume. Alex was more comfortable with her self-absorption, comfortable not to be stared at right at that moment and she drifted into the water through the shallow steps. It was pleasantly warm. She felt

herself beginning to relax. She started to swim a few lengths of
her own, keeping her injured face above the water and turning
away as Jo splashed past. Hanging by the waterfall, letting the
falling water massage aching shoulders, she realized how much
tension she had been bottling up. After a while she swam back,
her neck aching from the awkward angle, arrived at the shallow
steps and waited for a while until Jo came to rest some lengths
later, panting as she tried to catch her breath.

"That feels bloody marvelous, after the plane and the car.
All that sitting." She came behind Alex, only just hiding her
astonishment at the bruising with a sharp inward breath, and
even so a soft exclamation of, "Alex!" still escaped her pursed
lips. She straddled her legs with relaxed familiarity either side of
her back, sitting on a slightly higher step and gently massaged
her shoulders.

"Actually that feels really good too," Alex said quietly,
listening to the fall of the water and watching the ripples across
the pool.

"Who takes care of the place, when you're away?" She
ventured, keeping Jo's attention away from the injuries.

"Oh, Andy usually comes and goes a bit and there's a couple,
Zara and Yuri, who came with the house, practically. They're
very discreet. They've probably been in recently, I had asked
them to. But I'll ask them all to stay away while you're here. It
would be better, for our privacy and your peace of mind."

She bent and kissed her shoulder, then carried on with the
rubbing.

"Want some oil on that? I'll do it properly, carefully…"

She nodded a little cautiously.

"…this way. Look, you mustn't be afraid. I'm here, you're
here, because I want you to feel…unthreatened. The last thing
you need right now is…" She petered out, words failing her.

"Yes. I know." They stepped out and Jo threw her a towel,
drying herself simultaneously. She took Alex's hand. She was
perfectly aware of her reticence and obviously quietly fuming
inside at the bruises and invasive marks from the attack, although
apparently firmly resolved not to draw further attention to them.

"Just leave that, I'll tidy later." She led her back through the house, holding her hand loosely, their feet bare and noiseless on the hall tiles and feeling luxurious on the carpeted staircase.

"So, you haven't seen upstairs yet?" She led her briefly from room to room, each immaculate and welcoming, distracting her thoughts again. "Upstairs office with a garden view, guest room, guest room, another guest room and another, main bathroom, master bedroom, dressing room. It goes on and on. Upstairs—a bit of a library and a den to crash." She led the way to the largest bedroom.

"Lie down, if you want." She indicated.

Alex was happy to try out the massive bed with its dark blue, stitched eiderdown. It was deliciously soft and inviting. She slipped off the still damp costume and lay on her front, sliding her bottom half under the covers. Jo threw her a pair of silk pajama bottoms. "There. I don't mind lending them to you..." In an attempt to signify closure on anything too intimate, while she went into the bathroom to hunt down the oil.

When she returned, she stood still in the doorway and breathed, "You look so gorgeous there. I can hardly believe you're here. You're not going to evaporate in the night or anything?"

"Not planning to. Rather grateful to be here, too, actually," Alex answered sleepily.

She came over to the bed warming some oil in her hands to sit beside her. Familiar, yet not uncomfortable.

"How's that?" she asked, spreading the warm oil over her back and starting to work it in.

"Fabulous," she whispered, closing her eyes.

"Don't worry about anything. Leave it all until the morning. You can call Leanne, the agents, the lawyer, all of them, in the morning. I'll switch your phone off for you in a minute."

Her warm hands were the last thing she remembered that evening.

* * *

She woke much later in the night, briefly alarmed. The house was dark, except that Jo had left a soft light on, coming from the dressing room. She felt her breathing calm, remembering now. Jo was deeply asleep, warm beside her, one arm thrown up on the pillow—an apparently habitual position. Their bags were lying against the wall beneath the long window. She must have carried them up.

Alex crept to the bathroom, the thick carpet soft under her bare feet, hunted out a toothbrush from her bag, drank some water and admired the darkness of the night beyond the curtains. *So private, but with the bustle of the city only miles away.* The skyline was silhouetted by a distant orange glow. She was grateful to be somewhere so utterly obscure and away from the rest of the world. An oasis of calm. It felt…safe. Everything felt a little more removed from reality than it should, even allowing for the unfamiliarity of Jo's palatial house. *Weird that not a soul knows I'm here. Only one.*

She went back to bed and curled in next to her. It was so peaceful, childlike and comforting. Jo had not demanded anything from her. Apart from attempts to distract her. She had managed to forget the sick feeling in the base of her stomach for a while. She winced at the thought. She watched her motionless form, the barely audible breathing, long dark lashes closed over the resting eyes. Nothing could have been more of a contrast to the previous night and she lay back, ready to sleep again without fear.

CHAPTER FOURTEEN

At Jo's

The following morning, when she roused herself, Jo was gone, the space in the bed ruffled, but already cool. Momentarily anxious, her thoughts rattling in on her, until she heard noises somewhere on the lower floor and remembered again where she was. She borrowed a silky wrap from the bathroom and wandered down, going into the kitchen and helping herself to juice from the fridge. The regular click-click of the gym machinery drifted across from beyond the further door, strangely comforting. Meandering back to the studio with the piano, she found it was still open from last night. Placing the drink down on a nearby desk, she started to run over some scales and fiddly passages. It was pleasantly relaxing; companionable to know they were both preoccupied with their separate preparations.

After a while she went out onto the terrace, where the doors had been thrown open wide. The grass was cool and dewy as she walked onto it to explore. A pathway wound enticingly down the garden. Following it she discovered a slightly shabby looking tennis court beyond the trees and a well-cared for sizeable pond, with fish and tadpoles swimming around. She wandered back and found Jo seated at the terrace table, with a tray of coffee and toast, a newspaper and the revised script.

"Hi! I heard you were up. A few musical notes drifted through the house and told me. Coffee? You've made a column on the front page."

"Oh, dear."

"Not so oh, dear. It's in your favor."

Alex scanned it quickly. "I'd better make a few calls early this morning."

She fetched her mobile from her bag and switched it on. "Thanks for last night, by the way," she commented.

"You were shattered."

"Yes. I was rather."

"I came down to close up the house and check the messages after you fell asleep. It turns out I have to make an appearance at my agent's offices in New Bond Street, later this afternoon. I haven't been back since the Awards. They've organized a drinks bash for clients, in celebration." She looked apologetic.

"That'll be nice, though." Her phone beeped into recognition.

"Kind of. I'd hoped not to have to go anywhere for a few days. You'll be all right?"

"I have a load of practice to do for the weekend."

She picked up the revised script. "I'd better get onto learning this, this morning. You could wander up to Highgate if you wanted. I have a selection of large sunglasses, if you feel like a disguise. You said it was your old stamping ground. You don't have to go out, of course. But you don't have to feel trapped here either."

"Actually, that would be really nice. I don't suppose anybody will be looking for me around here."

"There's a café at Kenwood House."

"Yes, I remember."

The main phone in the house started to ring again and this time she went in to answer it.

Alex checked the messages on her phone: Leanne—*Have finished early. Can be back for agents on Wednesday. Better than Thurs/Fri for me. You okay where you are, or want to come to me?*

Then Jenny—her heart stopped briefly, before opening it. Josh's assistant. *Alex. I'm so sorry. I should have known. He hid himself away sometimes. I never questioned it. Camden-W. offering me a position, but taking a few days to consider. Funeral Monday, Beckenham Cemetery. Don't suppose you want to know that much.*

No. Don't suppose I do, she thought. *Oh, Jenny.*

Jo returned from the house. "Sounds like this 'bash' is growing. They've had enough interest to hire one of the rooms at the Ritz at short notice. I'll try to get away early."

"It's all right with me. You could show me how your home cinema works though, before you go."

"Sure, how about now?"

Alex went around the table and leaned down to give her a warm kiss: the first initiated by her since the whole drama of the rescue, since Los Angeles. Jo's lips were soft and warm, receiving her gently, gratefully. Something re-awoke, glowing deep inside her, almost guiltily.

"Less painful?" she asked.

"Yes," she murmured, lingering close to her mouth. Being with her felt right...complete, so completely different. "Thank you." Jo kissed her back carefully and then, holding her hand, stood up to lead the way to the cinema to fill her in on its mystical workings.

After a shower and change and a half hour's unpacking of her bags, Alex borrowed the sunglasses, which she noticed appreciatively were large enough to cover her bruised cheek, applied makeup in an effort to camouflage the worst of the injuries and a chiffon scarf to cover the bruising on her neck, was instructed on the house codes, given spare keys, grabbed a floppy hat and her bag and left Jo's ivory tower behind.

She hiked up the hill toward Highgate, slipping anonymously into shops to buy a paper and early strawberries, then strolled morbidly through the cemetery and out onto the Heath, eventually finding herself a table in the morning sunshine outside the café at Kenwood, where a waitress brought her a coffee. It was an opportune moment to sit and make calls, privately, in this quiet corner, trying to ignore the yawning vacuum where Josh's personality should have been: making the calls for her, ringing to inform her of the outcomes, bubbling with his interfering enthusiasm. The dog-walkers and joggers passed by obliviously across the pathway; their apparent normality contrasting with the abstraction of her current world. She confirmed an appointment with Camden-Waterhouse for the following afternoon, booked a table for two for lunch at the Ritz café, instructed the lawyers to deal with the police at Godalming, text-messaged Leanne and left messages for her dad, brother and Pauline. The practical action was reassuring. She found it hard to think of Nightingale's End. Even its name had taken on a more sinister connotation. The luxury of coming to Jo's had distanced her.

Thank heavens for her, she thought, gazing out across the heath and wrapping her hands around the coffee mug for additional warmth. *It feels so...secure. She needn't have been so good to me. She must have the attention of everyone she meets, all those beautiful actresses on sets or gorgeous girlies at stage doors with the potential to drape themselves all over her.* She did not particularly mind. For some inscrutable reason Jo had chosen to rescue her and that was sufficient. It restored her shaken faith in humanity.

Her phone beeped conversationally, like a little bird demanding to be fed. Vladimir—

Sorry to hear of your ordeal. I hope you are recovering. Take strength from your music. If my sources are correct, I believe we have a return date to meet again. Fondest regards x.

So sweet, in his own way. She returned a message of thanks and tentative reassurance, then paid for the coffee and decided to take the long route back. It was as if she had been strangely transported back to her student days when she had marched this area in a similar solitary fashion. Walking past the old bathing ponds, which she had never dared to try and through the woods, passing walkers and joggers and chided by chattering birds, she came out a little lower down on the main road, from where she could easily head back up to Jo's.

She let herself in quietly through the security gates, stopping to check they closed behind her, then up the driveway and silently through the front door, using codes and keys.

The house was quiet, too. She went through to the kitchen and dumped her bag on one of the counters. Through the glass at the far end, she could just see Jo, pacing out some scenes in the sunshine in the back garden and mouthing words to herself, then strolling over to the table to double-check the script. She grinned. *Is that how they do it?*

She decided not to disturb her. The walk had made her famished, so she rummaged in the fridge and found chicken and vegetables to create a stir-fry. The chopping and preparing was therapeutic. A search of the cupboards was fruitful and she added garlic, ginger, soy sauce and Chinese wine, until a tempting fragrance filled the kitchen. It must have stretched out into the garden, for soon Jo appeared in the archway between the rooms.

"Smells fabulous. I didn't realize you were back. How was your walk?"

"Relaxing thanks. Made the calls that needed to be made. But I must say the best bit was watching your performance when I returned."

"Ha! Not fair. Tickets aren't on sale for that one yet!"

They ate cheerfully together, perched on a couple of barstools and after they had cleared the kitchen, Jo apologized and went to change, returning in a close-fitting, pale blue shirt and slacks, casual and yet the picture of elegance.

"You look gorgeous!" Alex murmured.

She fetched the car keys.

"Where do you park?"

"The offices have some allotted underground parking spaces. They'll have one reserved for me today. Not bad, this fame lark."

Jo kissed her gently. "I'm sorry I have to do this, but it will be you I'm coming back to see tonight. You help yourself to whatever you need. Sure you'll be all right?"

She nodded, determined not to appear needy.

And she was out of the door and gone.

The house was peculiarly empty and silent.

Suddenly she felt very alone, aware of her isolation, the blank solitude for the first time since…she walked in a slow circle through the ground-floor rooms. The unseasonable, growing heat of the day was starting to feel oppressive. A burning pain was rising in her throat. The crunch of the car tires on the gravel was long gone. Suppressed thoughts began to surface. She realized that she had not had any time to herself to think. When she arrived at the terrace, she planted herself on the top step into the garden, put her face in her hands and wept, huge, shuddering sobs, which crashed over her like stormy waves breaking onto the beach, barely giving her time to draw breath before another one threatened to drown her.

Josh. You idiot. Why the hell couldn't you have done something normal. If you had to kiss me, couldn't you have heard me out and left it as it was? She remembered the webcam, the forethought that it must have taken. The keys that she had loaned him one day when she had needed a score from home in a hurry. *Oh, hell. What a bloody mess.*

And then realizing the ambiguity of the words, her emotions overwhelmed her again.

* * *

While Jo headed into town, to face the demands of her other life, back at her house, Alex had finally run out of tears, for herself, for Josh, for everything. She stopped rocking herself on the top step and pulled herself up to standing, shaking out her skirt. *This won't do. It won't do at all. It was sudden. It was shocking. It was unimaginable. But it had happened. Way out of my control.* She went indoors to the kitchen and drank more juice, cool from the fridge. It helped to clear her head. She felt ridiculous. Here she was in this beautiful house, the home of one of the most attractive women in the land. Jo. As she came. She had an independent career that intrigued her with its unattainability and opposition with her own. It did not totally depend on her being gorgeous, she just happened to be so. It was what she could do and the wit and intelligence that came with it that was so important and gave her a depth which was fascinating and irresistible to her. She felt a surge at the thought. Their egos weren't in competition. She wasn't sure any of this was a healthier motivation, it wasn't even easy to analyze the reasons, right now it just made perfect sense.

It was time to make the most of it and enjoy herself. Action was better than thought. She ran through the house, realizing she hadn't even visited the top floor, scampering up the stairs to the top rooms. She threw herself into a huge beanbag. Better. How many people would envy this? She browsed the bookshelves and DVDs, an expansive library. She wasn't in the mood to read, but lingered long enough to choose a couple of films for later. She ran down a flight and strolled from room to room, imagining living in each, ending in the room they had shared for the night. She found her swimsuit and started to pull it on, then thought. *Who's to see?* Her thoughts added—a little more soberly—*no webcams here.* But when she went downstairs, she did check the plants and pictures for any suspicious leads or holes. She plunged naked into the pool. Without the waterfall on, its surface was as still and reflective as glass, until she cleaved it, sending a bow-wave across behind her as she swam hard, liberated, length after length, until she was breathless and gasping and laughing back at the shallow steps. Her reverie was broken when she heard her mobile ringing from the other part of the house. She pulled herself out, grabbed a towel and was still chuckling and dripping when she picked it up, checking the caller.

It was Camden-Waterhouse.

"Hello?"

"Sorry to disturb you, especially as we're seeing you tomorrow," a polite, professional voice said, "Anthony here. Just quickly for you to think about, before we see you. *The Johnson Show* wants you for a brief post-Oscars party slot this weekend, some playing and a short interview, Friday night. We can advise they steer away from any particularly difficult subject matter. You might prefer to avoid it altogether or you might like to have an opportunity to say something appropriate. Would you like to have a think about it and call us back?"

She paused only briefly, a sense of growing self-determination beginning to replace her former anxiety.

"Alex, are you still there?"

The feeling of agency was a welcome relief from this self-imposed isolation. "Yes. I'm here. No need. Please say yes. Take it on. And I won't mind taking the interview as it comes."

"Many thanks. See you tomorrow."

"Bye." She flicked the phone shut and smiled. She could do this. *Life after Josh*. It wasn't her mistake. She went through to what she thought of as the piano studio and sat down, wrapped only to the waist in the towel, warm in the early, unseasonal humidity, hair still dripping down her back, and played, playing without stopping, covering everything she could think of; everything for Saturday, introducing a couple of new ideas in the cadenzas and anything else that might be appropriate for *The Johnson Show*. When she stopped, she realized it must have been hours, her hair was dry and the light was fading outside. She felt a little stiff and stood up from the piano, shaking her arms loosely by her side. She called Leanne, chatting for half an hour, firming up the plans for their meeting, comforted by the normality of her friend's voice and news. Continuing her plan of action when the call had ended, she grabbed a bottle of water from the fridge and went to try the gym.

Later, aching and starting to flag, she found a ready-prepared salad and some sushi in the fridge and went to explore Jo's cinema. She was all the way through an ancient, silent Laurel and Hardy and halfway into a modern romance starring Jo, when she fell asleep, where she was, in a comfortably cushioned seat, the film still rolling, still naked from the waist up, hair tousled, like Echo or a mermaid washed up on the beach.

* * *

When Alex woke it was to fingers gently over her hair and down her neck, reaching over the back of the seat to kiss her bare shoulder. She disturbed, gently, not startled.

"Oh, you," she murmured sleepily.

Jo went round to the front of the chair, taking her hands in hers, pulling her carefully to her feet and kissing her, drinking her in. Alex put her arms around her neck, still soporifically stretching herself and leaned into her.

"How was it? You feel sticky."

"Okay. Exactly that. Sticky, hot, crowded. Come on, I have just the thing."

Jo held one of her arms around her neck, a soldier helping a wounded colleague, but less like the soldier, put the other around her naked waist. The towel fell to the floor and Alex noticed vaguely that she didn't care.

Jo led her through to the terrace, letting go of her arm to flick on the lights softly. She lingered in the doorway.

"Hang on a moment." She went back to her, nestling into her neck and kissing her questioningly again there. "It takes a moment…"

Now more awake, Alex started to undo the buttons on the pale blue shirt, dark in places from the sweat of the party.

"It must have been hot…"

"And crowded…" She wriggled out of the rolled up sleeves, kicking off shoes as she helped her with the buckle on the slacks until they matched in their nakedness and they stepped into the warmth of the tub together. Alex felt a spark of interest low in her abdomen, this time she noticed without any misgivings.

"Oh, that is so…good. The perfect antidote. They made me do a speech."

Alex smiled at her and swam the few strokes over, sliding an arm around her neck to rub her shoulders. "And is that easy? Do you find it easy being that spontaneous?"

"Mmm." She laid her head against Alex.

"The speech?"

She spoke dreamily. "I'm practiced at it by now, part of the job description." She ran her hand along Alex's side inquisitively, who shuddered, pleasantly surprised with herself. Suddenly it was a matter of urgency, previous troubles laid aside temporarily to attend to the immediate situation; the sensuous warmth of the pool and their intimate proximity overtaking their senses and then, moving, dripping onto the rug in the living room and eventually heading upstairs into the spacious, graceful bedroom.

Freed again to enjoy each other, the burden of anxiety put aside, Jo was being supremely careful with her bruised face and particularly alert to cues from her, until they lay spent and devoid of further energy, chuckling occasionally and stroking each other's soft, receptive bodies, sometimes smiling and, moments later looking suddenly serious.

"I'm in deep water here," Jo murmured, kissing her hair, breathing her in.

"Not anymore!" Alex laughed at her.

"No seriously. Just so you know."

"Oh." Not quite sure what she meant. "Out of your depth? Or enjoyably deep?"

"Oh, enjoyably."

"Oh," she whispered again and rolled over to kiss her, smiling at her and stroking her ruffled hair, until she fell asleep in her arms.

After a while, Alex left her lying there asleep, and went down to the kitchen to make herself a drink. A gift, luxury bath products, was lying on the kitchen counter with the car keys. She read the card with a smile and went back up to the guest bathroom to fill the large corner bath adding some of the milky bathing fluid, which boasted of its ability to bring relaxation, although she didn't feel it was particularly relevant now. Jo's comparative tenderness had helped bury the more upsetting images in her mind, and she almost felt guilty to feel aroused again so soon after…but it was *different*. She blocked the thought. *It's okay to bring the curtain down on it, Alex.* She insisted to herself, *Healthier to move onward.* The mixture smelt expensive and intoxicating and she sank into the heat, soaking until she was sufficiently scrubbed and indulged to dry off and join Jo fragrantly in the huge bed, slipping in without her ever realizing she had been gone and falling asleep deliciously beside her.

CHAPTER FIFTEEN

Back to Town

She awoke first in the morning. Jo was still oblivious and now curled on her side. She slipped out from under the covers, grinning at the thought that she had helped to wring the energy from her. She hunted quietly through the dressing room and unearthed a light day dress with which to impress her potential new agents and a silk shawl to cover some of the bruises. She glanced at her watch as she attached it, eight thirty already. She needed to meet Leanne at ten. She fixed her earrings and hurriedly padded out of the room on bare feet, carrying heels in one hand and a bag of relevant material for the day in the other. It was pleasantly cool downstairs after yesterday's humidity. It appeared to have rained in the night, the gravel and paving stones darkened by moisture. She put the kettle on and filled a bowl with cereal, stretching the aches out of her muscles and replying to messages while the water came to the boil. Last night had been...delightful. It was...*of course*...still possible to live!

Having filled a couple of mugs with tea, she took one and went through to the piano, running through a few quiet scales, trying not to wake her. Afterward, while she was munching the cereal down quickly at a high stool at one of the counters, Jo drifted into the room, still looking docile and rubbing the sleep from her eyes and forehead, dressed in a T-shirt and hotpants.

"Morning!"

They grinned at each other, both remembering the preceding night.

"You left me." Her voice was deep, thick from sleep.

"It was a wrench. You looked that good. I have to be in town at ten, Leanne, Camden-Waterhouse etcetera."

"Oh, yeah. Need a car? How are you going?"

"I thought I'd just take the tube."

"Really? With your face on half the headlines?"

"Oh. Yes. I hadn't thought it through. I'm not used to—"

"Give me a sec and I'll run you in. I'll drop you somewhere in Mayfair, you could walk it from there, if you like."

"That would be great. There's a mug of tea for you."

"Thanks. I'll be back in a moment." She disappeared into the downstairs bathroom.

Alex cupped her hands around the mug, losing herself in thought for a while, but as she returned recovered herself to say, "By the way, thank you. I found your gift. I've treated myself already."

"See. I was thinking of you, while living it up at the Ritz." She rested an arm on her shoulders and kissed her lightly on the cheek. "If you call me when you're ready I'll pick you up later too."

After a brief interlude upstairs in the dressing room Jo ran her into London, with her mug of tea poured into a travel mug and sandwiched into a cup holder between the comfortable seats, looking simply practical, domesticated and still warm and placid from the lie-in. Alex alighted discreetly in a back street, just off Piccadilly, and disappeared around a corner with a brief wave to hunt down Leanne in the designated coffee shop, while Jo headed back home to work for the morning.

It was simplicity itself, a contrasting freedom, to meet up with Leanne who was already waiting in the coffee shop with cappuccinos and pastries lined up. As she walked over to her she stood up and welcomed her with an enormous hug.

"Oh Alex. Let's have a look at you."

She lifted the glasses off her face just enough to show her the bruising, now hidden a little by a layer of foundation.

"And your lip too."

"Yep." She moved the scarf to reveal the bruising around her neck.

"I can't believe it. I've met the man. What a bloody idiot." They were keeping their voices low.

Alex smarted at the reminder of her own words. "It's good to see you." Her legs felt weak suddenly.

They sat down; Alex fell gratefully into the chair.

"Sorry love, to bring it all up again," Leanne continued, "but really…what the hell did he think he was doing? After coming out to LA and lapping up your glory. You'd think he'd just want to expand and capitalize upon that, not…you know."

"Oh God, Leanne…" She felt her throat tighten. "I'm only just under control."

"Sorry love."

"It's just that he lost the plot completely. When it happened, he just lost it. He was…animalistic…predatory. I was terrified. But he'd been planning things…"

"…the little shit. What about the ramifications of all this?"

"It's in the hands of the Surrey police now and I've got a lawyer, but thank heavens, my part in this appears to be clear-cut to them." She paused. "There's video evidence, the webcams in the cottage, as I said." She gulped.

"What a madman!"

This response brought a glimmer of a smile back to her. "I suppose there'd be recorded evidence of what he'd been up to. Do you remember how upset I was in Vancouver? That creepy dream. Like a premonition. Those letters…all him. I dread to think. Perhaps he expected that he'd be able to watch what he did to me again, before the accident stopped that."

"Blimey. Oh, honey. Who'd have thought?"

"I know. It's just appalling. He's dead. It's hard to believe. I shouldn't say it, it sounds heartless, but perhaps it's simpler that way. What could have come after this? How the hell could... I've been a mess. Pauline rescued me, then this friend that I'd met in California."

"Yes. Who is this mystery friend?"

"Oh, Leanne, I promise I'll tell you...when I can. Everything's such a muddle now."

Leanne looked briefly ruffled, then reached out for her hand across the table.

"Okay. That'll do for now. You tell me when you can. But they must be worth having, if they snaffled you away from the limelight and helped you to stay this much together over the past few days."

"Yes."

"And you're okay there? You feel...secure? You can come to me whenever you want."

"I'm okay for a few more days, it's felt better being removed, but I might take you up on that later. I don't think I can go back to the cottage at the moment. How was Nottingham?"

Leanne nodded. "Same old, you know. How's the coffee doing?"

"Nearly finished. Shall we scoot in a minute? There might be a reporter lurking. It was in the paper that they were taking over."

"Yeah. I wondered." She delved into her bag and brought out a similar large pair of dark glasses. "What do you think? Matching starlets?" She laughed.

"Brilliant."

They left the coffee shop, both bespectacled, and headed for Camden-Waterhouse.

Sure enough, on the park side of the square, a couple of photographers were loitering, drinking from take-away cups.

"See them?"

"Yes. We'll march up the front steps. Take my arm." Leanne suggested.

To anybody else they would have looked like a couple of familiar friends arm in arm walking up the pavement, but the photographers were on the alert for their quarry and immediately downed cups and went into action, hurrying over the road for their shots of this pale, wan looking girl with a recently split lip and a tall, willowy girl, both in sunglasses, climbing the steps of one of the Georgian houses in a determined fashion and waiting to be buzzed in.

"Alex? Alex?" one of them called. "What's the latest? How are you dealing with it all? Where are you staying?"

The tall girl moved across to the other side to block their view and thankfully they were quickly buzzed in before they were harassed any more.

"Thanks, Leanne," she said, as they entered the rather splendid lobby, closing the door behind them, taking off their coats and smiling at the mutual intrigue and daring escape. "You're a perfect minder." She felt childlike. Frustratingly so dependent upon other people's kindness and initiative at the moment.

The receptionist hung their coats politely for them and indicated spacious armchairs and a coffee table stacked with magazines and today's papers. "Mr. Waterhouse will be with you in a moment, please take a seat."

They had barely sat and started to scan the headlines, with Leanne pointing out in a whisper that there was a column about Alex on page three of the *Telegraph*, when a smartly tailored, balding, late-middle-aged man came into the lobby from the inner sanctum and held out his hand.

"Good morning, Miss Palmer. I'm Anthony Waterhouse. Do come through. And this is?"

"Leanne Marson, a friend. She's accompanying me today."

"Come through both of you. Would you like coffee or tea?"

"Coffee please." She half-grinned at Leanne, feeling that they were already swimming in caffeine.

"Sandy," he called across to the receptionist, "can you arrange morning coffee to be sent up, please?"

"Certainly."

They walked through the inner security door, down a thickly carpeted hallway with doors off at various intervals and up a curling flight of stairs. Mr. Waterhouse opened a door at the top and held it open wide enough to allow them through.

"My office," he said unnecessarily, and they found themselves in a large, bright room with the same carpet as the hallway, many bookshelves, cabinets and a spacious curved desk with state-of-the-art information technology.

"Does Leanne want to sit in or would you rather take advantage of our comfortable staff room along the corridor?"

They looked at each other, considering. "I'll be along the corridor then if you need me."

Alex nodded. "Okay." She was feeling unreasonably edgy and knew it must be written all over her face. Leanne gave her a meaningful look. Alex nodded at her.

Mr. Waterhouse directed Leanne out of his office and then she noticed he left the door slightly ajar, as if sensitively indicating a possible escape route.

"So, Miss Palmer…"

"Call me Alex, please."

"Alex then…" He smiled pleasantly. "I think you'll find us very professional and highly organized, should you wish to continue with us after this temporary period."

"Thank you. You'll understand it's all a little…difficult at the moment."

"Yes. Of course. We have been in touch with the Surrey Police; they were part of our initial instruction. Would you like to pass on any other contact numbers?" He proffered letterhead paper and a pen.

"Yes. There's my lawyer, in case there are any issues and e-mail, and my accountant—but perhaps you have them on file. It's best to reach me on the mobile at the moment." She reached into her bag and copied down the contact details. "I heard from Jenny. I believe she might be coming here."

"Yes, well, we've made her an offer. Actually she recommended us to the police when they shut the office down. It works for both of us. She has knowledge of the clientele portfolio and we can offer her security."

"Yes. Of course."

"Back to business…" He pulled a file across the desk. A secretary knocked politely at the door and brought in the coffee. "Thank you."

After she left, he continued. "We have some letters for you." He passed them over. "Grammy nomination details, *Johnson* details for Friday, EMI contract, proposed East Coast and LA tour in October and the commission music for the principal Prom. It appears to have taken some time to finalize. The composer has enclosed a letter and might wish to communicate with you, for alterations."

She opened the score first. It was alternative, bizarre and fascinating, dotted with some unusual special effects.

"I might need to speak to him too. This looks cutting edge."

She went to the mail. "The Academy wants to award me an Honorary Fellowship. That's something of an honor!" And another, "The Grammys. Excellent. I'll have to play?"

"Apparently so."

"Do you know what they're expecting?"

He made a note. "I'll look into it for you."

This was all cheering, distracting news.

"And would you mind sending thanks to all the West Coast tour contacts, fixers, conductors and orchestras. I don't think Josh—" The name caught in her throat, guilt-laden, embarrassed. "Mr. Pembroke…got around to it…" She trailed off.

"Of course." He made another note. "Is there anything else that we can do for you, regarding Mr. Pembroke?"

"I don't think so. I'm afraid any overtures from me for the funeral will be inappropriate."

"We may be able to cover that in a sensitive fashion for you. May I offer my sympathy on behalf of the company? I must say that what happened is quite obviously not normal professional practice."

"Thank you." *Not normal! You can say that again.*

There was another knock at the door. An equally finely dressed gentleman, younger, dark-haired and handsome, entered the room.

"Ah. Alex, may I introduce you to my partner, Peter Camden."

She stood up to shake hands.

"Pleased to meet you."

"The honor is all mine." The mild pomposity was vaguely amusing and reasonably reassuring, a contrast to Josh's familiarity.

"Thank you, Peter," said Mr. Waterhouse. "We're nearly finished here I think."

"Anything we can do for you, anything at all, just call us," Mr. Camden boomed in a resonant voice.

"Thank you."

Anthony Waterhouse slid a wallet of company cards across the table. "There. Direct lines and full details. Copies should you wish to pass them on. Let us know if you wish to continue with us."

"Thanks."

They stood up and the two men flanked her to the door.

"Miss Marson is down the hall on the right. It's been a pleasure to meet you. We'll look forward to hearing from you."

They failed to close the door behind her.

"Stoical girl."

"Tough cookie. Fingers crossed." She heard their quiet comments as she turned, grinning to herself. *Musician's ears.*

Going along the corridor, she turned into the designated room. The door was open to a generous staff room with comfortable armchairs, more magazines, files and a small kitchen area. Leanne was engrossed in conversation with a dishy young man, smartly dressed like the main partners. She looked up from her discussion and grinned at her.

"Alex, hi! You all done? This is Nathan, one of the junior PR clerks here."

She winked discreetly at her and smiled at Nathan. "Hello."

"Well, lovely to meet you, Nathan. We must be off, lunch at the Ritz next," Leanne bubbled. Alex smiled, glad that their lunch was something to boast about. Nathan passed Leanne his card.

"Call me, as we said. We could continue our chat over lunch one day," he suggested.

"That would be fun, thanks. Bye."

They scampered down the stairs, arm in arm, giggling while they hunted for their coats, then dived out of the door, taking the photographers by surprise by sprinting along the street, losing them around the corner and a couple of rapid back street turns, before stopping, breathless and laughing.

"Hey. That Nathan looked all right...*call me*?" Alex gasped between panting breaths.

"I should say so. Mustn't lose that card." She tapped her bag, still laughing and gasping for breath. "How was the meeting?"

"Fine. Very polite and professional. Made a nice change. Come on. Let's go for lunch. I'm swimming in coffee." In the elegant comfort of the Ritz restaurant, they hunkered down for a meal and a friendly chat, relieved to have the business end of the morning out of the way.

"So do you think you'll stay with them?"

"So far so good. I think so. They seem very efficient and trustworthy."

"That's a good start. You mean, I might get to see young Nathan again?"

They laughed.

"He looked pretty gorgeous..." Alex offered.

"Oh, yes. And interesting. Cambridge degree, etcetera. He was at a neighboring college."

"I think you should call him."

"Yes. I will..."

"This friend, Leanne, that I'm staying with, they're rather... well, *very* famous. That's the difficulty."

She was intrigued. "But he's nice?"

Alex let the gender mistake go, for now. "That's the thing. They've just been great. They made LA, before and after I saw you, which was good too by the way, great fun. They're nothing like the media images. And...quite a bit of a hero the other day, whisked me away before the scavengers descended, when I wasn't even thinking straight…" It was a pleasure to talk about Jo, even in veiled terms.

"Sounds good. Look…" Leanne looked at her intently, "You don't have to tell me—it's fine. I just don't want to see you getting hurt even more, not by anyone, regardless of how famous."

She smiled at her friend. "I know. I was suspicious at first too. I know you're watching my back. Thanks. But there haven't been any demands. It's been all generosity and for now their place is the last place anyone would expect to find me."

"That's fine then. So…what about the cottage?"

"I don't know. I think I'll go down there tomorrow, see if there's anything I need to do. Even the idea of it gives me the creeps." She felt a moment's nausea.

"I bet." She paused. "Why don't we just go this afternoon? I'm free. Less buildup. Take it by surprise before you've had a chance to think. We could leap in my car, after this, it's in the NCP, get it over with, be back before the rush hour. You have your keys?"

"Yes. I do." She stared into her drink for a moment, wondering. "I think I'll be okay with you there too."

"Good. It's a plan. Here comes lunch." She squeezed her hand.

Two plates were delivered and they talked on.

Following a delicious meal, Leanne went to bring her car to the hotel and Alex waited in the lobby, fielding some sidelong glances from passersby.

They drove to Thurslow in a little over an hour, the roads fine once they had reached the A3. All was quiet in the village, with no sign of the police or reporters at that moment. The rain had started and any sensible photographer left waiting for days would have decamped to the excellent local pub by now. Leanne parked in the Waldrens' driveway to look less conspicuous and with sunglasses on again Alex scampered to Pauline's back door to knock. There was no response, so she cut across the gardens and beckoned Leanne over. They stood on the front step. Alex unlocked the door.

Leanne pointed to the stain on near the lowest step, "Is that…?"

"Yes. Don't." She shuddered. Leanne put an arm around her to steer her in as the door opened.

The cottage was eerie and silent. A pile of mail had been stacked neatly, clinically, on the hall table. Alex picked it up and shoved it into her bag. The house was clean, but smelled unfamiliar in some way. She went through to the piano room at the back and gasped. There was a huge array of flowers and bouquets, arranged in her own and unfamiliar vases. She started reading the labels, but then put her hand to her throat, feeling the rising heat, "I don't think I can…"

"Let me." Leanne took over, collecting the cards as she went. "Your dad—*See you Saturday. We'll come over for the concert*; LPO—*Wishing you a speedy recovery*; Vladimir—*Kindest Regards*; Camden-Waterhouse—No message, just their name; Jenny—*This should never have happened*. Odd, that message…but then Jenny had to be stunned with shock.

"Don't."

"Okay. There's more…but I'll just gather up the cards."

"That's enough. Can we go? This is horrible."

"Hang on. Fetch what you need. Just let me check your messages." Leanne went to the phone and switched on the computer on the way. "Quite a few hang ups. Media, probably. Friends…family…Godalming police, would you call in at your earliest convenience? They should have called your mobile."

"Perhaps they did. I haven't checked since breakfast." She rifled through her handbag.

Leanne went to the computer. "Password?"

"I'll do it." She tapped on the keyboard, then left Leanne to it and went upstairs to pack some things.

She came back down after a few minutes, carrying a bag of extra clothes. "Only a few e-mails…Nothing much really. Mostly junk."

"They'll have gone through to my mobile. Let's go now."
It was a matter of urgency. Suddenly she could barely breathe.

"Sure." Leanne shut the computer down and they left the
house. She had not looked at the piano for more than a moment.

"The whole place is creepy," Alex commented quietly then
jogged over to pop a hastily scribbled note through Pauline's
letterbox to thank her and suggest the neighbors might benefit
from the flowers.

"Yes. It is rather. Let's get Godalming over with and then
head back as soon as possible. What about your car?"

"Perhaps I drank too much at lunchtime. I'd rather be with
you."

They drove to the village. Luckily the rain was even more
persistent, so few were around to witness them parking up and
hurrying in.

The interview was brief, but not very pleasant. Leanne
stayed with her and held onto her hand from time to time, as if
comforting a patient, while they had to check and verify details
recovered from Josh's computer. There were various clips from
the hallway and bedroom, some too intimate, some they did not
want to bother her with and a selection of disturbing close-ups
from various TV appearances.

As they left, Alex's voice came out in an unfamiliar undertone,
"You can see why I can't bear the house at the moment."

"Completely. Next stop London. Shall I drop you somewhere
on the way back?"

"Would Hampstead or Highgate be okay? I can walk from
there."

"Sure." Leanne smiled at the mystery. "He'd better be good
to you, this chap, else he'll have me to answer to…I'm going to
book a ticket for Saturday. We'll have a drink together afterward,
maybe?"

Her stomach writhed at the deceit. "Lovely. Come to the
Green Room, backstage afterward. There are a few people
coming, just to warn you."

As the fields and rolling hills passed by, viewed through
the pouring rivulets of rain, Alex had the weird and contrary

sensation of her spirits lifting as she headed back toward London, leaving the cottage and all its associations behind them. It had usually been quite the opposite, that the approach of the brooding city oppressed her. Tangled in with that was the guilty feeling that she should be more open with Leanne, there was a lot still to tell her. It was just too much to do now with everything that had happened. She would repay her kindness when she could.

Acknowledging the feeling objectively, as if viewing herself from a distance, she played through the last movement of the Beethoven in her mind and on her thighs in an attempt to distract herself. She would have to knuckle down and practice hard tomorrow and Friday.

CHAPTER SIXTEEN

Safe Home

She arrived at Jo's bedraggled, but happier, her arms aching from carrying the bags from Highgate, and yet she felt washed and cleansed by the rain, distanced from the memory of Thurslow. She rang the buzzer at the gates so as not to surprise her and to avoid the hassle of rummaging for keys.

"Hello?" Jo's voice came cautiously through the intercom.

"Me. Alex," She responded, gasping, drowning in the still persistent rain.

"Oh, good." Sounding relieved, she buzzed her in and Alex trudged up the puddled, graveled path, dripping wet, listening to the clink of the gates behind.

"What do you look like?" Jo laughed at her, waiting at the door. "Thought you were going to call me!"

"Well, yes…I was. But the day turned out a little differently."

"Come on in. Want a towel?"

She passed her one on the way back from the kitchen and took her soaking coat to hang it up. "There."

"Thanks."

"Come and have a drink and you can tell me how it went." She disappeared back into the kitchen.

Alex towel-dried her hair and peeled off the damp layers, leaving them there and trudged upstairs for dry clothes, taking her bags with her. She changed into some warm slacks and socks and a pale sweater. After brushing out her damp hair, she grabbed the new score from her bag and scampered back down the stairs.

Jo was in the living room, stoking up the fireplace with fresh logs. A glass of something sparkled encouragingly from the coffee table. She plumped herself down on the sofa gratefully and Jo came to join her.

"There. Warmer?"

"Much. Thanks."

"So tell me about your day." She handed her a glass.

Alex related the trip to Camden-Waterhouse with Leanne, how Leanne had expertly fielded them past the photographers, the agent's professionalism, Leanne's brush with Nathan and the spontaneous escape to the Ritz, foiling the photographers.

"Sounds like a good friend. Perhaps you should stick with this agent."

"Yes. I might. They seemed a decent sort. Then we went down to the cottage, rather impetuously."

"Oh?"

"It was grim. There's still a bloodstain on the steps, despite apparent cleaning, loads of post and swathes of flowers. Horrible. And we made a visit to the police station, where I had to check some computer images that he's been keeping."

"Oh."

"Exactly. Horrendous, too close for comfort. To think he's... he'd been spying...I couldn't get away fast enough and leaving it all behind as we drove back to town was just a blessing." She paused for breath, wrapped her hands gratefully around her drink, peering into its depths for answers. "Strange really, it was usually the other way around."

Jo put her arm around her and she snuggled in. They leaned back into the sofa, comfortably. The silence, broken only by the crackling fire, helped to distance the memory.

After a while, Alex asked, "And you? How was your day?"

"Oh…fine," she said, too flippantly. "Just preparation to do. Couple of calls to make. The hotel details came in for next week, country house hotel, near Atlantic Bay, looks charming. And *Johnson* for Friday, some post-Oscars thing."

"No!"

"What?"

"Me too. I forgot to tell you."

"Crikey."

"I'll give myself away."

"No you won't." She thought for a moment.

"Here's what we'll do. Look…" Jo stood up and went to the door. "You be me…"

She mimed a drum roll. "And now…Alex Palmer!" She announced it like a dart game's score, "One hundred and eighty!"

She wiggled, imitating Alex walking down the stairs and smiling at the imaginary audience, sat on the arm of the armchair and pretended to play the piano, then curtsied and strolled over to where she was already giggling. "Stand up… now be yourself," Jo hissed in a comical stage-whisper.

She stood. "Marvelous, Alex." Jo imitated Johnson rather well. She shook Alex's hand politely, smiled briefly and sat down, crossing her legs, after tugging up her trouser legs with male precision.

"Very good." Alex laughed.

"Now you…I'll be me."

Alex copied her actions and when she came to shake her hand, Jo was cool, polite and convincing, kissing her on each cheek briskly, a very different, professional version of Jo.

"Not a smidge." Alex flopped down beside her, giggling and kissed her.

Jo kissed her back. "Do you have to play?"

"Probably."

"Oh good. We must get our story straight, just in case." She imitated Johnson again. "So did you two have a chance to meet, you know, two Brits in LA, at the same venue?"

"No, I'm afraid not. It was really busy and my schedule was crammed," Alex replied.

"Now steady you see, you make it sound like you wanted to…*I fear the lady doth protest too much.*"

"Give away, yes. Try again."

"So did you two meet up over there?"

"The party was very busy. I just played, part of the entertainment, you know."

"That's the idea. We'll work on it. Look, we can still drive down together, just go in and come out our separate ways."

"Fine."

"What about that pile of mail from the cottage?"

"Good idea." She hurried off to fetch it from upstairs, while Jo went out to the kitchen. When Alex came back Jo was waiting with a silver letter knife and a brochure.

"That's where we're booked into next week. Looks good doesn't it?"

"Lovely. I'll take a look in a moment. I'll just tackle this first…" She started on the pile. There were letters from friends, cards, an official letter from the lawyer confirming her appointment.

"Reassuring, I suppose."

"Yep."

"This is depressing. Like the cottage at the moment. I loved that place. It shouldn't have been turned into a morgue."

"No."

There was another long silence.

"Alex?"

"Mmm?"

"I was thinking…on and off today…and for a few days really. Would you…you could just…if you wanted to…stay here? For as long as you like. Experimentally at first. But if it works… longer term. We could still keep things quiet. See how it goes?"

Alex sat motionless, listening to the words settle in the room, surprised by her sudden offer and the careful forethought, flattered, touched by the vulnerability in her words. Momentarily apprehensive of the commitment. Also weighing how consistent this woman could be. It had been such a short space of time, a brief window through which to judge her. The flames crackled in the fireplace, starting to engulf another crispy log and the light outside seemed to dim a degree more toward nightfall.

"Look. I don't want to rush you. This might sound unlikely…unbelievable perhaps…but it's not actually an offer I've made before. To anyone. I'm far too proud of my privacy, usually happier on my own. But I like having you here. And frankly we're way beyond the possibility of any conventional dating opportunities given our situation. We'll have to make up for that later, somehow or other."

Jo spoke with obvious sincerity and her line about privacy chimed sympathetically with Alex's own thoughts on that subject. She searched her heart for a response and felt only relief to be away from Thurslow and pure pleasure at the thought of being safe, with her.

"I'd be delighted." She replied softly. "How can I refuse such an eloquent offer?"

Jo smiled, warming to her subject, encouraged. "I was thinking about it and I couldn't see how you could go back. You could empty the cottage of what you need. Bring your car."

"My piano?"

"Move it here, into the studio, plenty of space, room for a piano duo, if you like. If you wanted to, you could let the cottage out. See how it goes. How it feels. You don't have to go back there. I think there's enough space to fit you in."

"Steady on. It's quite a step, for you too."

"Yes. But as I said, I'm in deep already."

Alex hugged her. "Thank you. You are quite simply a genius."

"I thought that was you. Do you know what you're letting yourself in for?"

She smiled at her, embarrassed suddenly and decided to lighten the subject. "Do you?" She took out the modern score.

"Look at this. It's completely off the wall. I'm going to have to meet up with the composer to even begin to understand his intentions here."

"For?"

"The Proms. Oh yes. And on a brighter note, the Royal Academy, my old college, wants to grant me some award or other."

"That sounds impressive."

"Pretty cool as these things go. What shall we do for dinner?"

"There's an excellent Thai in Highgate that delivers. You'll need to acquaint yourself with these important local matters!"

* * *

The next few days passed in a blur of activity: Alex settled into the house, enjoying the elevated new status, still slightly in disbelief at the rapid changing of events, still shaken up, re-mixed like a cocktail waiting to settle. There were arrangements to make to transfer what she needed, as well as a huge quantity of practice to do and she worked through the first morning, breaking briefly for lunch and continuing into the afternoon. Jo had her own preparations for the coming week and on Thursday a new script arrived that needed to be read through for an unrelated project. They spent some of the afternoon companionably together, one day jogging across the Heath, choosing quiet paths, another swimming and working out in the gym. Or discovering surprises like Jo's penchant for collecting old 78 rpm recordings and theatrical memorabilia. Jo had to go in to town for various appointments, costume, agent, some weaponry coaching or other, sometimes the phones interrupted incessantly. Alex arranged via Camden-Waterhouse a session with Arnold Braithwaite, the composer of the new piece, for the following week at his house, and an appointment came in for a photo-shoot at the Savoy for *Salute* magazine, to do with the Oscars involvement. They spent part of Thursday redirecting Alex's contact details to Jo's house and computer.

"Okay," Jo said. "So we'll give it a go. You'll be all right next week when I'm away?"

"I must admit I'm a bit nervous about Monday. It's his funeral. Perhaps I'll arrange to meet up with friends."

"Well, I'm here until the afternoon, not actually on until early Tuesday. I'll take you to lunch before I go. And afterward, when I get back, perhaps we could get away somewhere…"

Evenings were spent in unadulterated bliss.

* * *

Thursday night she decided to risk taking Jo out to one of her favorite time-off haunts, a back-street comedy club in Islington, attempting to lighten her general mood. She did not want her to presume the dour patches were habitual. And if they were to attempt to make up for a lack of dating, wouldn't they have to actually go out somewhere together?

"It's where I go when I need cheering up. Occasionally if a performance has gone wrong."

"I can't imagine that happens very often."

"No, not often noticeably to the audience, but irritatingly to me and the other musicians. The club has some great names doing stand-up. It's launched a few national and international careers and they come back out of loyalty to the place."

Jo was understandably cautious. It was potentially an impetuous choice. She was more aware of the amount of furor that had been batted around in the media about the events of the previous days and what could have caused it all. At that point, apparently, Alex had been protected from much of it, little realizing her face had been all over the free newspapers handed out all over London, all the national papers and magazines. She was instantly recognizable and still the topic of ongoing speculation about the confrontation. It was hardly appropriate to be seen out, laughing, after the events of the week. And yet, why should they have to be cooped up as if Alex was to be imprisoned by an event not of her making? Jo had chosen to humor her.

They sidled in at the back of the club, into a dimly lit alcove, Jo partially hidden by a dusty, red velvet curtain and an uncharacteristic hoodie, having managed an unobtrusive parking spot and a discreet entrance, while Alex paid their way in. "...so there I was," the comedian continued in a rowdy voice, the audience already tittering, "standing in the middle of Victoria Underground concourse, vomiting profusely, with thousands of rush-hour commuters hurrying past. Actually two did stop to offer me packets of tissues. There is hope in the human race yet. Mind you, have you seen how hopeless a packet of tissues is when up against a bucketful of vomit? Unfortunately though, there was no bucket..." The audience was groaning. He had them eating out of his hand already.

"There's a corner of Victoria Underground that I'll always feel a strong bond with. Closest I'll ever get to a decent relationship of any kind...! I'll send it a bouquet once a year on our anniversary. Or a suitable gift...first year a paper hanky, second year a clean cotton T-shirt and so on...building up to the bucket."

"Okay. Here goes." He sat down at the piano on the stage, beginning a robust but rocky version of "I've Got Rhythm."

"Somewhere...I have rhythm, but I can't seem to find it today..." He checked his pockets. "Let me see...ah..." withdrawing a metronome and setting it, ticking, on the side of the piano. "That's better."

He started again. "No...still no rhythm." There was laughter.

"Don't you just love Morecambe and Wise and their Andre Preview, I mean Previn, sketch. An all-time favorite." He demonstrated the badly played Grieg. There was a ripple of applause in agreement. "Best music sketch of all time. Previn's a decent jazz pianist too, y'know...unlike me. *The piano has been drinking...*" He sang, quoting Tom Waits.

He stopped abruptly and shaded his eyes with his hand. "Talking of which...do I see our old pal Alex Palmer out there... up the back?"

Jo took a rapid dive behind the curtain as the spotlight swept their way.

"Now I know for sure, you've got rhythm, babe. You've showed us before. Want to come up?"

She shook her head decisively and waved her hands to indicate a firm "No Way!"

"Not tonight love? No. Well, I hear you've been in the wars this week. In recovery. Sure, sure, best of luck. Come and join us on stage again when you're ready and we'll try to bring a smile...Now where was I...?"

"Time to go?" Jo stage-whispered from somewhere near the floor.

"Maybe. Sorry. Well it was worth a try."

A couple of audience members had turned to look and one was standing up with obvious intentions to dig in their pocket for...what? A camera perhaps.

"I can see the charm, but perhaps not the best timing..." Jo groaned in discomfort, choking on the dusty carpet. "But it has brought a smile to your face!"

Alex was laughing at the sight of her crawling along the floor on all fours.

They escaped through the back, Jo on her hands and knees at first, keeping behind the curtains, torn between a grimace and a grin.

That was the end of that escapade and a premature culmination to their first attempted date. Not one to hit the headlines in any sense, fortunately.

Friday, late afternoon, they left together for the appointment with Johnson.

CHAPTER SEVENTEEN

Johnson

"As I've already mentioned, it's a night for homegrown stars and my next guest is Alex Palmer, who recently graced the Vanity Fair post-Oscars party with her delightful playing and is going to offer us up her own rendition of Gershwin's 'I've Got Rhythm'…"

She liked the private joke. It took the edge off her nervously pounding heart.

She walked down the steps, grinning at the personal reminder of their previous night's failed date, hoping she was cutting the right dash in the sequinned Oscar's outfit, while huge applause broke out, subsiding into shuffling from the band as she settled at the piano, the lights sinking a little and a spotlight settling on her. The performance was subdued at the beginning, but accelerated into high-speed in the middle and she sailed through it, enjoying the rush within the intricacies of the piece, finishing with a flamboyant flourish to more applause and shuffles.

"Fabulous! Fabulous!" Mike greeted her warmly, with his usual affable, mature style, as she retreated to their podium. The others stood politely. Harry Mitchell, the resourceful comedian, shook her hand and gave her an air kiss. Jo greeted her formally, kissing her politely on each cheek. She acted her part well, sitting down after this only moderate attention to Alex, adjusting her skirt. "And that's not all you do, is it Alex?"

"No, Michael. I'm at the Royal Festival Hall this weekend and available for any other engagement: weddings, birthdays, Oscar-parties, Proms, almost any occasion really, as long as it's paid," she joked, as Jo had primed her to do.

"Ha-ha. What a multitalented girl. So how was LA, in the heart of the Hollywood machine?"

"Mmm. Hollywood. As anybody who has been there will know, it's a city of contrasts and Hollywood is the district of the beautiful people. But I was largely on the periphery. The Oscars party was a treat, but I was still an employee, the entertainer for the night. I had little to do with the stars of the show."

"I'm not so sure," piped up Jo. "One might say she was among the stars of the show."

Alex did her best to cover her surprise.

"Of course. You heard her playing there?" Michael inquired.

"Oh, yes. It set the atmosphere really." Jo's eyes twinkled.

"Thanks." She smiled politely. She could sense Jo was teasing her a little, enjoying the intrigue.

"You met there?" Michael probed.

"I wasn't able to see anyone much," Alex replied. "It was pretty packed. I had my head down, concentrating! But it was a truly spectacular evening." She noticed Jo's nod of appreciation at either her acting, which was unlikely, or in her actual agreement.

"Of course. So, Alex," Michael changed the subject, "may I just offer my sympathy for the recent events earlier this week?"

"Oh...thanks." Her television bonhomie dissolved suddenly at the mention of the forbidden, her eyes instantly betraying their worry. Suddenly very aware of the bruises that the makeup artists had tried to hide. This was dangerous territory. She spoke quietly, "It's been a…terrible shock. I think for more people than just me."

"But you're out and about?" He spoke with sensitivity, gently, encouragingly.

"Well, trying. As they say, the show must go on." Quietly.

"And you're still carrying the scars."

Her hand went involuntarily to hide her lip. "Yes. You might say."

Mike sat tall with his arms tightly crossed against his chest. The others bristled at the subject, Harry tensing his shoulders up and crossing his legs, Jo's hand going to her own cheek abruptly.

"You can see from the body language, we don't approve. It's not right for a woman to be attacked."

"Thank you for the words of support," she said even more quietly, dangerously close to releasing unwanted emotions.

"I mean it. And so…what happens from here?"

She sat up, taking a deep breath and forcing the courage to look briefly toward the camera and out to the audience, "It's been a dreadful week, as you know, and my heart goes out to anyone else who has been disrupted or affected by this too or anything similar." She found her voice again and returned her full attention to the host. "New start. I suppose the show will go on, as I said."

"And any gentlemen friends to ease the pain?"

"Oh, Michael, are you offering?" She laughed, recovering her way forward, remembering Jo's advice as she lay in her arms last night: *Don't worry, it'll be fine, I'll help you if I need to, if in doubt: joke.* "I've nothing planned for after the show?"

He chuckled. "Okay. I deserved that. I think Mrs. J would have a thing or two to say to me about that. But seriously?"

"There's little time for all that. But I do have the opportunity to meet some great people along the way."

"Well Alex, we wish you well with all of it—the Proms, the Grammys and so on and we are all delighted that the Brits are traversing the Atlantic." There was a ripple of applause in agreement. "Jo, good luck with the new film and Harry, the American tour. It's been great to have you all here tonight and Alex, perhaps you'll be kind enough to join the band and play us out tonight."

"I'd be delighted." They all shook hands warmly. She received their polite kisses gracefully and then went over to the piano. This time the bandleader led the way in a rehearsed version of the show's theme tune with additional material from her. It had all been mercifully brief. She was quite relieved to be just the lollipop at the end of the show.

* * *

There was a small after-show party in the Green Room. Michael, selected members of the audience and the show's production and technical team met and chatted with the guests.

A slim, pale lady in a business suit approached Alex across the room.

"Hi. That was great. It's good to see you. I'm Olivia, representing Victim Support and Women's Aid. I wondered, I hope you don't mind me asking, I know it must be a difficult time, two things: whether we can be of any help, also whether you might be interested in helping us with a charitable appearance, given what you've been through and survived and what you said earlier. I mean once you feel ready. It was a brave response. It would help women who are in a similar or even less fortunate position?"

She nodded. "I'd be glad to help." She was feeling uncomfortable to be reminded again and scrutinized in such a way, but produced a card for Camden-Waterhouse automatically from her bag and handed it over. Old habits die hard. She tried not to flinch at the thought and the fleeting memory that the name on the card had only recently been changed. Fortunately, Michael had spotted the conversation, came over to intervene and politely steer her away, with a smile of acknowledgment to Olivia.

He had loosened his tie, ditched his characteristically crisp suit jacket and unbuttoned his collar. "Sorry." He apologized, running his fingers nervously through his silvering hair, "Certain members of the audience are asked in. Are you all right?"

"Fine thanks. Good of you to rescue me. It seems necessary just to get on with things as usual. I wasn't sure about making a public appearance so soon. But I have this concert to face tomorrow anyway. It's a trial run."

"Perhaps it's the best way, to press on, not to change too much. I tried to keep it brief tonight. The playing is fabulous Alex! Really lifts the spirits."

"Thank you."

"I suppose it's like a friend that you always have with you. Something of a comfort at all times. Will you come back and see us again soon, when things have settled down? We'll co-ordinate with an event for you, additional publicity."

"Of course. Thank you, Michael."

* * *

"That went well, don't you think?" Jo asked, as they met up quickly at the car having taken separate back routes. "Well played." She drove out of the car park.

"Well spoken. I heard you in the Green Room. Actually well-acted too. You teased me."

"It's my job."

"To tease?"

"No, to act, silly. I wasn't teasing much, just distracting the full attention away from you."

"Oh…yes. You did. Your interview went well."

"It's part of the job, as I said."

"Mine too, the playing not the acting obviously. Weird, huh?"

"Funny too. He pitched it about right for, you know…Josh. Kept it short. You held it together well."

"Mmm. Just."

"Alex?"

"Mmm?"

"What do you want to do about all that? The funeral?"

"Well...The funeral, I've left it to Camden's, to do what they deem appropriate. It eased my conscience and seemed right, simultaneously."

"You shouldn't have a conscience."

"But I do. I keep thinking if it wasn't for me he might not have gone over the edge with it all."

"Alex, he probably would have gone over the edge anyway, with somebody else. It's a personality type. Obsessive. Over-controlling. The man seemed pretty driven when I met him, albeit briefly."

"I could just see his angry, vicious face again when I went back to the cottage."

"Yes. I wondered about that."

"Thank you." She placed her hand lightly on the back of Jo's, resting it gently there as she changed gear. "For wondering. For thinking. I'm not used to people being that thoughtful." She paused. "By the way, how's Petra the professor coming along?"

"She'll do, I think."

"Good, it's just that you'll need to be really good to convince Leanne, my folks, my neighbors...when we all meet in the Green Room afterward."

"Oh hell, really? Nobody put that in the contract. I'll have to charge extra."

"Payment in kind."

"I'll hold you to that." She grinned cheekily at Alex. "But seriously, I'm not sure the makeup will stand up to close scrutiny."

"You could meet me at the car afterward. I might have to stay for a drink with everybody. See how you feel."

CHAPTER EIGHTEEN

Royal Festival Hall

The following day, Alex had to say goodbye to Jo and part company at midday. It was a wrench to have to return to a more public persona, on her own this time.

Jo attempted to reassure her. "But you won't be on your own…exactly."

"Yes, I know."

She borrowed the spare car and drove down to the Royal Festival Hall, parking up in the artists' car park. The rehearsal was unproblematic; both orchestra and conductor were in excellent form. She covered a memory slip quickly and attempted to ignore the looks of concern, trying to keep any emotional surges at bay and to accept the kind comments of sympathy with grace and gratitude, although dying a little inside again each time.

Just before six, she met up with Pauline and Bill Waldren at the front of the house restaurant, which was starting to fill up with a noisy background chatter. Although it brought a mixture of feelings to the surface, realizing she really had been safely hidden away and protected since she had last seen them, she rummaged around dragging out enough energy to thank them profusely for their help and for Pauline's continued care of the house. She apologized for her absence, but they cut her explanation short, understanding completely, the place was giving them an uneasy feeling too. She felt some of the eyes of the restaurant customers resting upon her. Quietly she suggested, tentatively at first, that it might be necessary to let the place out as it now had so many associations. Perhaps a family, young children running around would obliterate the past. They could understand that line of reasoning, had even been starting to wonder. She hoped Pauline might continue to keep half an eye on the place for the time being. They ate well and comparatively jovially, once the subject of the cottage was left behind and when she departed having settled the bill and directed them up the stairs, she felt some relief to have the plans for the house out in the open. She disappeared back through the partition door to prepare for the performance, stepping back into the familiar backstage wonderland of instrument cases, warm-ups and stage fright.

There, in the relative peace and quiet of her dressing room, she slipped into Jo's favorite gown, the green one-shouldered dress, superstitiously feeling it would bring her luck, and went to the piano to run over a few passages and to try to ease her more-than-usual nervousness. She would not cry in the second movement, she ordered herself. She would think of Jo as Petra Rahmanoff, the Waldrens, Leanne, her...family of sorts, out there, willing her on. This was a hurdle that *must* be overcome.

The distorted sounds of the concert beginning chimed through the intercom, the rustle of applause and the *Egmont Overture*, rapid and immaculate after its imposing opening, and she paced the room to pass the time and focus her thoughts. When the final bars approached her heart typically doubled its rate and there was a knock at the door to indicate her stage-call. The stage manager escorted her quietly to the wings and she waited, flexing her fingers, while the audience exploded into applause. *Follow that.*

The conductor bounded off the stage into the wings and stood at her side as the applause died down. "Ready?" He grinned.

She nodded, waiting as the leader offered a piano A to the oboe and the soulful pitch wailed out to tune the orchestra to her instrument. Her heart hammered in her chest and throat. She couldn't see the audience from there, obliterating them from her expectations almost as well as she usually managed. The leader took his place again and an anticipatory hush fell on the auditorium.

"Let's go. After you."

She led the way up the side steps and into the vast hall with the conductor following at a respectful distance, allowing her the recognition. Autopilot. Her professionalism clicked into place and she grinned widely, first at the orchestra and then out toward the audience, as they broke into welcoming applause. She shook hands with the leader and bowed deeply. The clapping still echoing all around her and her heart still hammering. As she lifted her head, she cast a glance at Jo disguised as Petra in the front row, close to the leader's side and directed her smile at her; Jo sat with her fingertips touching in front of her face, elbows on the armrests, and though looking solemn and intent, she winked at her.

Alex seated herself and looked around at the orchestra. There were some encouraging smiles. The clapping died and the conductor gave her a nod to assess her readiness. She nodded very faintly in return and he turned to begin the orchestral exposition.

She looked up at the boxes as the orchestra began, a little ominously, in C minor. The Waldrens could just be seen on the second row up. Pauline gave her an inappropriate, but endearing, little wave. She smiled and waited, falling into the swirling music around her and starting to forget the broader context. The front desks' playing was astonishingly dynamic and clear, right behind and to the side of her and her heart still pounded, but no longer dominated. She could do this.

At the start of the beautiful slow movement, she concentrated on Jo, somewhere beneath her elbow, not allowing any other thought to encroach. She tried to fill herself with her ridiculous, quirky appearance and had a reminding twinge of desire for the woman beneath the costume. She adored her. It was very clear to her. The sudden admission to herself filling her with warmth which she tried to pour into the opening passage, aware that she must draw her wandering concentration back again. She had taken her away, removed her from danger. She couldn't tell her yet, verbally, but this way she could indulge herself fully and try to convey it across to her by thin air. But finally, at the decrescendo of the final flourishes at the end of the movement, she couldn't push other thoughts out of her head any longer and as the strings sighed tenderly around her, the nearest members of the audience in the stalls could probably see the tears which were starting to fall, splashing onto her lap, darkening the satin fabric. She heard Jo's cough from the front row nearby, rousing her to reality. As the movement closed, she had to take a layer of her skirt to wipe the keyboard silently and her hands, before daring to look up and risk the fast finale.

The conductor turned to her and mouthed, "You okay?"

She nodded briefly and lifted her elbow to glimpse Jo who was looking concerned and intently at her. She nodded a tiny nod, imperceptible to anyone else and the matching movement gave Alex momentary confidence to continue.

She took a deep breath before launching into the Rondo theme after the brief orchestral introduction and its speed and vitality drove away the lingering dark thoughts from her mind. At that tempo, she could only live in the moment and do her best to translate the thankfully distracting Beethoven.

As the piece concluded, the audience burst into a rapturous reception and some of those in the stalls started to stand. The orchestra was cheering, the string players tapping their bows on the stands, the wind players shuffling their feet; she felt a little dizzy and distant, but went through the motions of bowing and acknowledging the orchestra and walked off with the conductor after he had kissed her hand gallantly.

In the wings he spoke gently to her, "They won't let you go that easily. Not tonight. That was fabulous. But are you able to go on?"

"I'm okay. I'll give them another if they want it." And she walked back on alone and trance-like, causing an apparently satisfied sigh and sudden hush in the packed auditorium.

She sat silently at the piano, considering what to play for a moment, then smiled and launched gently into a short, but softly flourishing version of "I've Got You Under My Skin"... It suited the moment and her feelings in the second movement of the Beethoven. *For Jo at the Oscars Party and in the front row, for the future.* It was not until the end that the ambiguity of Josh's furious face flashed through her again and she sat for a moment in silence, staring at her hands in her lap, the audience still drinking in the atmosphere. Her shoulders started to shake uncontrollably. The audience broke into ripples of applause, gathering apace until the house was echoing with enthusiasm and she stood to bow, wobbling, suddenly, feeling the stage fall vertiginously away. Immediately, the leader passed his violin to his number two and was there, gallantly supporting her and then he escorted her off. The applause died down as the audience headed for the bars and the orchestra packed up for the interval.

The conductor received Alex in the wings. "You were brilliant. Exceptionally rising up above all that you've been through. It's no wonder..." He loaned her his enormous handkerchief, and she dabbed at her eyes. "Congratulations, my dear. We weren't even sure you'd do the date this week." He kissed her on both cheeks. "Go and have a well-earned rest."

"Thanks. You were marvelous." She smiled weakly at him and trudged back wearily to her room.

There, she flopped, exhausted, into an armchair and guzzled a couple of glasses of water. When sufficiently revived, she stepped hurriedly out of her evening gown and hastily slipped on jeans and a T-shirt. *No reception tonight, thankfully.* Quickly brushing out her hair, she had just started trying to pour out half a dozen glasses of champagne with a shaking hand, when there came a knock at the door. She opened it to find her father and Leanne.

She hugged them gratefully.

"On your own, Dad?" she asked, raising her eyebrows significantly at him.

He fielded the question ambiguously. "It's a long story." Obviously it was not the right time for an explanation. "But you…you were brilliant!" he said, stepping back. "Are you okay? You look drained!"

"Yes. It's been quite a week."

"Perhaps it was too soon…"

"Well, I'm exhausted now. Anyway you made it! Have some champagne. Dad, could you pour? I'm celebrating getting through it at all."

Leanne hugged her and mouthed concerned words privately at her, while Dad continued, "I only arrived this afternoon. Where have you been? The phone's redirecting your number."

Leanne piped up. "It's fine, Mr. Palmer. She's been at our friend's in Highgate. She's had the phone redirected for now. The cottage is just…rather oppressive at the moment."

"Well, come to us, love. Now that we're back."

"No need, Dad. They're taking good care of me. I'm comfortable. I need to be close to London. I'll explain later." She smiled gratefully toward Leanne. Her father did not push the point.

There was another knock at the door. "Hang on."

Pauline and Bill entered the room and more glasses were distributed. The orchestral manager put her head around the door.

"Everything satisfactory?"

"Fine thanks," she replied.

"Great reception out there tonight. I hope we'll be seeing you again soon."

"Me too. Thanks for your help. Goodnight!"

The door went again. Petra put her head round the door, she grinned at Alex and her heart flipped. She had even done something to her teeth to discolor them.

"Aleex! Hallo!"

"Oh, hello!" she replied. "Come in. I'll introduce you."

"Oh, no, no, no, no! I just vanted to zay, maztervul! I vill zee you in zee bar for a dizcussion of zee technical detail?"

"Oh, yes. Sure. Give me twenty minutes."

"Okay. Good to zee you all!" And she was gone again.

It was impossible not to laugh at her. "Sorry about that. That's an old teacher. Well, I met her at a 'mazterclass' some years ago and bumped into her again earlier. She's a bit of an oddball. I might just have to go and see her after this. She helped me to crack a few problems. I owe her."

The others murmured their assent.

Her father came over to her. "You were brilliant, love. I'm with you all the way when you play. Are you really fine? I'm so sorry we were away at the wrong time for you. It must have been terrible. I met the man. He seemed reasonable then."

"Reasonable, but certifiable. The police have it all wrapped up. But his funeral is Monday. That's a horrible thought."

"I know you have this friend…but you can count on me, if you need to."

"I know, thanks."

Leanne raised a toast. "Here's to Alex for getting through it all and the Waldrens for rescuing her! Cheers!"

They clinked glasses. She went to Pauline and kissed her. "Thanks, again," she whispered.

Leanne edged over to her. "If you need me Monday, let me know."

"Okay," she whispered and gave her dependable friend a squeeze. The room settled down into an agreeable hubbub of chatter.

The Waldrens were the first to leave. "Well done, pet. And thanks again for the evening. You don't mind if we take our seats again for the rest of the program? We'll see you soon?"

"Of course. Go ahead. Thanks everyone for coming and making it a bit easier."

Followed swiftly by her father. "Me too? Do you mind?"

"Not at all."

"Come to see me soon. In the meantime," he looked pointedly at Leanne, "make sure your friends take good care of you." They all kissed and said their farewells.

She was left with just Leanne and hugged her again. "Thanks for coming. I don't suppose I would have made it through without knowing you were all there."

"You did though."

"Just."

"You can take confidence from that. How about the journey home?"

"Fine. I have a car. You? You staying?"

"Yeah. I brought the car too. I might stay for the next bit."

"Maybe see you next week then?"

"Good." Leanne smiled and they kissed goodbye.

She packed up her things and went to look for Jo. She was hunched in the now empty artists' bar.

Alex plumped down next to her. "How're you?" she whispered.

"Fine. You were great. You hung in there. Professional simply doesn't sufficiently cover it."

"Thanks. I did. Just. I was thinking about you all the way through the slow movement."

"That's the biggest compliment possible. I've been hanging around, trying to avoid getting into any discussions with anyone, trying to give off 'I'm a leetle bit strange, don't come near mee' vibes." She grinned. "Come on, let's go." The barman returned from loading the dishwasher and waved to them as they left.

"I came on the tube."

"You did?" Alex gaped at her.

"Stop it! Actually great fun. Method acting, y' know."

"Not exactly. But I get the picture. Must have been different." Her svelte figure was smothered in a shapeless, conservative dress.

"Fun to be unrecognizable. Well, I hope! You drive first while I sort this out."

They reached the car, she packed away her bags and they got in quickly, with Alex in the driver's seat.

Jo removed the wig and started to peel off her dress. "Ouch! Not enough space, I think." She discarded the badly fitting items, revealing tantalizing glimpses of her smooth legs, shrugging into a shift dress drawn from a capacious handbag and starting to look a little more like herself. She rubbed moist tissues over her face, smearing off the thick makeup and tidied up her teeth.

Alex laughed at her appearance. "Ah yes. Now I recognize you. It's you! I thought it was Petra this old teacher I met at a master class…"

"Oh. Very good. That's a relief to get that lot off. You actually okay really?"

"Just about. You were brilliant by the way. You gave me faith once or twice."

"Want me to drive now?"

"Please." She pulled up at a parking space in Tottenham Court Road and they swapped seats with Jo shuffling across discreetly inside the car, while Alex darted out and around. She fell gratefully, exhausted, into the passenger seat. It was done. She had made it through and proved that she could carry on. Perhaps the next one would be easier.

CHAPTER NINETEEN

Mastery

Sunday was wonderfully free and they did very little. It was unseasonably warm. They lazed in the sun and swam. After some early calls of congratulation, the phones remained unusually silent. At one stage Jo pushed a sun bed into the shade of the willow tree and generously offered to massage away the strains of the previous night for the best part of an hour.

"Under the tree. No one's safe with Google World, you see?" She chuckled.

"Mmm," Alex murmured. She was weary of all the cameras, the spying, the hiding. The novelty value of the game was waning.

"How do you tolerate it?"

"What?"

"The hiding...doesn't it ever wear thin?"

"Wear thin?"

"You know exactly what I mean. Hiding yourself away. The loss of freedom it involves."

"Of course it does. You know that. But, this is my freedom, Alex. It isn't freedom to be caught in a frenzy in a public place or to have some speculative photo plastered on the internet. I have people tracking me. There are websites out there, chatrooms, where they work out how to find me next. I know it sounds unbelievably narcissistic, but it's real enough. If I let it slip accidentally that I like...say opera...or in your case, comedy clubs," she raised an eyebrow at her, "then there's less chance of being *able* to go out to relax at one of those venues without someone somewhere looking out for you. It's not arrogant, it's an unbelievably wearying fact. It's not that I mind one autograph hunter catching me at an opportune moment, or a screaming hoard at a premiere launch, either of those go with the profession. But to have a trip out, a stroll, a holiday, an airport departure accumulating photographers or fans, when you're having what should be a private moment, frankly just in the mood to be alone, it's a whole different ball game. And I should be allowed to be private sometimes, not to always be aware of the fall of my facial muscles. That is allowed?"

"Yeah, it should be a natural right, of course." Alex was sorry for her growing irritation. Her mood had touched a raw nerve. This was heading into an argument.

"Humanity might live in cages of its own making, but you have to find a way to have your liberty." She softened her tone. "This is my freedom. Walking on the beach with you, being at home with you, without being spied on, without speculation. Being allowed a chance to choose and decide at *my* pace. I get that by being spontaneous, unpredictable, being Petra maybe, so there isn't a date and time chalked up somewhere. Or by shutting the doors tightly on the rest of the world for a while. That's how we've had a chance to...get to know each other. You realize that. You haven't been a witness to the frenzy...as yet. It's crowd hysteria. They fall in love with the character I've played, not me. When we're out in public, you'd have to be ready to share me, *I'd* have to share the way I want to look at you. I'm not sure *I'm* ready for that." There was an unexpected hint of sadness or loneliness in her voice, as if she was afraid that she would lose what they had once the reality set in. "I'm trying to keep it from you or you from it."

"I don't want to compete with a frenzy…yet." A memory of a dream fleetingly disturbed her. "I've had more attention than I like generally this past week."

She spoke quietly. "No. I didn't think so. I can't stay in one place for long before I'm being pestered. Or perhaps it's attention deficit. Now I start to wonder which came first. Keep moving on…keep working on different projects. I can't tell anymore."

Alex felt uncomfortable. She read her immediately.

"Work, Alex."

"Yes, I suppose I'm the same. It would be like being stuck on the same piece of music for too long."

"Or the same play, an infinite run where the words never changed." She paused in her outburst. "But not you. I don't mean that's how I feel about you. You must be starting to realize by now where I am with you."

She blushed. "What about…you know…coming out… publicly? Doesn't it bother you to bottle it up?"

She paused. "Well…of course. But I've become so used to it. It's become part of my most private self, that other people shouldn't know me completely. Part of the public act I suppose. It bothers me occasionally. Like, it would have been nice to be sitting with you at Johnson's show openly kissing you, holding your hand for support and I'm thinking to myself that *should* be fine. Then another part of me kicks in and says 'but think of the upset it would cause' and in our crazy world you just don't know where that will lead once people's prejudices kick in. Is our professional world up to coping? We both have work commitments to consider. It's not that you don't have your own fame either. Would it affect your bookings? I mean, the classical music world, it's pretty conservative…"

"From the outside maybe. It's pretty liberal, rampant even, within."

"I thought your world was a little more sedate, elegant, cultured even than ours. They don't stand at the stage door jostling in quite the same way."

"They would have a hundred years ago. Actually they do a little in some countries."

"Ah! That's exactly it. The film industry, it's one of the icons of our times. I want to spare you some of the hype. For now, at least."

"It seems like someone else has done a good job of exposing me this week."

"Exactly. That's why you're here now, isn't it?"

Alex stretched luxuriously, feeling the tension disappearing. "I wouldn't mind, if everybody knew how I felt about you."

"You think?"

"Well, yes. At least that's what I think right here, right now."

"Mmph."

"Don't you ever wonder where you belong? Is home here… or LA? Or is it like me, home is wherever the company is right, the work satisfying and profitable? Oh, I'm not sure where my home is since Josh's craziness."

"Your home can be here right now. If you want."

Alex rolled over and pulled Jo down toward her, the disagreement forgotten.

* * *

Monday dawned miserably. The weather had broken overnight and it was raining. Josh was being buried or cremated or something. Jo was leaving. Alex felt horrible, sick to the stomach, but hid it as best she could. The concert write-up in the Guardian was a saving grace: *Palmer Brings the Audience to its Feet and Beethoven to Tears, Royal Festival Hall, LPO, Saturday*. She dared not read the rest beyond the slightly unclear headline. Jo read on, summarizing it.

"The headline's only ambiguous for effect. They loved it. Although they weren't quite sure about the choice of encore." She looked at her pensively. "You shouldn't read reviews, you know. It's a well-known fact. If they're bad they're bound to be depressing, then you remember not to believe them, which leaves you where when they're good? You shouldn't believe them either? Very destabilizing…!"

"I was presuming it, the encore I mean, wouldn't be taken too literally." She smiled to herself, it had been her choice; why shouldn't she share some of the discomfort?

Jo went to pack for her week in the West Country. The world moved onward, she just didn't feel that she had quite caught up.

When the mail arrived, there were already some letters redirected from the cottage. A large foolscap envelope looked particularly interesting; sometimes she was sent new works or musical circulars directly to her home, as opposed to via the agent. When she opened it, however, the opening pages of the Beethoven concerto, torn out and cut jaggedly into four pieces, slid out onto the worktop. She yelped and dropped it, as if she had been burned.

Jo scurried in from another room, still pulling on her shirt. She looked.

"That's a bit sick."

"I thought I was done with all that."

"Apparently not. Right. Pick up the pieces with a rubber glove or something, put them back into the envelope and we'll send the whole lot off to your Surrey Police, okay? Right now. Turn something hateful into positive action."

She did as suggested and enclosed a shakily handwritten note of explanation. Jo looked at the envelope as she slid it inside another.

"You must call Leanne. Get her over to stay or go there. I feel rotten now that I have to go. Please…" Jo kissed her gently. "Don't dwell on it all today. If possible. Come on, I'll take you to lunch on the way. I'll get a private room somewhere. There's a great little place in Chinatown. I'm sure they'll be obliging."

She looked in her bag and brought out her mobile. "Leanne. Now," she urged. "Any trouble with this week going belly-up for you and I want you to book in here," she tapped her hotel brochure on the worktop, "with me. Same hotel and we can tiptoe to each other's rooms like teenagers for a few nights."

The insistence cheered her. "Deal," she said.

"I'm so sorry. We're going to have to go. Call her, while I load the car, leave a message, sort something out. This is a crap day to be left alone, but I have to go to this thing."

"You must. That's okay. I'll be all right. You've done so much to help me." She grabbed her jacket from the stool and her bag from the floor. "Let's do it." She sent a text to Leanne as she walked—*Can I come for the next couple of nights?*

As they went outside Jo asked, "You know how to lock up? Look here…"

"Right."

"Seriously. I want you to cancel everything and come down to meet me, if you have even a hint of losing it this week. Spend the week on a massage table. Sign up to play their piano if you need an excuse."

"Thanks."

"Let's go." She took her hand and led her into the car.

* * *

Leanne returned her text during the meal—*Come. ASAP. I'm working at home today.*

Fleeting guilt passed momentarily through Alex. At some point she would have a lot of explaining to do to Leanne.

"Great," Jo said. "Go home, pack a bag, take the car, shut up the house. It'll all be fine. You'll have company and I'll let Zara know the house is empty for a once-over."

It was a done deal. She had to leave. She tried to shake off the feeling that the veneer of safety was cracking: vulnerability, exposure was sure to follow. She saw her off politely, with little chance for more in such a public place. No one seemed to notice them and she did as planned; decamping rapidly to Leanne's for a couple of nights, with the prospect of therapeutic girly giggling sessions in the evenings and plenty of practice time in the days while Leanne went to work. With each change of location she was running away from Josh and distancing herself.

She had remained largely protected from the gossip-mongering and scandalizing that had crept into some of the newspaper columns and online blogs. What mixed signals had she given out to invite such attention upon herself? What had really happened that fateful night?

On Wednesday, toward the end of a slightly tedious day of maintaining a mask, being preened and posed for the magazine shoot at the Savoy, pretending the pretense with a peculiarly intense New York interviewer, her mobile rang. Fortunately, with Nathan on guard for the day from Camden-Waterhouse deflecting difficult questions with professional expertise and his distracting boyish smile, she was able to take a moment out to answer it.

Surprisingly it was the lawyers that brought her back to the real world with a little jerk. Thankfully, as expected, they informed her that the coroner's verdict was accidental death, but more surprisingly that during the ongoing full audit of Josh's personal and business activities and accounts, she had been awarded a preliminary settlement of around four million pounds. Her jaw all but hit the floor; fortunately she was standing with her back to her interrogator. Josh had been raking off more of the profits from royalty checks and fees than he was due, not only from her, and squirreling them away for some years in a rapidly appreciating property portfolio and a management company. The figure was only estimated at the moment, but with additional compensation for her to come from the estate, it would increase.

Alex was stunned. Josh. He had covered himself well, acting the jester, while planning for himself. She shuddered at the thought and with effort rearranged her features to complete the interview.

Surrey Police called at the end of the afternoon to confirm both the lawyers' message and the arrival of the Beethoven score package. They would be investigating, and had sent it immediately to the forensic department in Guildford to be scanned.

Her father rang to invite her to stay for a while, but the last thing she wanted was to be fussed over, infuriatingly, like a child, so she stalled him with a promise of a visit for Sunday lunch as soon as she could.

She did not much like the idea of chasing Jo around the country like some lap dog, and anyway being at Leanne's was fun, distracting. They always slotted in with each other like the couple of girls who had giggled and ached their way around the South Downs on that Youth Hostelling hike of so many years ago.

"We should do that again one day," they promised themselves almost every time they saw each other, even though they might have to be retired before ever fitting it in again. Both their jobs were demanding and time-consuming, with Leanne spending much of her time traveling and writing up reports, analyzing water supplies across the country. And yet, this time Alex had to hide a secret.

On Wednesday night, when Leanne returned from work, they sat in the living room cuddling mugs of tea after supper, discussing the surprising compensation. It was a huge windfall, equivalent to a lottery win, yet tainted.

"The least you deserve, if you ask me," Leanne commented loyally, "for going through that hell with Josh and having your privacy so exploited."

"Yes. I suppose."

"Think of the extra freedom it allows you. Buy a new place. Better security and privacy. A clean start, maybe sell the cottage."

"That's an idea. Yes."

"Such a prick. He had no right to think he could encroach upon you like that and smuggle away earnings that rightfully belonged to you and all his clients. I know one shouldn't speak ill of the dead but in this case…!" She paused, softening. "By the way, what's happened to your friend?"

"Away working. I'll go back to the house tomorrow, don't want to put upon you for too long."

"Don't be daft. I don't mind. I offered didn't I?"

"Yes, I know. I didn't fancy rattling around by myself there, especially on Monday night, following that letter and the funeral. You could come over…"

"Mmm. What, you mean I'm allowed to come and see it? If he's not back yet?"

"Sure. Why don't you come and stay tomorrow night, stop me from rattling around! It's a big place."

"That'd be great. I have to be away for the weekend following that anyway." Leanne kicked back into the sofa, her long legs spread-eagled out. Her long pale hair, the sort that didn't require taming with hair-straighteners, splayed itself all over the cushions.

"Have you rung your Nathan yet, by the way?"

"He's not my Nathan. No, not yet, I haven't."

"So? What are you waiting for?" She nudged her toward the phone. "Where's that number?"

"My bag."

"Go on Leanne. I'm here for moral support, you know. And I'm fed up with thinking about myself!" She grinned at her friend.

"Oh, all right. It should be the other way around though. He should ring me."

"What century are we living in? Anyway, does he have your number?"

"Er, no."

"So?"

So Leanne rang Nathan's number and Alex covered her face, hugging a cushion, to mask her amusement as Leanne chewed her lip, staring at her friend as she waited and then he answered. As the relief flowed through her expression and it became apparent that he must have recognized her, had even been waiting for a call and sounded pleased. After the tentative start, they ended by fixing a dinner date for the following week and Leanne hung up, laughing nervously.

"He wanted to."

"See! How long has it been since you had a boyfriend?"

"Couple of years."

"God, it's you who deserves that compensation!" They both fell about laughing, which rapidly dissolved into a cushion fight, the dust spiraling into the evening light.

When things calmed down, Alex continued, "So, pack up a small bag later. I'll take it back with me in the car tomorrow, after I've met this composer. Come and meet me in The Curiosity Café, just below the church, you know, on Highgate High Street after work. We'll have a small bite to eat and I'll walk you to where I've been staying. There's a fabulous pool and hot tub."

"Sounds wonderful. You know, I think I'll go and pack now!"

She left the room doing a silly dance to entertain her friend. Alex sat in the candlelight, still hugging the cushion and dwelled on all the continuing changes. It was almost faster than she could keep up with. She felt a stranger to her life of just a couple of months ago. There were times, it seemed, when life simply could not be pinned down, but ran away with itself, a river in flood, sudden twists and turns to be ridden perilously, barely under control until the waters might calm themselves again.

* * *

Thursday morning arrived and the two women said farewell to each other. Leanne headed off to work via the Underground, dodging the threatening black clouds and opening hints at a downpour. Alex took their bags in the car and headed out to Chorleywood in the rain to visit Mr. Braithwaite and discuss his composition, which, all in all, turned out to be a rather entertaining experience.

There was something of the mad professor about Mr. Braithwaite. His large, disheveled house hinted at a decayed former glory, grand and roomy, but dusty, unkempt and probably not redecorated since the early 1950s. He served tea in chipped bone china teacups while Alex demonstrated the work for him and they discussed his intentions, the special effects and the possibilities of her interpretation, including pegging some of the strings of the piano during the slow movement. It was fun and creative being adventurous with something so new and unpredictable. He explained he had incorporated a couple of possibilities for improvisatory moments and Alex showed him her suggestions. By the end of the morning they had earned a certain amount of each other's mutual respect and the composer suggested, a little shyly, if she would like him to dedicate the piece to her, as he had anticipated. She said it would be a great honor and they parted on excellent terms, looking forward to the rehearsals for the Prom premiere.

* * *

Alex had been blocking the thought of Josh's funeral from her mind, suitably distracted by her week. It had been a subdued event, she learned. Only the closest friends and family had been invited, the whole affair clouded further by the untimely and contentious aspects of his death and more literally by the gathering bad weather. There were a considerable number of beautiful flower arrangements, more for the feelings of the family than specific love for Josh, and just two official cars, with a small following. Unfortunately, a couple of television crews and photographers had tracked down the location and hovered at a barely acceptable distance to record footage of the relatives passing through the cemetery gates, who were even more distressed by their presence. It made the later news closing headlines, along with more clips of Alex and further speculations.

* * *

On Thursday night, as planned, Alex met up with Leanne in Highgate, then they walked down the hill, sharing an umbrella through the pouring rain, eventually turning in to Jo's house. Alex had been back earlier in the day, following her appointment with Braithwaite, and had spent some time pottering around erasing obvious signs of Jo's ownership, so as to keep the mystery intact for the time being. She sidestepped the discomfort that it caused her. It would have to do for now.

Leanne was amusingly and suitably astonished with the size and grandeur of the place, it had to be *some* guy that her friend was seeing, with exquisite taste, but she made a point of not prying. They swam in the pool, relaxed in the hot tub, warm while the rain poured down beyond the protection of the overhang, and then collapsed in front of a film. It made everything a little more believable for Alex, to involve her friend within the magical bubble of this secluded existence.

* * *

On Jo's return Alex did not disappoint; she had prepared a hot casserole, playing the role of hypothetical wife, having heard something of the Cornish weather and her ordeal this week. They lazed on the sofa together afterward, watching the crackling fire, Jo working her way through a box of tissues and a hot lemon with honey and whisky.

"Don't let anybody ever tell you it's all glamour in this business. There I was freezing my fucking backside off in the rain and gales, time and time again. You can't even get a double for a close scene like that. Then there's your line of work, where the worst weather conditions might be that the air-conditioning is on a bit high or the heat's making the orchestra doze off. Hardly dangerous. You didn't miss much by not coming down."

Alex laughed at her and Jo laughed at herself, good-naturedly. "I didn't need to," she said. "Leanne was good company. Poor you, though."

"I was thinking…why don't we disappear for a while? Maybe give me a day or two at home to try and shake this thing off." She waved a tissue in surrender, like a white flag. "Then hop on a plane, leaving the debris behind, to somewhere considerably warmer where no one's going to bother if we wander around arm in arm and warm the cockles of our hearts."

"Good plan. It's about time we did that. How's your schedule looking?"

"Free, until next week in Vienna, thankfully. Yours?"

"Amazing! We coincide. Free until next weekend, Birmingham."

"Excellent."

"Mail, by the way…" She placed a pile on Jo's lap.

She started opening letters. Partway in she stopped and stared at a handwritten sheet.

"Fuck."

"What?"

"Andy. He's resigned, effective immediately. Or until I make my mind up about you. That's a bit melodramatic don't you think? Thinks it's all too close for comfort…he wouldn't want to 'get in the way'! He could have a long wait on his hands. Where's the solidarity in that?"

"Oh God. Sorry Jo."

"It's not you…he's had his moments when he can be a bit of a center stage prick. Perhaps that's why he didn't make it in the business…control freakery." She flung the rest of the mail down.

"But you're old friends. He's probably had a crush on you for years. Look, I'll help you, I never meant to cause…"

"Yes, I know…thanks. But he's supposed to be gay! Not a crush, perhaps rivalry though. It's not like you've replaced him, you get busy too. I'll rope Harold in a bit more, at least until I get the time to sort this out or talk him round. Maybe later we'll look online for our trip, but for now don't mind me if I just rest my eyes a bit. I've had enough drama for one week."

Alex felt awkward and made to move.

Jo grasped her thigh. "I don't mean you. It's just the other crap that goes on."

It was the first obstacle thrown up by Alex entering her home. She went thoughtfully to the piano and played through a selection of her softest jazz tunes, until when she returned she found Jo had dozed off on the sofa, the whisky tumbler still balanced dangerously on her stomach. She rescued the glass, pulled a throw rug gently over her and sat down nearby to read a volume of Clive James's poetry, which she had been dipping in and out of when time permitted.

Andy had been perfectly pleasant to her. Charming even. But that was before…was it too much to ask for him to share Jo?

But it wasn't an even share. Perhaps it was just a phase, a prima donna moment as Jo had mentioned.

It wasn't possible to control everything or everyone. She of all people should know that by now.

* * *

The following day she decided to confirm her arrangement with Camden-Waterhouse. They had been nothing but professional with her and anyway, anybody needing to book her would want to know who to contact. They were suitably delighted and offered to courier the documents to her immediately, which suited her, although she preferred it would be to her legal advisor rather than giving away Jo's address for the first time. Jo, who had spent the day so far miserably on the sofa wrapped in excessively wintery clothing, in front of a roaring fire, suggested she ask them if they could fix her anything in Vienna from the twenty-fourth.

When the call ended, she realized that she had not confessed to Jo about the windfall yet.

"By the way, it seems I'm rather richer now than when you left for Cornwall."

"Mmm?" Jo inquired vaguely. Money had not needed to be an urgent issue for either of them.

She told her.

"Wow! That's a lot of squirreling away!"

"Yes, that's what I thought."

"You'll have to consider what to do with that."

"Just live off the interest? Or I could build a soundproofed room at the bottom of your garden so you don't have to listen to me all the time."

"But I like listening to you. It never fails to send me to sleep. Ha!" She tackled her playfully to the sofa as she passed.

"Feeling better?"

"Come on. Let's book that trip. Let's not fret about Andy. Three would have been a crowd. I'll write back and send him a final check, but leave it open-ended, explain he can come back, if I can find a tactful way of saying 'when you get your head together.' We'll still be mates when the dust settles. I'll sort something else out…or get the agency to."

They went to the computer and after a bit of hunting, she secured them a private villa with its own pool, in Southern Italy, even a private flight to avoid any fuss.

"I hear it's good. From colleagues."

"Perfect."

* * *

While they decamped to the Mediterranean, the offers of work continued to roll in. While Jo shook off her cold, reading a novel as she lay in the sun on the terrace, she was initially secured for a Stratford season, a perfume advertising contract and discussions for another leading film role in Hollywood. While Alex swam in their little pool and watched a lizard stick to the wall, her new agent was being inundated with bookings from both national and international orchestras, exclusive music clubs, chat shows, awards ceremonies and even the private wedding party of a couple of well-known British actors.

They knew about none of this, having asked their agents to hold all but the most urgent calls to them, until after they arrived home, having made a pact to switch on their mobiles for only ten minutes during dinner to pick up anything important.

Leanne was acquainting herself with Nathan, Jenny was being installed at the Camden-Waterhouse offices and a fixated, semi-stalking fan of Jo's had been frustrated that the trail had gone cold in her hunt. Andy had disappeared somewhere to lick his wounds. Alex's dad had woken up to the artifice in which he had landed himself and was separating from Cruella, despite the fact that it would mean splitting the house. Alex received only one message that concerned her. Pauline had rung to say that there had been an attempted break-in at Nightingale's End, but that the intruder had not made it into the house, having been disturbed by a neighbor who heard the sound of breaking glass. This only confirmed her feelings about the cottage and she resolved to contact various estate agents as soon as she could and put it on the market to be sold.

They passed their week away in contented, isolated bliss, wondering whether such a life would be possible or even desirable in the long term, able to leave the rest of the world behind. Toward the end of the week, reality started to press home and Alex went to play the neighboring hotel's piano, starting to pine for it a little. Jo took out the next scenes for the film and made sure she had absorbed the lines and moves. They packed their bags and headed off to the airport with some reluctance, knowing that when they returned they would again be charging around. But it was who they were, what they had become. What had made the meeting of two unconnected worlds a possibility. They had made their choices, their decisions to be at such a point. For a week they could imagine they had it all in hand. But in real time some of the decisions were being made for them, beyond their sphere of control.

CHAPTER TWENTY

The LSO at the Barbican

Alex's second Sonata series had been given a final date and contracts were signed; a second cocktail CD was also urgently in the pipeline. She was relieved in a sense; she thought the adverse publicity over Josh might have finished her or at the very least caused some inertia, but on the contrary—ironically and with a lingering feeling of guilt by association, the exposure had served only to publicize her more. The physical and mental scars were fading, the circumstances of her new beginning replacing the sour memories. She and Jo both continued to travel, but did manage to coincide, first at Vienna and then elsewhere, surreptitiously smuggling each other into their respective rooms or suites at night, when all was quiet.

At times the subterfuge was thrilling, at others a little wearing.

For Alex's Fellowship award, Jo dressed as Petra again and hung around in the audience, trying to hide her pride of association with artificially aged stooping, while Alex thanked past piano teachers and professors for their invaluable help, unconsciously inspiring the listening students and the worldly professors that their goal was sometimes a realistic possibility.

In June she was working again at the Barbican, rehearsing with the London Symphony Orchestra with a tied recording contract, and Jo was in Hollywood securing some deal or other. She had a suitable offer on the cottage, the settlement money had come through and Alex had sent a chunk of it to the kind neighbors who had managed her rescue. She and Jo were planning to chat about their future arrangements after this patch of work.

Jenny, who was now finding a niche at Camden-Waterhouse, had taken on the slightly irritating self-imposed role of Alex's protector. Alex felt it was probably tied to some inner guilt about her part in the Josh drama and had postponed making a point about it to either her or the agent. She would have to choose her moment. Perhaps this weekend could provide the opportunity.

On this occasion Jenny had turned up, not for the first time, to specifically coordinate Alex's part in the event and smooth her path. These reappearances of Jenny's had a nasty habit of reminding Alex about what had passed, rather than soothing the memory.

The Proms loomed, with Mozart and Braithwaite to prepare, the Beethoven series was under her belt and in the hands of the recording company. Leanne had resigned from her role of accompanying companion whenever Alex visited Camden-Waterhouse, seeing as the media were no longer an intrusive presence, and anyway she could now see Nathan at her own leisure. Alex was pleased to see her friend's relationship blooming. Alex and Jo's secret was still secure. They had played a consummate, professional game of cat and mouse; and anyway, who would have thought that a phenomenally rising film star and a talented concert pianist would have found the time or the attraction to bother to be together?

* * *

Alex had barely rested her hands on the keyboard for the opening statement of the concerto that evening in the packed concert hall when there was a sudden commotion behind her and an alarming crash across the quietening music. There was an audible intake of breath from the audience and sudden, inappropriate talking from behind her. At first she continued to prepare for her entry with oblivious professionalism, cutting out the distraction, but then, when she looked up for her cue and saw that the conductor had put down his baton with startled eyes and the orchestra was petering out, she turned to look to where all eyes were staring. The leader had fallen right off his chair, throwing his violin to the stage, smashing the bridge and the valuable bow in two along its length, as he twitched and convulsed. At first, she thought he must be having an epileptic fit. Other front section members were on their knees next to him, loosening the Victorian collar and bowtie. A St. John's Ambulance first aide attendant was pelting down the central aisle, anxious to help. The front row of the audience were up on their feet, murmuring. She made to stand up and suddenly felt breathless and constricted herself; she couldn't seem to breathe, her head felt light and dizzy and as she leaned forward to put her weight on her left leg to stand, the hall slewed sideways. She knew nothing more, crashing the keyboard noisily with a helpless hand as she too fell to the floor with a resounding crack which echoed around the hall when she hit the wooden stage.

* * *

Musicians Collapse at Barbican ran several of the headlines in the morning newspapers. *The leader of the London Symphony Orchestra, John Shillinworth, and the pianist Alex Palmer are in intensive care at Guy's Hospital after their sudden collapse at last night's Barbican concert. Both are said to be in a serious condition. Initial discoveries appear to indicate a type of poisoning. Detective Superintendent Ashworth of the Metropolitan Police described forensics' early identification of the presence of a powerful neurotoxin at the venue, concentrated at the piano on the stage. Members of the audience were ushered quickly from the hall, but anyone concerned about possible exposure should telephone the emergency hotline listed below. The co-leader of the orchestra, Nadjia Brown, was in tears as she reported that her desk partner crashed dramatically to the ground toward the end of the orchestral introduction, not long after tuning the orchestra from the piano at the start of the concert. Alex Palmer, who was said to have barely touched the instrument and turned around to witness Mr. Shillinworth's collapse, passed out on the stage shortly afterward. Sir Matthew Eldridge, conducting, praised the rapid action of the St. John's Ambulance crew at the concert hall. Mr. Eldridge and the surrounding orchestra members were only partially affected, reporting symptoms of mild dizziness and shortness of breath. The police are investigating a similar collapse of a member of the public in the Sunningdale area. Continued on page 2.*

* * *

Camden-Waterhouse contacted Alex's father. He contacted Leanne. No one contacted Jo. She was in LA. Her parents, who might have made the link, were away in France, not bothering with the news headlines that day. Leanne still did not know who the mystery partner was in order to be able to make contact.

Her father stood vigil all through that first day, periodically in tears, watching as the doctors and nurses fidgeted with her drip, the machines, set her broken elbow, watched the heart monitor and waited for the results of the scans. Across the room in a separate curtained bay the leader of the orchestra lay, also unconscious, attended by his wife. Toward the end of the day, there was a sudden flurry of activity, with the consultants coming in to administer more drugs to the two patients.

"We may have found the cause," they explained hurriedly, while scuttling past to deliver possible antidotes.

The visitors went to the waiting area and flicked on the six o'clock news on the television in the corner of the room. The broadcaster reported, "Police have traced a connection with the collapse of the two respected musicians at last night's Barbican concert. A young woman died in Sunningdale last night from contact with the same neurotoxin that has been discovered on the grand piano of last night's Barbican concert. A broken vial containing the poisonous substance is believed to have been found at her flat. The area has been sealed off. Police believe the woman, who has not yet been named, may have been wandering out into the street for help while the chemical was taking effect."

They all looked at each other, stunned into silence. Who could it be?

* * *

The intensive care unit was relatively quiet. The evening settled in, but the lights stayed on in the unit. The nurse adjusted the sheets and it was at that point that Alex's eyes flickered open and squinted painfully at the light, bringing instant tears to her eyes.

She felt nauseous and barely able to move. Her muscles ached and when she tried to flex her hands, pain shot through her left arm. Everything felt heavy and distant. Where was she? What had happened?

Hearing something, the nurse returned to check her monitors. Alex groaned slightly in an attempt to attract her attention.

"Oh, you're back with us, love. You've had a bit of an attack, been unconscious for nearly twenty-four hours now." She pressed a buzzer.

Alex blinked at her, unable to formulate a word.

"It's okay, love. Your body's just had a traumatic shock. Do you remember the concert at the Barbican?"

Alex frowned a little, then nodded faintly and blinked at her again.

"Would you like some water?"

She managed another faint nod and the nurse lifted her a little and plumped the cushions up, then held a plastic cup to her lips and Alex sipped a little. Everything tingled.

"You've broken your left arm in the fall. So not to worry if it feels strange. You're plastered to the shoulder."

Alex looked down at her arm and flexed her fingers a little.

"Mmm," she managed faintly.

"Well done, love. That's better."

One of the doctors came in.

"Ah! Back in the land of the living. That's excellent news. There'll be a lot of people relieved about that. Can you feel this?" The doctor began to test her systematically, touching fingers and toes, gently checking for responses.

"Yes," she managed weakly. The doctor summarized the events of the previous evening, omitting the details about John Shillinworth, the woman in Sunningdale and the full possibilities of the attack. "Your body has been in a state of toxic shock, so you need to rest up. You've had us worried. But this is positive news, that you're back with us. Very good news. How are you feeling?"

"Sick," she whispered.

He filled a syringe and ran it into one of the tubes. "That should help. Just give it a minute. The nurse will put the call button in easy reach and you can call us when you need us, any time. Sleep if you can." He nodded and smiled at them both and went to check on the other occupant of the cubicle.

Alex smiled weakly at the nurse, then gave up on the effort and, surrounded by a hazy feeling and an inkling that if she tried anything else she really would throw up or break into pieces, closed her eyes and disappeared into unconsciousness again.

* * *

Someone placed some flowers at the bottom of the bed. With a lurch to her heart Alex saw that it was Jo, dressed as Petra Rahmanoff. Jo checked the blinds were closed and bent to kiss Alex, warmly, softly.

"You!" she said quietly. "Oh hell, look at you. This shouldn't have been allowed. I hope someone's head is going to roll over this. This shouldn't have happened. Isn't there any security?" Jo seemed barely able to contain her anger at the sight of her.

"I don't make a habit of this. Honestly. The police are all over it like a rash," she said quietly.

Jo stroked her hair flat, making a point of calming her breathing and ran her fingers down her unbruised cheek. "But really, it's outrageous. Life can't dish out this much trouble!"

Alex leaned her face into the hand, safe in their privacy. "I don't know. I tend to feel life finds its own equilibrium. There has to be a counterbalance to the good fortune of meeting you."

Jo rolled her eyes.

"Contrary to appearances, I don't make a habit of this. I've never had a year quite like this one. It really isn't normal. You were in LA."

"Yep. Now I'm here. As fast as possible, given the time delay and the lack of instant British news on CNN. You had me frantic."

"Funny. You're not the first person to say that."

"Why? Who else has been charging halfway around the world to see you?" Jo smiled and squeezed her right hand. "How you doing?"

"Better. I only woke briefly yesterday evening. I was out of it for the whole day. They weren't sure how it would…John still hasn't come round, but they're optimistic now that they know what it is. Now that I've woken up."

"What it is? What is it?"

"You're still a bit behind, aren't you? They located a vial of the stuff at this address in west London and a woman has died from around there. It had been painted on the piano at the Barbican."

"Oh, my…but really?" Jo seethed for a moment, her anger gaining the upper hand, until she could take another deep breath. "It's like an Agatha Christie. Honestly you're not doing all that well for luck at the moment."

Alex smiled at her. "Oh, I don't know…"

"And the arm?"

"Just a hairline fracture. I fell on it badly, unconscious you see, so you don't put your hand down to stop yourself in the right way. They've made a meal of plastering it, only because of what I do and what might follow if they made a mistake. Not that there would be any legal action by me, of course. I'm just grateful they got us out in one piece. And I've been scanned Lord knows how many times."

"And your cheek?"

"I hit the deck rather hard."

"I had this horrible flight. Both turbulence and worry."

Alex squeezed her hand back. "You came, though."

"As fast as possible."

"That isn't always a bonus…"

"Oh, you are feeling better aren't you…?" Jo kissed her lips slowly, smiling close up.

"Did you have to cancel anything major?"

"No. It's fine. Just a postponement. I have to be back for the launch later in the week."

"Thanks, Jo." She knew Jo would make light of anything awkward anyway. She felt deeply grateful. It was a sign of how much it all mattered to her, although it was more than she could say without openly tipping the delicate balance. She reached for her hand to hold onto it tightly, reluctant to let her ever go. She was her protective layer. "My dad's been here. He'll probably want to spirit me away."

"What do you want?"

"If I'm up and about, I'd rather be up and about at home, our home."

"Yeah. Me too. How are we going to manage explaining that? Shall we tell him, just him. I mean…my folks know. It would be fair."

"Yes. Let's. He'll be okay about it." *I should think.* The thought delighted her, even through the soporific, numbing effects of her treatment. Other than the sheer entertainment value of seeing Jo dressed in character, the subterfuge was wearying: the need for truth and accuracy having become clarified by the close brush with danger. "Come tomorrow afternoon.

Visiting starts again at two p.m., I think. He'll be here. If Leanne or anyone else is with him again, I'll lose them for us. Send them on some fictitious errand. Come as you are now and we'll find a way of explaining. Would you mind flicking on the news?"

Jo obliged. Other headlines had precedence this evening, but at about the fourth story in they announced—*The Metropolitan Police have identified the mystery woman linked to the toxic attack at the Barbican. Miss Jennifer Mathison, recently an assistant at the agency Camden-Waterhouse—*

"Jenny!" Alex exclaimed.

—*and previously at the offices of Joshua Pembroke, was found dead in Sunningdale from a fatal dose of the same toxin discovered at the Barbican on Friday night.* The item cut to part of an announcement from the police, "We are working on the possibility that the incident may be connected with the previous attack on Miss Palmer." The news reader continued: *Miss Palmer was attacked at her home by Joshua Pembroke earlier in the year, resulting in his accidental death.* The news item cut again to one of the orchestral members.

"That's the principal viola…" Alex murmured.

The bulletin continued with the viola player saying: "She had been hanging around at the rehearsal. I'd stayed behind to run through a few things and she was fussing around the piano, polishing and spraying…"

"I didn't know…" Alex whispered.

The item continued—"*John Shillinworth is still in intensive care, but is said to be stable and doctors are optimistic following the revival of Miss Palmer late last night.*" The news cut to the next item.

Alex had her good hand on her chest as if to slow the racing of her heart. "Jenny! Did I ever tell you about Jenny?"

"Yes. I think you mentioned her in passing, but nothing particularly problematic."

"No. She was fine. She'd always been helpful. But she had started to become a bit of a pain, constantly hanging around and checking up on me. I thought it was guilt…to do with Josh…I can't imagine why she would do this…"

"Starting to sound more like jealousy and bitterness. Perhaps she did the Beethoven letter."

"Oh!" She paused, speechless for the moment, tears stinging her eyes.

"Do you think this might be the end of it all?"

She nodded. "Could be." She winced at Jo. "I must go and check on John tomorrow. I feel it's all my fault. If they can get me into a wheelchair or something I'll go and sit with him."

"If you're up to it."

"My life isn't usually like this you know. If it wasn't for the more positive aspects of this year—such as you—it would be the curse of living in interesting times."

"Yes, but you could say it's the interesting times that have caused our paths to cross. I'd better go, before the ward sister comes and boots me out. I'd stay the night if I could...but it would incur the wrath and not to mention suspicion of the staff, no doubt."

"You should get some sleep too."

"I'll be back tomorrow afternoon, as planned. Okay? We'll make a spectacle of ourselves to your father. Call me anytime. I'll bring you some things. Anything that you want in particular?"

"A book or two please."

Jo leaned over and kissed her again. "Do you want that TV off?"

"No. Leave it on. I don't think I can sleep. I've had a double dose of it recently and I'm still feeling pretty foul. Pass me the remote. Thanks. I can't tell you how glad I am to see you. I couldn't remember where you were at first."

"Oh." She frowned. "I was furious that I hadn't even thought of wheedling Leanne's number from you. I had no one to call, nobody who knew to call me, the hospital wouldn't impart any information, just the newspaper headlines to go on. I had to phone the LSO, pretending to be 'Rahmanoff, a close friend.' It's at times like this, when the cover-up doesn't seem worth it."

"You're a love. I'm trying to imagine the effect you'd have on everyone if you weren't disguised. Now, get in role Petra, before you're seen. I'll see you tomorrow. I'm sorry I don't have much stamina." She managed a grin, although her insides were still in some turmoil. *Jenny!*

"Stamina? I'm just pleased you're intact." Jo grinned back with considerable relief, stooped into character, gave an aged wave and disappeared through the door.

* * *

The following morning, after very little sleep, but some attempt at breakfast, Alex asked to be helped down to visit John. He had apparently awakened late in the night, similar to Alex. She took Jo's flowers with her. Intensive care was unpleasantly bright and the electronic noises from the monitors disturbed her, bringing returning associations with nausea and pain. John was propped up in his bed, very pale, but awake.

"John?"

He turned slightly and spoke quietly. "Alex? I only found out this morning that it was you too. Look." He held out his hand a little. It was shaking, trembling uncontrollably. "Automatic vibrato, see?" He smiled weakly.

"It's okay. It will go. I felt terrible when I woke. I was shaking a bit too. It was some awful substance. It's the shock. It was directed at me. I'm so sorry. I feel responsible. It was on the piano. You touched it for longer than I did." She paused between each phrase, unable to be more fluent with him, not wishing to repeat information that he had probably heard already.

"That's the last time I attempt to tune the orchestra." He managed a faint smile. "They're moving me to a room later."

"Good. That's a good sign. You've come out of the woods. Flowers. I feel I owe you." She held them out and put them next to him.

"You don't owe me. But if you insist, if they're able to put my violin back together and if I'm still fit to play after this, we'll do some duos together."

"You won't be able to bear seeing me."

"Oh, I think I will."

"Anyway that's getting off a bit lightly, for me."

"Not when you see the fiendish repertoire that I had in mind." He smiled weakly and gulped a little.

"I'll leave you now. I just wanted to see if you were okay."

He nodded. She gave his hand a squeeze and left him to rest.

That afternoon, her visitors arrived promptly at two o'clock, her dad carrying a bag for her.

"Feeling better?" Leanne asked. They each kissed her.

"Much better today, thanks."

"Honestly, you had us worried. You're having a bloody awful time of it." She didn't often hear her father swear.

"It hasn't been all bad."

Her dad put the bag on the bed and started to unpack it. "Chocolates, grapes, other essentials, Leanne's choice, not mine…" Leanne grinned.

"Thanks. You're all so sweet. Did you see the latest?" She explained about Jenny. "Josh's assistant, you see? She must have been bottling it up since Josh's death, or something."

"Don't worry yourself, love. The police are onto it."

"I went to see John, the leader. He's awake, but pretty shaken up. I feel like it's my fault."

"It's not your fault. You've just been unfortunate enough to run into a couple of total lunatics," Leanne chimed in, clearly annoyed about it too. "I thought music was supposed to be a safe choice, a peaceful career."

"They say you could be out in a day or two." Her father lifted the conversation. "There are no long-term lingering side effects apparently, once you've shaken it out of your system in the first few days. Just the initial tiredness. You're going to have a hassle with that arm for a few weeks. It's only a hairline fracture. They reckon they'll take it off in a week or two. The plaster, not the arm, obviously."

"I can see you've been talking to the doctors. Thank heavens. 'You shall go to the Proms, Cinderella.'"

There was a brief knock at the door and the scruffy head of Petra poked around the edge of the door.

Jo had made a thorough job of her image; the old tweed skirt and jacket looked decidedly ill-fitting and threadbare in the light of day.

"Hallo," she said, her voice thick with an accent.

"Hi!" Alex called cheerily. Everyone looked startled, a little offended by the sudden intrusion. "Leanne, Dad, let me introduce you. This is my friend—"

"We've met before," her dad interrupted, "Petra isn't it?" He went forward to shake her hand. "At the Beethoven concert? I'm Michael, this is Leanne…" They all shook hands. Another knock at the door and a hospital porter came in, carrying a large pile of cards and letters for Alex.

"Thanks." He went out again. "Fan mail," she explained, apologetically. "It's rather nice, actually. They say really kind things, most of the time. Apart from the one that said 'despite not liking your interpretation of Rach two, and that your idea of rubato is outdated, I was sorry to see that you have been taken ill'!" She laughed. "I've had a few romantic offers too." She saw a frown pass fleetingly across Petra's face, and smiled.

"Leanne could you do me a favor? I could do with some thank you card responses, a couple of dozen, the agency can deal with anything more. Would you mind hunting some out for me? I've been meaning to ask."

"Sure. I'll go now."

"You're an angel. Bring back some teas if you can. I'm going to owe you big time after this."

"No way. I still owe you for the trips abroad. And Nathan." She grinned at her friend. "See you in a min." She slipped out.

Petra closed the door and was already tilting the blinds. She flicked the lock quietly and stood with her back to the door, so that no one could open it suddenly.

"What are you doing?" Alex's dad asked nervously. He threw a glance at Alex and straightened himself up to his full height.

"Dad. It's all right. We haven't got long. I've got to do this while Leanne's out of the room. I've been meaning to tell you something. You haven't exactly met Petra properly. Petra is an actress, sorry, actor I mean, she's been a good friend. We met in

LA on the tour. She was at the Oscars and I ended up playing for that private party at her beach house. It's she who's been my heroine and kept me in hiding during all the Josh saga. I've been at her house in Hampstead."

She faded out, tired from the effort and brushed her hair away from her face in a faintly defiant gesture. Jo was nodding through most of this and standing in her own relaxed posture, arms folded across her chest as she leaned against the door, strangely opposing body language for the look of the character.

She stepped forward now, tugging off her wig and glasses, smoothing her hair down and offering her hand again. "Hello. Yes, my name's actually Jo, not Petra. Joanne Davison."

The penny dropped immediately with her dad, along with his jaw, as he made a poor effort to cover his surprise, "Jo! Davison! As in *One, Two, Four*? Well, hello. I'm very pleased to meet you. You had me fooled."

Jo was shaking her dad's hand again, grinning at his response. "Fooled? Well I didn't mean to fool you. It's just that this…It gave us a chance just to be and work things out." She indicated the outfit.

"Work things out?"

Alex rolled her eyes. *Here it comes.* She watched the next penny dropping.

"Dad, I know it's news to you…but Jo…well, she's my…"

"We're girlfriends. Seeing each other…dating," Jo chimed in helpfully.

"Dating? Any chance of that would be a fine thing!" Alex murmured.

Jo grinned at her. They both stared to see what would happen next.

Michael swallowed quite deliberately, then nodded once. "I see. I think that makes a lot of sense to me, in more ways than you can imagine. Your mother once told me something…"

Alex raised an eyebrow at Jo. "She did?"

"You must excuse me, I shall try not to be an old-fashioned fool." He stopped.

Jo carried on, unperturbed, "Well…it meant, this," she indicated her outfit again, "that I could come to some of Alex's engagements without it becoming some huge hysterical thing in the media."

"It's very good."

"It's my job, the acting…" Jo smiled.

"Of course. I just meant, very convincing."

He had apparently gathered his wits. "Thank you. For taking care of my daughter. I've been wondering what was going on…I mean, obviously she has her own life now. But I would have called you to let you know what had happened, if I'd known."

"Thanks. In retrospect that would have been a good thing. I had to depend on the news, secondhand, as it was. I was in LA until yesterday."

"But how on earth have you coordinated everything? You must both be impossibly busy."

"Yes it has been a bit of a game," Alex answered for them both. "The thing is, I'd rather go back to the house in Hampstead to recuperate, I don't want you to be offended. It's where I've been living really, since the whole saga started. I've moved my piano in." It was an awkward moment, surprisingly teenage for a couple of full-fledged adults.

Her father frowned briefly, struggling to understand, apparently left behind by some feminine leap of logic. "Of course. I wasn't expecting anything else, I'd thought it would be Leanne. You would have been welcome, but I'm hardly able to get a grand piano up to the eighth floor of my new place."

Alex smiled at him, relieved. Jo was grinning at her a few paces away, enjoying the dramatic moment. She raised her eyes to the ceiling in an ironic gesture, laughed out loud and came over to stake her claim beside Alex.

"Now if you don't mind, Alex, and if you don't mind," she said to Alex's father, "being accompanied by a hairy professor, why don't the two of us go down to the canteen and get some coffee, leaving Alex in peace for a bit, and we can…get to know each other…well, sort of, under the circumstances?" She indicated her outfit, struggling to replace the wig effectively.

"And the subterfuge has to continue?"

"For now, I think. I hope you don't mind. You can help us to keep the secret for the time being. Would that be possible? Even from Leanne for now? It's not going to be forever."

Something skipped inside Alex at this welcome news. She felt she must push this discussion further.

"Can you imagine the fuss for Alex, as she's already plastered, pardon the pun, all over the news headlines at the moment? We'd have camera crews and photographers queuing at the house and at every venue she had to appear at, from the hairdressers to the concert halls, over and above what's usual for her. It takes a bit of getting used to and perhaps right now isn't the time?"

Her dad raised his hands in surrender. He nodded. "See you in a little while, Alex."

Jo slipped back into character and altered the blinds again. "I vill zee you a leetle later? Ve vill maybe tell zee best friend later too?" she said as she exited, leaving Alex alone, chuckling to herself. She would have some explaining to do when finally they did tell Leanne.

CHAPTER TWENTY-ONE

The Aftermath and the Outing

It was unadulterated bliss recuperating and relaxing at Jo's.

It did feel like home now. The toxin attack had left her feeling less shocked than at Josh's assault, the first one having emotionally trumped the other, and perhaps this latter one had been less traumatic; it had been less confrontational in that respect. Or at least she had been unconscious this time. She shuddered whenever such thoughts flicked across her mind. There was only one way to deal with a second catastrophe. Lock it out.

Her father came to stay for a couple of nights. He swam in the pool while she watched from the side, amused as her dad luxuriated in the surroundings. He had to agree with her reasoning for wanting to be there, one way or another, giving her a mischievous smile. Jo was in and out of the house, apologetically, caught up with the launch work for a film premiere, the related interviews and social commitments, but invited her folks over to meet Alex's dad on his last night.

A brave move, to be sending such signals.

Still with a prickling conscience about the events at the Barbican, Alex invited John over when he was sufficiently recovered, having been kept in hospital for a little longer than her.

"This is all your own work?" he asked amazed, as she let him in.

"Not exactly. A friend."

He stood on the tiled porch, looking for all the world in his crisp, pale chinos, open-necked shirt and mop of fading blond hair as if he should feel at home in such a place, but apparently not. He twiddled his long violinist fingers nervously, then nodded. "Ah. We're quite well paid toward the top of our tree, but not *this* well paid."

"Precisely. Come in."

They sat and drank coffee on the terrace and discussed possible plans for recitals and maybe even recordings. Neither of them could play yet, but Alex was doing a pretty good line in right hand piano practice. Thankfully, John's shakes had calmed down although he had taken a break from work to recover. She was still feeling incredibly guilty despite the financial compensation that there would be to cover this. On the plus side, there was the bonus that it was looking like the start of a friendship that could overcome its awkward beginning.

This time she felt relatively distanced from the police. Perhaps it was more self-evident what had happened? Not at her home this time, but blatantly contrived in public. She preferred not to know too much about it all, carefully avoiding the claustrophobia of scrutiny or the agoraphobia of ever going out again in public that it might bring.

* * *

Four weeks after she had first been admitted to hospital, Alex returned to have the plaster removed, with great relief. She could get on with her life and put the past few weeks behind her. Her arm felt a little stiff, and progress needed to be slow at first, but after a few days of intermittent, gentle playing, the muscle memories began to revive.

One day following this, while she was working on the *Symphonie Concertante* for the Proms, Jo bowled in on her waving a card.

"Wedding invitation, Kate and Andy, friends since RADA, you may have seen them back at the LA house?"

"Yes. I think so. I know of Kate, anyway. You know I've been asked to play?"

"Nope."

"Didn't I tell you about that one?"

Jo scanned the invitation. "No, I don't remember. But...oh, yes, here it is. *Live music featuring Alex Palmer and The Pasadena Roof Orchestra*. Small print at the bottom. But gold lettering."

Alex scowled playfully at her and doodled on the piano. "Uh-huh."

"Well, great. We'll see each other there. You know, we never had that chat. What with everything that happened."

"I know. It occurred to me, the other day. What were you thinking?"

"I had a couple of sketchy ideas that I wanted to put to you." She was in a short, flimsy skirt for a change, the material fidgeted against her legs as she came over to the piano and rested an elbow on the side of the music desk. "How's the arm feeling, by the way?" She had a light tan from the improving weather and had grown her hair into a slightly shaggier style, with a reddish tint, for the approach of the next part. She had hardly any make-up on, just a little eyeliner that matched her irises. Alex thought it suited her.

"Not bad. It aches after a while...but the ideas?"

"What would you say...and it's just a bit of a mad idea at this stage...to pooling our resources a little, some of your compensation, some of mine, and buying a place in LA that we could decamp to. Stay at when one of us is over there and the other is free, or we're both working. I bet you could get a foothold in the music market out there. I even heard a rumor about you while I was out there about the soundtrack to a new film called *The Forgotten Pianist* or some such title." She dropped her eyes down and nonchalantly polished a small smear off the side of the piano as she said this. "It's just...I heard that our beach house was going to go on the market—that's what I'd been meaning to tell you—it would be in addition to this place, of course. I couldn't part easily with this place. Wouldn't want to." She paused, waiting for a response to her speech, glancing up at Alex expectantly.

She sat quietly, thinking it over, but watching the excitement in her face.

Jo continued. "I think we'd need to get everything in writing too. Legally binding."

Alex looked at her pensively and the edges of a smile began to blossom. "It sounds...absolutely brilliant. There are days when I'm passing Covent Garden when I'd like to be a thousand miles from where Josh used to be. We could. We could simply buzz off when necessary, or even when we felt like it." *And not least, having a concrete connection with each other...*

"Precisely. And the American media don't care nearly as much about a two-bit English actress, we usually play the villains anyway, and a pianist who isn't interested in Hollywood guff."

"I wouldn't exactly say that." Grinning, she ticked off on her fingers, "One, you're not a two-bit actor and two, Hollywood guff is what brought us together."

"But you see my point."

"Uh-huh. It's brilliant. Can you find out about the beach villa? It *was* particularly special..."

"Exactly. I even know who to call. I made a note. Just in case. And then all the other stuff intruded upon us. Anyway, it's *real estate* as they say. It could always be sold again, if we felt like it, no doubt for a profit."

"Hold your horses. We don't know if it's still available, haven't bought it yet and it's being sold again?"

Jo stepped toward her and placed a delightfully soft kiss on her mouth. "I love you." She pulled back suddenly as if surprised at what she'd said, thought for a moment. "Yes...I do love you.

It's felt…cataclysmic each time there's been a drama for you and harder to part with you each time I have to…"

Alex watched her closely. "And I love you. You know. For as long as I can think. It's just been creeping up on me and then one day, a while ago, I knew for certain."

Jo ran a finger down her cheek, a slightly ragged sigh escaping her and leaned forward to plant another kiss. "I think I've been overprotective of you. I'm sorry. And still it wasn't enough to prevent you from being hurled onto stages."

"Hardly within your control unfortunately."

"I'm turning over a new leaf. I'm going to make a couple of calls then." She nodded and wandered back out of the room, happily. Alex doodled thoughtfully on the piano and stretched out the recovering arm.

* * *

Only once was Alex's reverie of recovery disturbed. On a day when Jo was out in London, the buzzer went on the front door. She had taken to answering callers freely on the intercom, although anonymously, in the newfound confidence of a shared home, and scampered to the door to answer.

"Hello?"

"Hello," came a forced female voice over the intercom. "I'm looking for Jo."

"Can I help?"

"She's expecting me. A lady friend. I'm here to help as requested."

Alex's skin crept a little. "Oh? She's unavailable at present. I'll pass the message on. Leave your card in the letter-box, please."

"Well, tell her I'm looking great. And I'm ready, willing and able."

"Er, fine. Bye."

That was all. When she checked the security camera, all she could see was the departing figure of a thin, blonde girl.

Peculiar.

She recounted the conversation to Jo, her stomach tensing ominously. The storm clouds gathering on her horizon.

"Crank caller," she said, turning the unhelpful card over in her fingers and then dropping it significantly into the bin. "I'm really sorry, Alex. It happens sometimes. But I'm sorry it had to be you answering after all you've been through lately. They have ways of finding out where you are. It's fine. Actually, I'll pass this onto the local constabulary, or the *Talent* security office, on second thought," she said, and fished the offending article from the bin and pocketed it. "Don't worry."

* * *

Kate and Andy's wedding reared itself quickly, perhaps to avoid too much fuss in the buildup, early in July, the first Saturday, before the Prom the following week. They traveled together, but as Alex was not invited to the ceremony itself, Jo dropped her at the massive country house to prepare in the ballroom with the band while she went on to the event alone. With the band, she frittered away the afternoon having a ball of their own, busking through a few numbers and some silly additions such as the *Dambusters* and *633 Squadron*. Several of the players had started to take advantage of the flowing refreshments by the time the wedding guests started to arrive back from the ceremony to canapés and champagne. A couple of photographers from one of the glossy magazines which had been given, or more accurately paid for, the rights to the occasion, flitted through the accumulating guests, taking pictures where they pleased of the colorful outfits and entertainment.

At first, having taken time out to change into her black cocktail dress, Alex was free to watch from the wings, sipping champagne slowly, trying to keep her head for the performance. It was clearly reminiscent of the Vanity Fair Oscars party and her heart twinged briefly as she saw Jo arrive with a glamorous British actor hovering near her. She was cutting a dash in a clinging pale orange dress, with a plunging neckline held up by impossibly narrow straps. Alex was all too aware of the distance between them. By not allowing themselves to be recognized in public at an event like this the gap was made apparent again, but Jo was searching for her this time and spotted her in the wings. Apparently remembering the same event she sent Alex an apologetic shrug and a reassuring grin. She waited with the band while the line of welcome formed and the new bride and groom shook hands with all the friends and family. Subsequently it was their time to be announced to the stage, while Kate and Andy were invited to the floor for the opening dance. The musicians settled themselves at their instruments and started "It Had to Be You" and the newly wed couple took to the floor, wrapped elegantly around each other, while the watchers applauded. At another time it might have been too sugarcoated, but they looked so charming and she managed a brief glance to find Jo, who was being distracted by a beautiful woman. She looked up and batted her eyelashes. The gesture made Alex grin and she inserted a sparkling arpeggio to indicate she had spotted her. On looking again, Jo was laughing at her and the woman was looking bemusedly toward her. Then the music took flight and there was little time to dwell on anything else. The first general dance number involved the band too with a game of musical tennis developing as they enjoyed themselves batting versions of the "In the Mood" theme around, playing at musical flirtations with the trombones, copying their explosive low notes and slides. The bandleader was engrossed, practically dancing between the trumpets and saxophones and laughing back as he wove faux-sexily around. Alex looked out into the massive room which was heaving with energy now and caught only a glance of Jo as she was thrown out and back by a lively partner. Gosh! She could dance. She hadn't had a chance to witness that one. This was followed by the "Six-five Special," then a slow one, "The Way You Look Tonight," for recovery time for the dancers and eventually the buffet was announced to all. They settled into some more background numbers while the guests ate, and finally were able to take a break for the speeches. Alex retired to the wings, still giggling with the band as they made suggestions for the next set. Maybe "Back in the Saddle Again" or "Making

Whoopee"? They were ushered out to their own buffet, in a rear room near the kitchen and they tucked into it with enthusiasm. When they returned and took their seats again, Alex scanned the room for Jo. She was not to be seen anywhere. *Oh well. C'est la vie.* At the end of the night they would be back in the same car heading for home. The bandleader whispered over, "Six-three-three Squadron." She mouthed back, "You're kidding? I thought that was a joke!"

"No. Special request from the groom's father."

"Okay then."

The buildup of the introduction was quiet at first, amusing to them and caught the diners by surprise. *Oh, the band's back.* A few took to the floor, standing at the edges while others lay back to listen, a couple of the children starting to fly enthusiastically around the room like spitfires. After this they switched into some dance tunes to "Rock Around the Clock," "Shout!," "Twist and Shout" then more quietly "Embraceable You," "Mind if I Make Love to You" and "When I Fall in Love," at the start of which, Jo suddenly appeared at the side of the stage and leaped nimbly up next to the piano. She held out her hand expectantly and Alex looked up startled, first at her and then to the bandleader who shrugged and nodded.

She stopped playing and as the band warmed it up a little to cover her absence, with the conductor urging the saxophones to take over, she stood up to take Jo's outstretched hand, looking quizzically at her for an answer.

Jo pulled her close and whispered, "Are you ready for this?"

Her heart was pounding. "As ready as I'll ever be."

"I can't think of a better time."

"Are the hosts ready for this?"

"I've cleared it." She grinned at her and jumped lightly down from the stage, grasping her on either side of her waist to swing her down. Some did not notice, many did not care; a handsome young man who had been paying special attention to Jo shrugged, wondering how he had been usurped, but the photographers flitted around them as Jo brought her close and nuzzled in, swinging rhythmically and gently across the floor with the others. Alex's main preoccupation, beyond the flutter of nerves inside her, was the sensational feeling of Jo's dancing, leading her instinctively and easily through the melee. Jo looked up as she passed her friends. Kate was shaking her finger lightheartedly at her, in a "You! You old cad!" way; Jo raised her eyebrows at her and pulled Alex around to kiss her neck as they danced.

"I think I may have outed us," she whispered into her ear.

Only too delighted by her courage, Alex laughed at her and kissed her back as the photographers snapped away. She danced "Misty" with her too and then handed her back to the stage to rejoin the band. Jo shrugged at her friends, who called her over to them for further information.

"Need a room?" Andy called into her ear, above the volume of the band.

She nodded, laughing. "If there's one going!"

"Fine. There's a spare four-poster on the first floor. Rhiannon can't stay over!" They gave each other a high five. "So that's the mystery girl! Since when?"

Jo backed away from her friends, tapping the side of her nose and laughing. Alex watched this as she played a few minimal chords, her head still spinning, recovering from the shock. Andy chuckled back, squeezing his new wife around the waist. Jo beckoned to him, offering a spin around the dance floor. Kate released him and pushed him encouragingly forward.

The party went on, until the dancers could dance no more and the children had long since departed for their beds. The guests cheered the band and the bride and groom, having disappeared to change, returned to say their farewells and were seen off in an immaculate silver Bentley. Back inside, sandwiches were offered, but most of the guests started to drift off as the musicians packed up. Alex closed up the piano and hugged some of the band members and the bandleader goodbye, complimenting them on how much fun it had been and hoping to see them again for a rematch. Stretching out the recently healed, now slightly aching arm, she leaped delicately off the stage and went to find Jo, who was on the garden terrace steps finishing up a conversation with another actor that she recognized. She was balancing a plate and a glass in one hand, while gesticulating with the other. It felt pleasantly odd to be able to slip an arm around her waist as she greeted her in a public place, wonderful for it to be acceptable. She put her spare arm over Alex's bare shoulders and pulled her in to introduce her to Anthony, who stepped forward, lifted her spare hand and kissed it. Alex smiled at him and Jo turned and kissed her neck lightly.

"Well done. That was great fun. The band were good weren't they?"

"They were hilarious."

She whispered to her, as the friend turned to say goodbye to someone, "We have a room here. Is that all right with you?"

"Perfect."

"Let's go then." They said their goodnights and farewells to various people, crossing the hall arm in arm and mounted the graceful staircase.

"I sneaked off and put our bags in there earlier, not that we have that much with us."

She led the way to a solid, oak-paneled door, just past a couple of plaster busts, far down the corridor on the first floor and swung the door open to reveal a beautifully indulgent, red-velvet upholstered room with a queen-sized, four-poster bed. "Not bad for a spare. I wonder what the master bedrooms are like?"

"Absolutely. What happened to Kate and Andy?"

"They've disappeared to a little cottage, well more of a villa, in the grounds somewhere, for some peace."

"Sounds good. Hey! You outed us, without warning!"

"Yes, I did rather, didn't I? Like the surprise?"

"In some style." Alex closed the door behind them, flicking the lock and went over to put her arms around Jo's neck and drink her in.

"I don't know what I've started."

"No. But the rewards are great."

Alex backed her toward the bed and keeled them both, in

slapstick style, onto the satin eiderdown. Jo lay there passively while Alex released the clasps and zip of her dress, kissing each new patch of skin as it became exposed, so pleased with her that words could not cover it.

"You really don't mind?" Jo asked.

"Does it look like it?" Alex managed between kisses.

Jo chuckled.

"It may have been a touch theatrical..." Alex added.

"I'm known for that..."

"And maybe I'm a tad nervous too...but I couldn't be more proud to have you stand by me, stand up for us, take the risk." And with that she continued her route until Jo could not bear being still any longer and felt urgently through Alex's clothes for contact of her own, even though Alex wanted to take the lead and show her how much it all meant to her. She leaned gently on Jo, kissing her on the neck and down past each hollow and notch she could find, tracing the collarbones, sternum and out toward each breast and nipple, taking an eternity in the process. Jo lay mesmerized, following the journey with each nerve ending, waves of hope and expectation that this could only continue. And Alex was in no hurry. She paused only to sit up and free herself from her black evening dress. Slowly dealing with it all herself, releasing straps and her zip, eyes locked with Jo's.

"Isn't it just marvelous that no one but us gets to see *this* performance," Jo added softly just smiling, her short tousled hair spread on the pillow, enjoying the spectacle, allowed at least to raise a hand to stroke Alex's cheek as she returned to the bed, pulling the red velvet bed curtains slightly across, and follow the line of skin, across her jaw, slender neck, brushing escaped curls behind her shoulder, pursuing the contours of her until she could stroke Alex gently at the apex of her breasts too. Alex sat next to her enjoying this, the tremors of Jo's touch sending excruciating thrills into the core of her as she controlled herself, attempting to wait, while she released her hair until the rest of the curls cascaded wantonly across her shoulders. She smiled humbly back at Jo, who was staring almost in awe. She continued her journey along Jo's skin, kissing, caressing, delighting in its softness and warmth, the tautness of her toned stomach. Surely it shouldn't be possible for anyone to be this incredible? She felt herself think, all but briefly, her firing emotions making it less possible to think at all, Jo's hands now caressing her too, trying to repay the compliments. Alex followed the lines of smooth skin, smiling at the landing strip of hair left by the French waxing that Jo had complained about, necessary due to a close-fitting costume for the next round of filming.

"I can see you smiling at it..." Jo managed between breaths.

"Yes, but for all the right reasons," Alex murmured and kissed Jo's inner thighs very gently, letting her tongue lightly trace a path upward toward the center until Jo shuddered.

* * *

Suddenly their decision had freed them to wander the streets of London openly, or book a table without worrying, a conscious opening of the sluice gates that in hindsight, they ruefully agreed, may not have needed to be kept locked. There might be some flak still to come, but it would be dealt with if and when it arose. There would be doubters and dissenters. But why should their opinions and prejudices win out?

They had even managed a night out at a highly-rated new club Ultra-Violets, mostly happily tucked away at the back of the VIP bar with a few of Jo's close friends, enjoying the entertainment, undisturbed. Jo surprised Alex again with some impressive salsa moves, though why she had not expected Jo to move as freely as a snake at the hips was more of a mystery to her.

To them, it meant that Jo could attend her Prom, hanging around backstage for the end of the rehearsal with the BBC Symphony Orchestra, meeting the composer and conductor. Her presence turned a few heads and invited a few comments from orchestral members, although most were polite enough and anyway were enough used to famous faces passing through their rehearsals not to care. They dined lightly before the concert and Jo took a private box to enjoy the zany, but evocative piece, joining Alex proudly afterward at a drinks reception, doing her best to avoid being cornered by anyone.

Despite all this, nothing hit the press that week to preempt the approaching magazine article.

CHAPTER TWENTY-TWO

Camden and the Globe

Just before the story broke on the newsstands, Alex phoned Leanne, as she had promised to herself that she would, and told her the identity of the mysterious friend. The call was reasonably brief seeing as Leanne became incapable of speech, having to readjust her perspective beyond an astonished, "*Wow, Alex! Dark horse. That explains a lot. I hope I get to meet her at some point?*" She indicated that she would need a few days to digest it all. Alex couldn't blame her for that.

When the magazine published its article, she jogged very early in the morning up to the nearest shop to buy a copy and they sat on the terrace at the house, flicking through and laughing at some of the photos, including one of Jo scooping her off the stage and a closeup of them dancing, with Jo nuzzled into her cheek. The captions read—*Joanne Davison surprised the onlookers by stealing the pianist Alex Palmer away from the stage*—then—*Jo lays claim, getting to know Alex more intimately.*

"Hah! Little did they know how intimately I knew her already. You know what this means today?"

"I think so."

"They'll be camped outside the gates for a few days, until they get the shots they want."

"So? You're more of the expert with this stuff…"

"Not quite so expert with this particular event. However, two possibilities occur to me. We pack a bag, book short-notice flights, hurl ourselves out at top speed in the car and go and seal the deal on the LA place or we go blatantly out of the front gates for a long walk down to Camden Market, coffee and lunch and let them snap at our heels, satisfying their hunger while we satisfy ours, so to speak. Meanwhile I can make a call and get the agent to seal the deal on our beach house and courier the documents over."

"Mmm. You know what I fancy? Why not Plan B? I think I've had it with hiding."

"Fine with me. If we just stroll out and give them what they want, they'll be sated. And the interest will die down eventually. If we hide, we'll be chased. And anyway, I've had it with hiding too, I'm rather proud of being with you. Isn't it about time that everybody knew? And I like the intellectual street-credibility of having a talented pianist on my arm."

"Very funny. Although I must say that it doesn't exactly do me any harm to be accompanied by you. Will they turn up here do you think?"

"From past experience, I should think it won't take long."

"Let's do it. Let's have a swim or something first, give them time to stir up a hornet's nest and then do as you say, enjoy the freedom of just strolling out in public, regardless."

"Excellent idea."

So after swimming and choosing their clothes with deliberation and minimal baggage, Jo crept to the bend in the drive and peered comically through a bush, to check the lie of the land. She tiptoed back exaggeratedly.

Alex giggled helplessly at her, carried along by a cocktail of adrenaline, nervousness and excitement.

"As expected," she whispered in mock-Inspector Clouseau, "we 'ave company."

"Shades?"

She returned to relatively normal. "Yes. Good idea. Shades."

They donned their best sunglasses and their bags, stuffing in a few essentials.

"Phones to silent. Put in a toothbrush and spares, I don't know quite how this will work later."

"Really?"

"You'll see...nice to travel light for a change, isn't it?" She locked the front door, but didn't need to set the internal security, as Zara and Yuri were pottering around the house, tidying. That had been another advantage.

"Ready?"

"Ready!"

"Sure? Last chance to back out? Countdown to launch-time...twenty, nineteen, eighteen..." Jo counted as they strode down the driveway, the gravel crunching at each step, giving them away, arms linked, "three, two, one, we have liftoff." As they rounded the blind bend in the drive and crunched their way onward, the waiting photographers, of whom there were about five, began to realize they had their scoop and struggled into activity.

"Jo! Alex!" they shouted and Jo squeezed her arm. "How are you both? When did you start seeing each other? How long have you been here Alex?" they chorused, a cacophony of voices, the words becoming lost in the noise and click of camera shutters, as Jo let the two of them through the gate and secured it behind, positioning herself to fend them off from jostling Alex.

They smiled at them, but only said, "Hi!" and strode out down the hill, as the hunting pack struggled to gather up their belongings and follow.

"This is practice," Jo murmured into Alex's ear. "A rehearsal."

"For?"

"When you keep me company walking down the red carpet at the Oscars, if we get that far again next year."

"Oh, Lord. That *would* be a performance. No actually, I'll be rehearsing at the after-party venue, they've booked me again."

"Excellent. You can do the red carpet, do both somehow and then I can whisk you out of the wings this time to dance the night away with you, in between your performances! Or something!" She chuckled at her, put her arm around her shoulders, as if bracing them for any future controversy and steered them a sharp left onto a path through the Heath, cutting off the corner of the journey. The photographers hurried behind, stumbling over tree roots, encumbered by their gear, attempting to take photos while jogging in mild-mannered pursuit.

"Let's have the photo shoot and be done with it," Alex suggested, as they reached a particularly attractive clearing.

"You are a lamb to the slaughter, aren't you? However..." Jo nodded appreciatively, "we could give these guys the best story they've had all week, but do you think that will be enough?" She stopped and lounged elegantly against a tree and Alex tucked herself under her arm and smiled at the photographers, as they gathered around like a flock of starlings that had just spotted some decent scraps.

"You're teasing us!" one called.

"No, just being cooperative," Jo said through a smile.

"Where are you off to?"

"Enjoying a stroll."

"How long have you been together? Since Kate's wedding or before?"

"That's a little cheeky," Jo replied, relaxed. Alex squeezed her hand behind her back, anxious that she might say too much.

"Alex! When did all this happen? What about all the trouble you've had this year?"

She grinned. "A knight, or perhaps I should say damsel, came to rescue me."

And with that they set off on their way again, quickening the pace and laughing as the photographers scampered to get themselves together again with all the photographic baggage that it entailed. When Alex peered back, a couple of them were on their mobile phones as they jogged to keep up.

They broke into a sprint, discovering how hard it is to run while holding someone's hand, laughing and letting go. With a couple of sudden turns, they found themselves climbing Parliament Hill. They stopped only briefly to catch their breath and admire the panorama, London unrolling itself into the distance, then jogged down the other side. Only two of the fittest of their pursuers were to be seen at this stage, but as they turned out of the park and took a couple of unexpected back street turns toward Chalk Farm, they lost even those, temporarily. They slowed to a walk, enjoying the momentary privacy.

"That was almost fun," Alex said.

"Yeah. It was actually. I wonder how long they'll be hanging around the house?" She thought for a moment. "Oh great. I thought so. It's market day."

As the photographers started to reappear behind them, Jo took her hand and dived into the crowds of Camden Market, losing their pursuers easily in the melee. They even had time to browse the stalls. Jo bought a T-shirt for herself and a bangle for Alex and then they carved out a way to a reputable pizza place, where they sat and watched lunch being made in the clay ovens. Halfway through their meal though, they were spotted through the window of the restaurant, but at least the reporter had the decency to stay outside. An American couple sitting at an adjacent table, noticing the attention, started to peer inquisitively. After a moment, the lady leaned toward Jo, asking, "Excuse me, honey, would I have seen you two in something recently?"

"Well, one of us, maybe," Alex replied, smiling, "She's the actor, not me."

Jo grinned at her, shrugging apologetically, in that gesture that she had grown to love. So much.

"Could I have your autograph?" The lady offered a pen.

Jo signed a napkin with a flourish. *Jo Davison, Camden Town* and dated it.

"Many thanks. I am a bit of a collector. Enjoy your pizza."

"We will. Thanks." Alex grinned. "A collector of napkins?" She giggled under her breath.

Jo beckoned over the waitress and gave her best smile, tucking a generous tip under a saucer on the table, "Excuse me, do you have a back door here?"

"Sure. This way..."

They gathered their things suddenly and left quickly from the back of the premises, through a courtyard filled with bins and out onto Arlington Road. On Parkway they were lucky enough to catch a cab almost immediately and were being whisked away to the south, while the photographers were still searching Camden.

The air-conditioned taxi was a cool contrast with the increasing heat outside. Alex's heart started to settle after the sudden dash, until she felt her mobile vibrating again which sent her scrabbling in her bag. She checked the number.

"Just Camden-W," she explained to Jo. "Do you mind? Excuse me." She took the call. "Hi? Yes...I know...I can imagine...Perhaps you can do your best with that. I'm sorry for the extra work. Uh-huh...Wow...Really? Yes thanks. That would be great. Yes. See you."

She turned to Jo. "You were right. Potential work in LA."

She raised an eyebrow quizzically.

"*The Forgotten Pianist.* They've sent a score through. Would I like to consider it?"

"See? The grapevine was right. Our LA house will come in useful!"

"That's fabulous. Perhaps I *could* get more work out there..."

* * *

Jo nodded sagely. She had been flicking through her messages and was frowning. "Two things. Now that the cat's out of the bag, Mike Johnson wants us back. Both of us. What do you think?"

She thought. "Don't see why not. Might as well be seen publicly and get it over with. What say you?"

"We'd have to think it through. It wouldn't be bad publicity either. I mean, it wouldn't do either of us any harm, as long as we pitch it just right. I'll run it past the agency's PR rep. You and I can do some plotting."

"And the other?"

"Andy. Wanting forgiveness…mmm…I'll have a chat with him…seems he didn't really get it. Perhaps saw you replacing him."

"Well, a bit strange, but perhaps I can see the confusion. That would be your call. But I liked him when I met him." Alex said, "I'm wondering what effect it will have in reality? All this…"

"The fuss will die down after a while. Hopefully quicker than you might think, especially if we don't stoke it up accidentally."

"And how would that happen?"

"Appearing on a chat show together?"

"Some of that's inevitable."

"One of us doing something way out of our boxes…like you taking to acting suddenly or me appearing as a pianist somewhere…"

"We're safe then. That's highly unlikely for me."

"Me too. There are plusses too. Like going out today. Or being able, expected even, to go to official dates together."

"And we already have some planned. You won't lose work over it?"

"I don't know. Surely the scales will balance themselves. There'll be those who like me less because of it, those who like me more. No one's telling me I'll be refused a romantic lead on these grounds. Won't there be people curious about this? And I can name you a dozen rom-coms with complicated intrigues that walk that line. *In and Out, Kissing Jessica Stein, Sirens*…"

"I don't know those."

"Oh babe, we have some fun to come then." She paused, thinking, then suddenly launched herself: "'Once more unto the breach, dear friends, once more, or close the wall up with our English dead'…see? I've started already. Wrong play of course. Actually, I might need your help, learning the right one."

"Sure. If I can. What do I do? Read the cues?"

"That and play other parts if you like. Test me."

"Oh, I like the sound of testing you. So have you been with the Royal Shakespeare Company before?"

"Yep. Some years back, before I became rich and lazy…"

"Ha, ha."

"There are vast soliloquies aren't there? That must be a bit different from a few words here and there on screen. I mean in the play, the words must count even more than on screen, where it's the fall of your facial muscles and the action that matter, and you have somebody to edit it all?"

"Only the words do count too, obviously. Careful there, you're giving yourself away! *Pianists, know your place!*" She laughed.

Alex scowled at her. "Time for some homework, Ms. Davison, get back in the groove. Watch some perhaps? Is that the sort of thing you do? It would look great on your cinema. I love it anyway, *Henry V, All's Well, As You Like It, Midsummer Night, Othello*, there's a famous Olivier one isn't there?"

Jo leaned over to kiss her, having patiently tolerated her enthusiasm. "*Mais non…*" she said, "it is not a fashion for the maids in France to kiss before they are married."

"Give over."

"Oh, okay."

After a while, they found space to speak again. "So how come you're such a Shakespeare expert, then?" she murmured as she nuzzled Alex's neck.

"A-level English literature after music college. Sorry. I've studied it twice."

"Oh don't be. You are useful in more ways than one! I officially appoint you as my personal trainer…"

"What, now?" And she pushed her hands inside Jo's shirt. "Ooh. Can I start testing you out now? We need to work on those pecs and abs, helps vocal projection. By the way, what about that singing…?"

The cab driver was glancing at them in his rearview mirror.

"Later…" Jo smiled.

CHAPTER TWENTY-THREE

Out of the Den and into the Lion's mouth

"Alex Palmer and Jo Davison…" The audience for the *Mike Johnson Show* erupted into applause and whistles as the two of them came down the famous staircase to the band's "It Had to be You."

"Sorry, about that," Mike commented, indicating the band with a twinkle in his eye. "We couldn't resist. Forgive us, we can't help ourselves when it comes to a little real-life romance."

Jo rolled her eyes and grinned at him.

"So you two, welcome back." They thanked him and settled into the capaciously comfortable chairs. "First I have to ask, were you already an item, last time we met here?"

The two of them looked at each other. Jo gave the hand clasped in hers a gentle squeeze.

"That's a provocative first question…" Jo twinkled at him. "I'm not saying when this happened, sorry…"

"All right. Alex. How on earth does a concert pianist's schedule dovetail with a busy actor's?"

"Well, Michael...not always. However, you'd be amazed. We often both work evenings. We both have to prepare and well, in all honesty, still learning. See?" She tapped her back. "Learner Driver, can't you see the signs?"

"And you're both going to be working in Hollywood some of the time?"

"It's starting to look that way."

"Jo. Alex, a pianist? How did you meet? It can't be that easy choosing when you're surrounded by gorgeous people in the film industry?"

Alex did a humorous impression of pretending to be huffed with him, crossing her legs and folding her arms. The audience was enjoying itself.

"Sorry."

Jo laughed at her. "To say too much as to why, would be giving too much away, but what Alex can do is different..."

"...ah, the pianistic talent." Mike clarified with amusement. "And you both decided to make it public at Kate and Andy's wedding via *People* magazine."

"Well, *she* did!" Alex interjected. "Swept me off my feet without a by your leave." She laughed.

"That was good wasn't it? Nobody wrote that one for me." Jo laughed too. "But seriously, I'd had enough of hiding. I don't suppose you'd know that I was pacing outside the hospital when Alex was ill after that outrageous LSO attack, dressed as a mad, old woman, wondering whether I'd be able to get in to see her."

"*Really*? Was it really that necessary? The old woman, the intrigue...not seeing her, obviously."

"Absolutely. I wondered what would it be like if the might of the nation's paparazzi queued up for an interview outside Guy's Hospital or climbed the walls for a glimpse of either of us while she was that sick. I really don't mean it to sound self-important, I just know from experience that they're clicking at my heels if there has been a whisper of anything. And Alex was already front page news." She seemed to feel more vehement, sitting forward in her seat. "It's like a global disease. A surreptitious, but invading presence that affects the way people feel and look, without them even realizing it's controlling them. Less reputable sources are always ready and eager to stick the knife in, influencing a country's view of you. And the news spreads so fast now with mobile communications that a crowd will gather if you stay in one place for too long. The explosion of gossip magazines in the past few years speaks for itself. Although the career choice may have started it, you don't actually ask to be caught unawares off-duty so to speak. You wonder if it's possible to have a line drawn somewhere for the sake of decency. Perhaps I'm making a plea."

"Passionate words, madam."

"Yes, sorry. I mean, that is part of what I do, perhaps even helped me on my way, one has to accept that, but it can go too far when they're camped outside your house...or the hospital. It crosses the line of decency. I'm all for consenting to a photo-shoot, but is it really necessary to be caught off guard? It's lost a sense of proportion, a sense of reason. It's become a legitimized version of curtain-twitching, where the targets are considered fair game. Just imagine if a neighbor spent that much time attempting to photograph you, it would be good cause for legal action. One doesn't have the option of privacy at times." She sighed and sat back into her chair. Alex squeezed her arm. Jo looked over slightly apologetically from beneath her long lashes.

"And Alex, you could see the point?"

"We had a chance to get to know each other, find out if it was real or spur of the moment, without the world clamoring for an answer to that question too." She spoke more calmly.

"Actually," Michael continued, skillfully lifting the mood, "it must be fun to venture into the different spheres."

"Yes, it is. I have a chance to be introduced to conductors, players, composers, fabulous musicians, some great people."

"And I've met quite a few people I've only seen on the screen. That size or that size," Alex illustrated by drawing screen sizes in charades fashion.

"I know what you mean. That's been my experience too. They do actually exist..." Michael added, which produced a chuckle of appreciation from the studio audience.

"You should come round to ours and meet a few more then," Alex suggested.

"Thank you. I'd like that. Future plans?"

"Plenty. But preferably kept quiet at the moment, although you'll be hearing soon enough when the next film hits the billboards. Shortly, I can't say much but it's based on an old legend with a new twist. And Alex is booked up a long way ahead, you'll be hearing her in a soundtrack too, soon." Michael drew them into some shop talk for a time, until heading toward a conclusion he asked: "And the two of you?"

"Definitely private and no billboards, once this initial furor calms down."

"But we'll be able to see you together now, out and about. I mean, can we look forward to seeing you looking glamorous together on the red carpets with each other?"

"Without a doubt."

"You know, I am pleased for you. You will give courage to many. Thank you. You are both charming company. And Alex I'm delighted that you've had some moral support during a particularly trying time. Even though you kept us in the dark," he added graciously. "Alex, do you want to play?"

"If you like…"

"Do we like?" Michael asked the audience. They cheered and whistled. "I think that's a yes."

Alex kissed him and went over to the band to begin a rehearsed version of "Someone to Watch Over Me," which halfway through became fully orchestral and Jo went to the piano to take her hand and lead her in a gentle dance, which ended with them disappearing back up the stairs, arms around each other, reminiscent of the wedding party and a touch of Hollywood.

CHAPTER TWENTY-FOUR

Festivities and Retribution
Giocoso, ma subito Con Fuoco

Their apologetic party for deceived friends and family was a roaring success. In the end they had decided to book the ballroom at the Hilton, Park Lane, managing to fill a cancellation, and arranging a buffet underneath the glorious chandeliers. As the evening wore on, The Pasadena Roof Orchestra again, some of whom were starting to become regular friends including the bandleader, raised the roof and the tables were cleared for some lively dancing. Actors and actresses rubbed shoulders with musicians, talk-show hosts and family; they all heard Jo's unexpected, initially shy speech, thanking them for tolerating their deception and for their support during difficult times, a reference to Alex's attacks and the media obsession. "However, let the champagne flow and the dancing blow us away," she concluded, "prizes by the way, later in the evening, for best footwork etcetera. We have a panel of appointed judges!" She ended to a cheer, making a gazelle-like leap off the stage, grabbing Alex and launching her around the room.

Later, Andy, Leanne, Nathan, Alex and Jo were at a table together at the side. They had all been in deep conversation, occasionally interspersed with laughter. Jo looked at Alex and gave her a nod.

"We were wondering, only wondering and stop me if you need to…we have been looking for a couple of additional assistants, PAs, you know, to alleviate some of the difficulties and duties, diary booking, hotel checking, 'help I need a red dress, a short-notice holiday, someone to organize me, get me to wherever, fight off the teeming hoards'…that sort of thing. Paid positions, obviously. To assist Andy. We've discussed this with him. He was finding it a job and a half."

At this point Andy nodded and grinned. "And then some. Not that I communicated that particularly well." He hinted at the storm between them that had now passed and been explained away.

Jo clapped him on the back and continued, "And that was when it was just me. Now with both of us, it's giving us a headache working everything out and keeping what's going to be at least two major properties, our work and us organized. And while thinking, we realized we'd need someone trustworthy, reliable, valuing privacy, some people we'd like to be around. We wondered, if it's not too much of a long shot, if it might interest you two?"

"Wow," Leanne uttered. "Give me a moment to think. Okay moment passed. Yes, absolutely. Nathan?" she asked, looking at him searchingly.

"Tentatively: that would be fabulous. I'd have a lot of questions for you. I'd need to sort something out with Camden's. And make sure I wouldn't be treading on Andy's toes."

Andy smiled. "No worries there, it would be good to have a sounding board to work things out."

They all lifted their glasses.

CHAPTER TWENTY-FIVE

Finale

Eventually, on the plane to LA, it seemed they had a moment to call their own, a new start, leaving some of the discomfort and intrusion behind. Against the drone of the engines and constant hiss of the air-conditioning, they whispered softly to each other.

"I may not have told you how much I love you," Jo murmured quietly.

Alex kissed her gently, nodding sagely.

"You know already that I'm the same. There is no doubt, this has been a year of...violent extremes."

"Yes. Exactly. Since, you know, everything that's happened, I was thinking I should do something worthy. It's piqued my conscience, prodded me about the value of life and opportunity. Do a bit more good with some of these vast fees. It's just that I've been thinking, since the attack on you and the lucky escape, I should do something more substantial...more concrete. Frankly, the whole thing, the acting, it's a bit of a temporary ego-trip, isn't it? To be standing up and lapping up the applause."

"You could say that about my field. But is it? It depends if you're doing it to lap up the glory or because there's something greater to be said through you for the sake of art or the deeper meaning, and you're just the conduit. You're taking people to a different place. Escapism is sometimes more important than you realize. Oh! I'm starting to sound—"

"Yeah, quite! Couldn't have put it better if I'd tried! Ha! What I mean is, the first time you're paid ten million dollars as a fee, and get an advertising deal because of it…it's easy to think, wow—I must be something quite special!"

"But actually, it's just some lunatic or other who is so desperate to have you that they'll be willing to pay silly money." Alex was chuckling at her. "The competitive market. Disproportionate fees. And the fact that your face becomes public property."

"Precisely. Really it should be the heroes, the lifesavers, the volunteers, the unrecognized stalwarts who get that. Our world seems to work in reverse. But do it for fifty pence and you wouldn't be taken seriously anyway. But wouldn't it be superb if we could organize a massive philanthropic, as you put it—good word, by the way—fund, supported by only a percentage of the income of the high earners, footballers, city multimillionaires, celebrities and so on, which could really make a difference. Give it a name that makes the contributors proud to be a part of it, makes others obliged to join or be left out as part of the Scrooge brigade. I don't know…fund a hospital, or something. It's about time we realized we could live without one million of the ten million fee, for the sake of a new hospital, and obviously once you combine a chunk of those millions, or a decent re-employment scheme or some such thing. Has it not gone somewhat by the wayside since Victorian times? Big money, new money was new enough then to provoke an individual conscience. Perhaps because they were more visibly running ramshackle over the country, putting up heavy industry."

"Yes. It should be done. One that specifically provokes the high earners and goes to the right places. It would need an organization, administration. It's not something you or I could run from the garden shed. There's probably such an arrangement out there already, plenty of charities needing support, pick the right one if possible and once you've found it, we could simply help it along with a massive injection of cash and enthusiasm. Putting your name to it would certainly help. We could do some research."

"And isn't it ironic, that the higher up you get, the easier it is to forget how it really feels to be in need? How it feels to be desperate for help. It's only when you have a shock like…well, events like there have been this year…that you realize what a tiny cog in the machine you are…how the world will exist quite happily if you leave it…and what exactly are you leaving behind if you do?"

The light of the setting sun was catching the tips of the high clouds as Alex looked out.

"And the higher up you get, they're the people in charge of it all. Scary. Easier to forget, to become removed from the reality of it all. Mmm. Good topic of conversation over dinner at Ken's."

"It would be. He's only too well aware of the egos of actors, I should imagine." Jo paused for thought. "Alex, I know this is not the place…" Her voice dropped even lower in dynamic. "I'm sure I should be doing this somewhere more romantic than this, but please marry me?"

"What? That came out of nowhere!…Sorry…hang on a minute…one minute we're philosophizing about world philanthropy and the next…not something I expected to hear on a plane, halfway across the Atlantic. Sorry…wait a moment while I compose myself." She caught her breath, fanning her face in a comical manner.

Jo's shock at her initial response was fast dissolving into laughter. "I'm not playing games. Let's make it official."

Keeping her voice lower, realizing she had caused at least one turned head, Alex answered quietly, in total seriousness, "Absolutely." Then, lightening her expression, added, "Incredible of you to ask. But it does depend upon what you mean. It would be churlish of me not to admit that's the best proposition I've had this year…actually this lifetime. But I can't wear a ring. I can't play with one. Look at this—la, la, clunk, la, la, clunk." She illustrated playing the piano with such a handicap, while Jo sat amused, watching this performance. "Buy something subtle, but fabulous, that I can wear round my neck on a chain all the time and never take it off. We'll know what it represents. And for goodness sake don't make me walk up some aisle somewhere in front of massed cameras. Not anywhere public, where they can have a field day on us. A secret marriage, that can't inspire any more lunacy. Somewhere, somehow where nobody knows about it, just you and I and our nearest and dearest. On a boat or a remote island in the Pacific perhaps? And I won't wear white or anything like that. And you shouldn't wear a ring, it would get in the way of the acting and give the game away. Spoil the available image."

"Not shouting it from the rooftops?"

"We can do that later when we feel ready and able."

"Any other stipulations?" She laughed, barely veiling her earnestness.

"That's probably the last response you could have anticipated."

"But the most disarmingly honest. And perhaps it was the least romantic place to be asked. The world need not know. And we can find a way to placate or involve the parents…I wonder how long that could be kept a secret? One would have to swear communicant, solicitor, registrar etcetera to silence, somehow."

"Try Oscar tickets, or something."

"Ha!" Jo picked up her hand and kissed it, looking sideways at her and whispering, "I love you. I really do. I really, truly, madly, deeply…"

"I've seen that one, too," Alex giggled at her. She paused, aware of the gravitas behind the next words. "Me too. It's been creeping up on me it seems, forever…"

They attempted to link their arms, in the manner of a pair of copulating seahorses, or courting swans, laughing as they tried to drink from their wineglasses, but the plane hit a bump of turbulence and they were both splashed.

"We're a catalogue of disasters." Jo chuckled.

"Not any more...I hope. I pray."

* * *

The beach house nestled in its own idyllic surroundings, an oasis of calm, completely as they remembered it, as if stepping back in time, but now theirs, still, quiet, secluded, leaving the recent catastrophes of the other life far behind. Their friends, and now new assistants, had paved the way; it was stocked and prepared seemingly without effort. They had encouraged Leanne and Nathan to use the small guest wing while Andy helped them to become acquainted with the Hollywood machine, but for now they had taken some time off and one of the cars to explore the region. It was a good opportunity. There were plenty of visitors, Jo had made many friends on this side of the ocean and Alex was pleasantly surprised to find how easily she was automatically welcomed into this too. Millie was still there, almost part of the furniture, to cater for their needs, apparently flexible and fond of the new arrivals, one of the few key witnesses to their early meeting, and a capable housekeeper.

The Forgotten Pianist proved to be enjoyably challenging. It was Alex's first experience of precision music-spotting since providing the sound track live on stage for some slapstick comedies at a charitable performance for Comic Relief a few years back. However, this was accuracy of a new kind, exacting timings to coincide precisely with the finished film material. Despite the hours of timed practicing from the cue sheet and communications with the composer already put in, it was painstaking work.

Between their professional engagements, they were inundated with visitors and went out to eat with friends, invited to palatial properties, hospitably wined and dined, enjoying refreshing conversation, in-depth discussions on new projects or finding ways to put the world to rights. Jo was invited in as a partner in a new production company, a chance at which she leaped, reminded of the potential shelf life of the profession, the fragility of the "action" years. It would be a practical investment in the future, which could be managed largely at arm's length for the time being.

Returning to the tranquility of their new home, grateful for the safe warmth of friends, they sometimes spent the rest of the evening lying in the beach house or elsewhere, pleasantly exhausted.

On such an evening, they were lounging on the rug in the poolside house, the doors to both the pool and the sea wide open, damp from swimming, still tacky as they dried slowly in the warm evening air.

"Bliss," Alex murmured, her eyes closed, listening to the gently breaking waves in the distance.

Jo rolled onto her side with an effort and stroked her back. It never failed to amaze Alex that her touch could leave a trail of fire blazing on her wherever it went.

"It's hard to believe this is where it all started, not even a year ago. Do you ever think about it? So much has happened," she continued, remembering her doubts too and smiling at them as she watched the fading light.

Jo nodded. "Not exactly where it all started. I remember it all precisely. The first time I was able to touch you was when we shook hands in the lift on the night of the Academy Awards. And the eye contact from behind that curtain. That's a huge thing for actors you know, eye contact. You had no idea what that meant to me to be able to look you directly in the eyes for the first time. We're coached to deliberate over it. It's hidden deep within the inner psyche." She held Alex's gaze, grinning at her own arch sincerity.

"And musicians, to a lesser extent. Not to deliberate over it, but you create it to begin accurately or convey decisions or changes in the performance."

"Of course."

"Ah, yes…But no, I didn't know it meant more than it was. I was just shocked that it was you."

"And I'd seen you before that."

"I remember that handshake. I thought at first I was experiencing some sort of static electricity."

"Mmm. And this is what I'd looked forward to, tentatively, hopefully."

She kissed Alex's back and neck. She rolled over obligingly, linking her arms behind her neck and pulling her down.

They lay together, forgetting conversation, their hands traveling. Later they lay collapsed on their sides, still gasping, still connected to each other. Then Alex rolled away from her gently, giving her the space to recover and allowed her free arm to splay out across the floor, as she stared into the night sky beyond the doors, catching her own breath.

The year was beyond belief, so much change. But for now, she stroked Jo's arm peacefully as they lay in the warm evening stillness, close to where it had all begun.

"Was it really that tenuous?" Alex asked.

"How do you mean?"

"Had it not been that you had stepped into that lift, this would never have happened?"

"You're joking? Perhaps had you not been invited to that original party, then it would have been more difficult. But still you were here, in LA. I think I would probably have found a way."

"A way?"

"To meet you. You looked so alone that night. But not exactly unhappy to be alone…it was something I recognized. Anyway I left the party just before you. I was in the lobby when you came in."

"You were?"

"As I've said, adept at hiding when necessary. TWYC. I was a member of the wanting you club. There was little chance that I wouldn't have stepped into that lift, although I nearly didn't catch it in time…"

It was mystifying, to have been stalked. Perhaps that was the wrong word…hunted out maybe…by this Venus of a woman. Alex studied the face she knew so well, reading the person within. Once she may have thought that it was only skin deep, that it was only the instant attraction of the beauty that brought such success. That perhaps she had learned to like it and depend upon it. She understood her better now. She was trapped within this to a certain extent, given that it came with handsomely paid luxury and labeled, pigeon-holed by it too. It wasn't something that could be backtracked, the instant recognition brought confinement with it, but she carried it with magnanimity, unspoiled by the fuss.

"I like you wanting me."

* * *

Jo performed in *Othello* at Stratford that autumn in front of packed crowds. Rehearsals had begun in London, as the first leaves had begun to fall from the plane trees, finishing later in Stratford, the schedule increasing in intensity, while Alex dashed around Britain performing a short national tour, by which time leaves lay in snowdrift-sized piles, inconveniencing the traffic in some kind of arboreal revenge. She headed down to watch as soon as time permitted, staying at the cottage they had promised themselves, tucked into the privacy of the Cotswolds.

The instant gratification of a live audience was a pleasure, a contrast to the delayed praise from film work. The nights without social commitments were spent fatigued, back at their rural retreat, relaxing in the comfort of an easy familiarity in front of a roaring fireplace and by morning, sometimes, still lying there wrapped in blankets, dozing together, the yule-sized logs still glowing softly.

The release of *The Forgotten Pianist* at the beginning of November was a well-timed marketing success, playing to packed cinemas and creating a media current that circumnavigated the commercial globe. While their own Christmas remained a private affair, the soundtrack went global and viral as it hit the market at the same time as the film, just in time for the closure of the Oscar nominations.

Walking the red carpet, arriving at the Academy Awards the following March, they were told by an interviewer that they made a glamorous, relaxed couple. Perhaps so, although it may have been the tight security that helped to ease the process and the reassurance that Nathan and Andy hovered nearby, looking impossibly immaculate in their tuxedos.

For a change, their appearance was on an equal basis, both as invited guests this time, with Alex scheduled to perform as part of the original music nominations for light relief during the ceremony. As they headed toward the entrance a ripple of applause broke out, gaining momentum as the reason spread like fire among the gathered crowd: *"Alex and Jo! What a year!"* They were encouraged to take a curtain call among the flash photography even before they went in, their hands grasped tightly together for mutual support.

During the ceremony itself, Alex had to take to the stage unexpectedly a second time to assist in receiving the award with the composer for his Best Musical Score. Jo had been nominated again in the Best Actress category for a harrowing role in one of the summer's blockbusters, *Abandoned*, although she was, she felt not unreasonably, pipped at the post by Meryl Streep. Still, the evening was rewarding, they could sit together and Alex at last had the opportunity to meet Ellen. There was no need and indeed no notion of escaping from the back door. Colleagues and the crowd were eager to press congratulations and good wishes upon them. It seemed that something better had come from the mayhem of their ridiculous year.

Most importantly, the government at home had announced an inquiry into the use of photographic material and finally the legal reforms required to catch a reputable legal system up with the fast-changing world of modern media. Complicated issues of privacy, stalking and illegal pictures were being confronted: that pictures other than security-related CCTV would not be published without the consent of the person unless judicially overruled as being necessary and beneficial to public safety. In the cases of articles of public interest, only photographs taken previously or currently with consent could be used to support an article. The Prime Minister had concluded that although visual freedom may be considered as a human right, given the extent of interlinking of media, the speed with which media can now be transferred and the widespread misuse of images, privacy now needed to be considered and counterbalanced with these issues.

* * *

This time, at the after-show party, there was no hiding in the wings or behind curtains to be done. They arrived together and when Alex had finished the opening set, she was able to participate as a guest, circulating, mixing and dancing, as welcome as any other and laughing with Jo at the memory of their first meeting, seemingly so strange now, precisely one year ago, at the beginning of that three-week tour. The apparent boundaries between them had been permanently crossed.

Only the most ardent fan or observant critic would have noticed the attentive, possessively passionate way that Jo caressed Alex's back as they danced or the pair of beautifully tiny, discreet sapphire and diamond pendants that they had each taken to wearing on a fine chain around their necks whenever possible like some type of matching good luck talisman, as if it meant so much more. They had first appeared around the end of January, representing a very private event, and had not parted company from each since then, unless Jo's work demanded it.

And perhaps the lucky charms worked. They seemed to be doing just that. Perhaps their personal lives would be no less exciting and busy from now on, just considerably happier.

Bella Books, Inc.

Women. Books. Even Better Together.

P.O. Box 10543
Tallahassee, FL 32302

Phone: 800-729-4992
www.bellabooks.com